KAPITOIL

HARPER  PERENNIAL

NEW YORK • LONDON • TORONTO • SYDNEY • NEW DELHI • AUCKLAND

KAPITOIL

A Novel

Teddy Wayne

HARPER PERENNIAL

P.S.™ is a trademark of HarperCollins Publishers.

KAPITOIL. Copyright © 2010 by Teddy Wayne. All rights reserved. Printed in the United States of America. No part of this book may be used or reproduced in any manner whatsoever without written permission except in the case of brief quotations embodied in critical articles and reviews. For information address HarperCollins Publishers, 10 East 53rd Street, New York, NY 10022.

HarperCollins books may be purchased for educational, business, or sales promotional use. For information please write: Special Markets Department, HarperCollins Publishers, 10 East 53rd Street, New York, NY 10022.

FIRST EDITION

Designed by Justin Dodd

Library of Congress Cataloging-in-Publication Data is available upon request.

ISBN 978-0-06-187321-8

10 11 12 13 14   OV/RRD   10 9 8 7 6 5 4 3 2 1

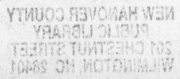

To my grandmother, Bess

There it is a definite social relation between men, that assumes, in their eyes, the fantastic form of a relation between things.

Karl Marx, *Das Kapital*

OCTOBER 1999

The Atlantic elongates below us like an infinite violet carpet.

However, the American teenager dividing me from the window does not observe it. He is plugged into earphones and recreates with a video game simulation of an airplane flight. It is strange that someone would focus on a minimal flat monitor of artificial flying when you are truly flying and have a big-picture view of the world. Possibly it is because he has traveled in an airplane multiple times and this is my initial experience.

His name is Brian, and acne covers his face like islands on a map or discrete red points on a graph. After we relaunch from London, he asks if I have any games on my computer.

"No," I say. "I use it merely for programming."

He unplugs one earphone. "What do you program?"

I am still in the brainstorming phase for the programming window currently open, so I have coded only a few lines. "I work for Schrub Equities at their office in Doha, Qatar."

"Really, for Schrub?" He unplugs his other earphone. "You make financial programs for them?"

"I sometimes create programs."

He looks at my screen. I reach for the airplane's consumer magazine in the chair's netting and intentionally contact my laptop so that it rotates away from the angle of Brian's eyes. "What do they use them for?"

"I typically do not show them to my superiors," I say.

"Why, they don't work?"

"It is complex to describe." I minimize the programming window. "Sometimes programs require—"

He shifts through different channels on his personal television. "Then what are you coming to New York for, if you're not a real programmer?" he asks.

"I am here until December 31st to help them prepare for the Y2K bug so their systems do not malfunction." It sounds less impressive than when I practiced stating it at home.

"So that's why you're in business class," he says, and I think he is complimenting me until he replugs both earphones and adds, "Only the serious businessmen fly in first." I restrict myself from telling him that it is in fact critical work and they are transporting me because I am the cream of the cream Y2K specialist in Doha, and instead I look outside, where the ocean mirrors the plummeting sun like toggling quartz in concrete or an array of diamonds, and reminds me of why our mother gave Zahira her name, because she parallels a diamond in various ways.

When I retrieve my new voice recorder/electronic dictionary from my pocket later to certify it is functioning, Brian inspects it and asks how it works. I explain that if it detects human voices nearby it records for up to 12 hours, and if it detects silence it powers off. He asks if I am also a reporter. "I am recording a journal while I am in the U.S., and this will help me to study the American voices I hear and to transmit their conversations without error."

Brian laughs loudly enough for the people behind us to hear. "You keep a *diary*?" he says. I wish his parents were on the airplane, but he seems like the class of teenager who does not adjust his behavior even in front of his parents. "The only person I know who does that is my sister."

Several of the American financial magazines I read advise recording a journal for self-actualization, and I am additionally doing it to enhance my English, but he will not appreciate that or my two other motivations: (1) I hypothesize that writing your thoughts is a way of deciphering precisely what you truly feel, and it is especially valuable if you have a problem, similar to how writing a computer program helps you decipher the solution to a real-world problem, and (2) recording my experiences is also integral to remembering precise ideas and moments from my time in the U.S. I have a robust memory for some details, but it is complex to continue acquiring data and archive them all, and even I now am forgetting some older memories, as if my brain is a hard drive and time is a magnet.

The captain says we should complete our customs forms "ASAP," and I research the term in the book I contain a copy of in my other pocket, which I also gave to Zahira: *The International Businessperson's Guide to English*, which self-defines on the reverse cover as "An indispensable compendium of English financial jargon and idioms for the global businessperson, from *actionable* to *zombie bonds*." There is also a void in the rear for the owner to record more jargon terms, as I do frequently, even though my knowledge base of English financial jargon is already broad for a foreigner because of my nighttime classes in programming and mathematics and economics.

The chief flight attendant commands us to power off electronics. We angle down to New York City, and the skyscrapers of Manhattan aggregate like tall flowers in a garden and the grids of orange lights look like LEDs on a circuit board.

The previous landing from Doha to London slightly panicked me, so to reroute my brain I reinitiate conversation with Brian, although my ideal partner for logic problems is Zahira.

"I have an interesting math problem," I say. "Is an airplane a greater gas-guzzler per passenger than a car? Here are some data that I received from the captain when I transferred, converted to American measurements: (1) We will consume approximately 17,000 gallons of gas on this flight; (2) it is 3,471 miles from London to New York; and (3) there are 415 total passengers and employees."

Brian yawns, but I continue, as sometimes people become stimulated by a subject once they learn more.

I write the equation on a napkin for him:

$$\frac{(415 \text{ passengers})(3{,}471 \text{ miles})}{17{,}000 \text{ gallons}} = 84.7 \text{ passenger-miles/gallon}$$

"Therefore, if a car has four passengers, what must its gas mileage be to equal an airplane's per-person efficiency of approximately 84.7 passenger-miles per gallon?"

"I don't know," Brian says. "I suck at math."

It is frustrating when people do not have faith in their skills, because this is a simple problem he could solve if he tried. I explain that a car must consume 21.2 miles per gallon to be as efficient with four passengers, and that a new hybrid car from Honda is more efficient with just two passengers.

"But there is no car that is as efficient if you are solitary," I say.

Brian opens the airplane's journalism magazine as we descend. I tell him there is an article on Derek Schrub, which delighted me to discover and which I am saving for Zahira to practice her English comprehension, but he is reading about an English actor's preferred restaurants in Tokyo. I especially enjoy the beginning:

Yo Ho Ho and a Two-Liter Bottle of Soda
On a windswept, perfect-for-sailing Saturday at the Indian Harbor Yacht Club in Greenwich, Connecticut

(lat. 41° 00' 40" N, long. 73° 37' 23" W), Derek Schrub—founder and CEO of Schrub Equities, the financial services and investment goliath whose net revenues topped $29 billion last year—makes an executive decision: asking his wife, Helena, to buy a two-liter bottle of soda for their day on the yacht. "It's cheaper than the six-packs," he rumbles as he checks the tides. A man of such impressive wealth doesn't really count cents when it comes to carbonated beverages—does he?

"That's how I grew my company," says the tanned and salt-and-peppered 64-year-old, who resides in an Upper East Side penthouse in Manhattan during the week but chooses the subway over cabs and limos ("The subway is fast, cheap, and entertaining; a car is none of those"). "Counting cents."

Known in business circles as "the Hedge Clipper" for his innovative hedging strategies in the 1970s, when his fledgling company soared while nearly everyone else faltered, Schrub is the closest thing the financial world has to an ambassador. Confidant to senators and celebrities alike, board member of dozens of charitable organizations, and the face of perhaps the most successful financial company of the last quarter century, he ranked first in a recent poll asking graduating MBAs which business figure they sought to emulate.

For now, though, he is looking forward to an afternoon on the high seas aboard his relatively humble—by Greenwich standards—35-foot yacht (named *Clarissa*, for Schrub's mother) with Helena and their two sons, Wilson, 21, and Jeromy, 19, on summer break from Princeton. "Sailing is my passion," opines Schrub, "but I don't need a fifty-foot boat to prove that to others. I'm not one for conspicuous consumption. There's nothing inherently wrong with accumulating money, unless that's all that matters to you."

The rest of the article is about sailing, and it does not indicate if the soda is Coke, which would interest me more than sailing does, but I like the last quotation, and I consider mailing the translation to Uncle Haami, because of what he said one year ago when I had the opportunity to labor at Schrub's Doha office. He was eating dinner at our home on a Friday and we were roundtabling my job offer. After being polite for the majority of the meal, Haami finally became upset when I discussed Schrub's recent record growth. "You will be divesting money from Qatar and into the hands of greedy Americans," he said as he swallowed the hareis I had cooked.

I was very prepared for this argument. "First, how are they more greedy than Doha Bank?" I asked. "They both aim to create more wealth. Schrub merely possesses more equity. Second, how are we paying for this lamb?"

"It is not money I object to," he said, which is slightly different from Mr. Schrub's quotation but has some intersection. "It is the imbalanced distribution. And it is the American economic policy of imperialism."

I said that companies like Schrub create the largest pool of money, and they can do so only because there does exist an imbalanced distribution of equity, so that the innovators, e.g., Derek Schrub, have enough capital to impact the world around them. I did not say it then, because it might have negated my argument, but the article is correct when it calls Mr. Schrub the Hedge Clipper. It would of course be optimal if everyone infinitely produced wealth, but sometimes only a zero-sum game is possible, and you must hedge to create wealth while others are losing it. And I agree with Mr. Schrub: I am trying to earn impressive wealth not for conspicuous consumption, but to certify that I can pay for half of Zahira's tuition and so our father can retire from his store before he becomes very old.

"And the correct word is not 'imperialism,' but 'globalization,'" I said. I believe I pronounced the English translation as well. "Globalization creates more trade and jobs for everyone, in both the U.S. and Qatar."

"I will not argue with you anymore in your father's home," Haami said. "What do you think, Issar?"

My father breathed on his gunpowder and mint tea and drank from it and scratched his gray beard before he replied. He looked at my uncle although he was discussing me.

"Karim is a grown man," he said. "He can make his own decisions."

He did not say another word then about Schrub, and he has not said anything about it after.

I appreciate that Zahira supported me by saying that I was not designed to labor in a garage, like our uncle, or to sell food and items people want that they cannot purchase elsewhere, like our father, and although that is true and I have more robust plans for myself, I told her after dinner that she should not devalue their jobs, which are integral even if we desire more from life than merely waking up, eating breakfast, laboring for someone else at tasks most people could do, and repeating the same actions daily without personal growth.

The airplane contacts the ground with force, and I close my eyes and contain my breath until the wheels smoothly merge with the concrete and we decelerate.

After I retrieve my luggage, which is minimal because I do not have much clothing and only one additional suit, I see a black man holding a sign that displays "KARIM ISSAR" with large quotation marks and at the bottom is the logo for Schrub Equities of a flying black hawk transporting the letters S and E in its two feet, which infinitely makes me feel proud, but especially now, when I see my name publicly linked to my company. He is approximately 15 years older than I am and has a full mustache and a mostly voided beard, probably because he shaved in the morning.

"I am Karim Issar of Schrub Equities," I say. I put down my luggage to shake his hand. The name sign on his left pectoral displays BARRON without quotation marks.

Barron does not shake my hand but picks up my luggage. "This all?" he asks.

I nod, because this is the first American here I have talked to besides Brian and the airplane workers and the customs official, and I am nervous about making an error even though his own sentence is incomplete.

"I can carry them," I say. But Barron is already leaving. I follow him out of the automatic doors of the airport onto American concrete, and my lungs consume the cool air that is like the initial taste of a Coke with ice.

Barron drives a black car, but it is not a limo, and the interior leather is the color of sand and feels like Zahira's stomach when she was an infant. A photograph inside the sun-protector over his head displays a little girl with braided hair, although it is unlike the fewer and less rigid braids my mother sometimes used to produce for Zahira when our father was at the store.

In the front mirror I see Barron has a small scar above his right eyebrow, which looks like his left eyebrow in the mirror. It is like debugging a program: Sometimes you do not truly observe something until you study it in reverse.

We are on the highway now, although there is not much to see and the sun has already descended. The speedometer is at 55, the optimal rate for consuming gas, so I recall the problem on the airplane. This car is probably not efficient enough with two people to be as efficient as the airplane, but I am curious.

"Excuse me. How much gas does this car guzzle?" I ask.

"Guzzle?" Barron says. "You mean its fuel efficiency? I don't know."

"It is not 42 on the highway, is it?"

Barron laughs, but it does not make me feel the way it did when Brian laughed. "Not even close. But if you find one like that, let me know. They make us pay for our own gas."

The car zooms through the streets of Manhattan like a circuit charge, and the buildings maximize as we get closer. From a distance I identify my new apartment building, Two Worldwide Plaza. On its top is a glass pyramid, and pyramids intrigue me for four main reasons:

1. The Great Pyramid of Cheops is one of man's superior ventures, yet we do not know with 100% certainty how it was constructed.

2. The perimeter of the Great Pyramid divided by its perpendicular height approximately equals 2π.

3. The circumference of a circle divided by its radius also equals 2π, which may or may not be a coincidence.

4. Pyramids are elegant images of best practice hierarchies for organizations.

Barron deposits me at my entrance. He exits the car and angles his head back to see the building, although his perspective is from the ground, which is inferior to an elevated view. "Not bad."

"My company is paying for it," I say.

He removes my luggage from the rear, and I give him a gratuity. "Thank you," I add. "I hope I have not interrupted your dinner plans."

"No, I've got dinner waiting at home," he says. "Have a good night." He reenters the car and drives away.

The material in the entrance is made of dark wood and brass or possibly gold. All the surfaces mirror light, and there is a guard in a suit of greater quality than Barron's behind a desk. My room is 3313, which makes me think of the RPM of records, and the record to the CD is an analog for the pyramid to the skyscraper, and although the modern invention is of course more efficient, there is still something intriguing about the obsolete device. E.g., I have positive memories of my mother playing the few Beatles records she was able to acquire in Doha when I was a child and of the sound of the instruments merging with the interference and especially of how she played them at higher volume when my father was not at home, but I do not have any positive memories of CDs, possibly because I have little leisure time now to listen, and also I do not know anyone who loves music as much as my mother did.

ASAP = as soon as possible

On Monday, when I exit the elevator on the 88th floor of World Trade Center 1 (the floor number there also delights me, because 88 has perfect symmetry, as the most elegant objects and ideas do), I immediately see the *S* and *E* and the black Schrub logo of the hawk attached to the wall, as if it were trying to fly away. In the Doha office the logo is not so large and it is merely painted on the wall. This is a three-dimensional plastic object, and before I enter the office I touch the hawk briefly when no one is nearby, although a sharp corner of its wing slightly pains my finger.

A hallway curves around the main circular laboring room, and there is a small nucleus in the center of six desks in a circle. The sides of the room have sections divided by walls like the lines connecting to numbers on an analog clock, and in fact there are 12 sections called pods. Each section contains four gray desks and workers arranged in the shape of a non-compressed staple. Therefore, the workers in the center, who are the superiors, can observe the other employees at all times.

My podmates are Dan Wulf, Jefferson Smithfield, and Rebecca Goldman. Jefferson stands up to shake my hand and Dan shakes my hand from his chair and Rebecca waves. The desk assignments are:

```
 ⌐ ‾D                                  R⌐ ‾
 |  A      JEFF      KARIM      E|  |
 |_ N    |_____|    |_____|    B|_|
```

Jefferson is the pod leader. He is very short, possibly even shorter than Rebecca, although he wears shoes that have thick soles and when he took them off later that day I saw additional cushioning in the interior, so with them he equals her vertically. His pale face has acute angles and looks like it belongs on a sculpture and shares some features with Taahir's from Doha Human Resources, and his hair is between blond and brown. His forearms are highly defined with muscles and he frequently rolls his sleeves up to type but I hypothesize also to reveal them. Multiple postcards on the wall over his desk display the posters of Japanese movies with translated titles such as *Akira* and *Seven Samurai* and *Ikiru*. Sometimes during work he writes in a small notebook and counts with his fingers five or seven times as he moves his lips and mutely reads it.

Dan is slightly taller than I am, potentially 75 inches, although he constantly minimizes his height by not standing 100% vertically, and his dark hair is already slightly voiding on the top. He is plugged into earphones most of the time. Over his desk a framed image of the top of a mountain displays:

THE **ART** OF BUSINESS:
ANTICIPATE, DON'T WAIT
REACT TO THE FACT
THRIVE, NOT JUST SURVIVE

Rebecca wears glasses like a turtle's shell I once located for one of my father's customers and her black hair is not short or tied up like the hair of the other females in the office, although you can still see her earrings, which are in the shape of dolphins. One lower tooth is misaligned with the others. Her only desk decoration is a small photograph of her with her younger brother.

Jefferson and Dan complain frequently to each other about

our "minor league bitch work," which is partially true of the Y2K project because it is repetitive and Jefferson commands me to "piggyback" on the team's previous work and not create anything original, although I believe it is inappropriate to complain in the workplace and demoralize your coworkers. They sometimes quietly discuss other programmers and financial analysts ranked above them that they believe they have superior skills to. Rebecca does not make any negative comments about the project or other workers except on the first day when she says, "Don't expect to receive any kudos. We're essentially vassals here."

However, I can tell she is not stimulated because she frequently puts her lower face in her hands shaped like a V and stares at the divider wall above her monitor.

Jefferson and Dan also recreate with a game called fantasy baseball. When they arrive at work, they analyze the previous night's performances of the players they "own." Typically I do not listen to them, because I do not know the players and have difficulty understanding their jargon terms. Rebecca tells me they converse about it even more now than they did during the summer because they are in a special playoff fantasy baseball league and the winner receives more money. They also make daily bets of $10 with each other on the stock market's performance.

But I do listen to one integral conversation on Wednesday as they are leaving.

"Book it," Dan says as he clicks his mouse. "I just traded away Bernie Williams for Scott Brosius with Tim."

Jefferson cleans his mouth with a toothpick from a box he stores in his desk. "You was robbed."

Dan points to a newspaper article on his monitor. "Nope. The *Post* said Williams has never had a consistent playoff run—he always burns out. Brosius was consistent in every series last year. The data's out there. Tim's lazy, he never looks it up."

After they leave, Rebecca rotates her chair to me. "Do you ever just sometimes genuflect and thank Jesus that we're privy to such scintillating conversation?" she asks.

Although I can detect most of the idea from her voice and face, I do not know the definitions of some words, so I say, "I am uncertain what you mean."

Her small smile deletes. "Forget it, dumb joke," she says, and she leaves so quickly for the restroom that her chair makes a 270-degree rotation afterward.

I take the subway to the Museum of Modern Art after work to utilize my free access as a Schrub employee. The business section of *The New York Times* is on the plastic subway seat next to me, and I read about a merger on Tuesday between two start-up companies that raised their stock. A merger is similar to a mutually beneficial trade, although of course there is no way an investor could know about it before it occurs without insider trading.

But possibly there is a way to predict news like this without insider trading. E.g., what if I can decipher that a merger or another major transaction will take place, via public data, and then predict if the stock will rise or plummet? Dan performed normal research for his trade, but all financial workers do this for stocks and companies, so it is difficult to gain an advantage. I can merely hope my research is the most accurate.

My brain continues to evaluate this idea as I walk through the museum exhibits. The paintings of the Dutchman Piet Mondrian intrigue me, as they look like city streets, and one of his famous paintings is titled *New York City*. His lines are perfectly straight like geometric Islamic designs and would extend infinitely if the frames did not restrict them.

Then I enter an exhibit on the American Jackson Pollock. At first I do not enjoy his paintings. They are too chaotic and have no logic and organization like Mondrian's. I could have painted the same thing, and so could many other painters, only Pollock was the originator and therefore he receives all the kudos. Paintings of this class make me feel like I do not understand why people appreciate visual art.

But then I see some quotations by Pollock about his paintings, such as: "I don't use the accident—'cause I deny the accident." And I reevaluate that possibly Pollock's paintings have more value, because he has a philosophy similar to mine, which is that life is ultimately predictable. Many people believe it is science that controls life or Allah or some other spiritual energy, and in my opinion also we do not have true free will, e.g., my conscious decisions are the product of my neurons and not my will as an independent agent. Therefore, the variables that appear to be chaotic in fact exist in the environment for us to collect and analyze and make predictions from. This is how many systems function, like the weather, and, although some people believe it is impossible, the stock market.

When I was 11, my friend Raghid kicked a soccer ball through the window of our elderly neighbor Mamdouh's apartment. All the other children, including Raghid, ran away, which upset me since my team required only one more goal to win. But I forgot about the score and remained because the pieces of glass on the ground looked like icicles, which I previously saw photographs of exclusively, and I studied their shapes for several minutes as well as the patterns of cracks in the window that looked like spiderwebs and the parallels between the cracks and the arrangement of glass on the ground, and that is how Mamdouh detected me. My father commanded me to labor at the store until I could pay for the window. He knew I hated laboring there. I frequently complained as a child that it was too small for me to run around in, and when I was older it always bothered me how disorganized the items were.

I said it was not my fault. He asked who kicked the ball. Raghid's family was poorer than ours, so I said I kicked it. But I also innovated a clever explanation: I argued that because events are predetermined as Qadar in Al-Lauh Al-Mahfuz, where Allah writes all that has happened and will happen, it means that it was not truly my fault.

My father said that everything we do belongs to Allah and to us equally. He also said something that I have always remembered, because I read later that it was a strategic technique for parents, as it makes the child want to enhance his behavior, and I used it with Zahira on the few occasions when she did not perform well in school.

"I am not angry with you," he said. "I am disappointed."

Then he made me labor twice as long at the store so I could not only repay for the broken window but also buy new Korans for both Mamdouh and me.

But merely because something is predictable and destined does not mean it is logical outside the world of numbers, e.g., a scientist with infinite resources could have predicted my mother's breast cancer by analyzing her biological properties and her environment, but she was not personally responsible at all for becoming unhealthy, even though my father argued we are responsible for everything.

In the museum there is another Pollock quotation that intrigues me even more: "My paintings do not have a center, but depend on the same amount of interest throughout." I read it just after I notice that it is difficult to focus on his paintings.

And then I have an idea, and although the typical image to represent having an idea is a lightbulb powering on, for me I visualize the stars slowly becoming visible in the nighttime sky, because (1) like a strong idea they were always present; but (2) it requires the correct conditions to observe them; and (3) make connections between them. My idea is: I can use Pollock's ideas about denying the accident and about there being no center for a stock market program. Everyone else who writes programs to predict the stock market concentrates on the most central variables and incorporates a few minor ones. But what if I utilize variables that no one observes because they seem tangential, and I utilize *exclusively* these tangential variables? I would have an advantage like Dan had in his fantasy baseball trade, where he used tangential data instead of central data. And because I am a tangential foreign banker in the U.S., possibly I will have a greater chance of locating these tangential data, e.g., as a parallel, because I am not a native English speaker I must pay closer attention to its grammar, and therefore I detected the error Dan made that most Americans also make when he used "data" as a singular noun.

And possibly I will predict events that other people consider random accidents.

On Saturday morning I have my first opportunity to call Zahira when I am not too taxed and she is still awake.

"Karim!" she says. "I was wondering when you would call."

She is probably in our living room, next to the window that overviews our courtyard and the other apartments, and sitting on the brown cotton couch which we have had since I was a child and whose material needs to be repaired.

"I have been very busy. And I have emailed you," I say.

"Yes, but that is not the same. It is nice to hear your voice."

It is nice to hear hers as well. She does not remember it, but her voice sounds like our mother's: clear but soft and loud simultaneously, like warm water poured over your head. I ask her how she is performing in school, and she tells me about her biology class. It pleases me that she is engaged although I do not understand most of the jargon terms and ideas and cannot respond, except when she discusses viruses, as I mostly self-taught computers by studying viruses at night for a year when I was 18, and I was always the employee at the Doha branch who healed viruses. Biological viruses are of course not perfectly equivalent to computer viruses, but they share some theoretical similarities, and I find it intriguing that they are all self-replicating, as if they have their own brains, and it is dependent on my brain to contain and destroy them.

"Certify that after you finish your introductory quantitative analysis course you first take microeconomics, as it is important to understand individual motivation, and then macroeconomics for the big-picture view," I say.

"I know," Zahira says. "You have told me a million times."

"And if you enhance your English, we can converse in it more frequently."

In English, she says, "You tell me one million times."

"You *have told* me *a* million times," I say. "But I can tell you are studying idioms. If you read and practice as much as I do, your skills will broaden."

I talk about the airplane and the ways midtown reminds me of Al Dafna and the West Bay, and how rapidly people walk when transferring subways, especially the professional females, and that everyone's aggregated earphones in the subway sound like machines striking metal. I inventory my apartment: a high-end television and stereo; a quality couch of black leather; a bed that could contain three of my bodies; a silver refrigerator of spacious storage capacity; a white carpet that feels like a horse's hair; a square black table with four chairs; and an invisible glass coffee table that is elegant although when I arrived I did not observe it and crashed my knee on it.

She makes jokes that amuse only us, e.g., when I tell her how efficient the subways are and she says, "I would like to see Aunt Maysaa on the subway. She would complain even if it transported her from one station to another instantly."

I say, "And if it paid *her* money as well."

She adds, "And if the conductor told her she was the most important passenger."

We find similar concepts humorous, although she produces jokes at a greater and more successful rate. Business manuals explain how valuable it is to have a sense of humor, so I am studying how others produce jokes, such as making a statement that is clearly the reverse of what you truly mean and using a tone of voice that indicates the reversal. But it is not a natural response for me, minus sometimes with Zahira, and I am unskilled at intentionally adjusting my voice.

"I am working on a prototype of a program for the stock market that I will soon present to a superior at Schrub," I say.

I explain the concept, and how it employs complex algorithms, which are parallel to instructions or a recipe. Although she does not have my math or finance skills, she is intelligent enough to decipher the main idea.

"I am certain it will be successful," she says.

"Why?" I ask. "I have not completed the program yet."

Then she says what I always said to her when she was in school and was having difficulty with an assignment: "Because you are very smart and you labor very hard, and if it is possible to achieve, then you are the person to achieve it."

"Where did you learn that idea?" I ask.

"From a stupid person I know."

It is the class of joke she produces rapidly which takes me longer to think of, if I even do think of it.

She asks if I want to speak to our father. I pause, then tell her to transfer the telephone. Zahira yells for my father. In a minute he greets me.

"You have been away a week without any calls," he says.

Without attempting, I convert to the voice people use when speaking to an automated telephone menu. "As I told Zahira, I emailed immediately to inform you I arrived safely, and the time difference makes it difficult to call during the weekdays."

"Your sister was worried," he says.

The windows in my apartment have a partial overview of Times Square. At the top of the chief building is a neon-green Schrub logo of the hawk transporting the *S* and *E* in its two feet, with a thin horizontal monitor like an electronic ticker tape that displays a scrolling font of news, e.g., METS TAKE 2–1 DIVISION SERIES LEAD . . . YANKS LOOK TO SWEEP RANGERS . . . The monitor travels around all four sides of the building so that it is visible from every direction. It is enjoyable to watch the words angle around the corners.

"I will contact her more, but she is also very busy with her schoolwork," I say.

"Her work is not so important that she cannot take a few minutes off."

My hand tightens on the cellular and I walk in a rectangle around the white carpet. "I would not know about regular university courses. I know only about the nighttime courses I paid for myself."

He is mute for several seconds, then he says, "I have to leave for the mosque. I hope you have not been too busy so far with work to find one near you."

I tell him I have been to one already, and we disconnect. I spend the rest of the weekend working on my program and thinking about what Zahira said. If it can be achieved, then I have faith that I possess the skills to do it.

book it = make a transaction official

genuflect = angle the knees into a position for prayer

kudos = praise

minor league = inferior level of play in baseball; also applicable to
   other skill sets

piggyback = add on to previous work

pod(mate) = workstation (workstation coworkers)

privy to = have access to

scintillating = stimulating

vassal = inferior worker in the feudal system

you was robbed = usage of incorrect second person to indicate an
   unsound transaction

I stay up late Monday and Tuesday nights programming and email Zahira a longer description of my program. It is difficult to translate into words what is a very rigorous mathematical process, but it is still like scanning a Pollock painting. There are so many layers and colors and patterns of paint that it is impossible for an art critic to analyze all of them, just as there are so many data in and surrounding the stock market even for a computer program to evaluate, and in fact it does not help the program to evaluate *all* the data, because then it does not know *which* layers, colors, and patterns of data are truly important. So other programs typically weight the obvious variables more, but because they are all using them, they produce similar results.

My program magnifies variables that I believe other programs are underutilizing and creates links between these and other variables that do not seem to relate. It is like scanning one minimal corner of a Pollock painting and studying only that corner carefully, and then scanning another partition of the painting somewhere, or even another painting, or data from Pollock's life, and discovering how the different partitions of data are equal or different. Then the program repeats this comparison with more partitions and more paintings, which computers are of course more efficient at than humans are.

While I labor on the project, I power on the television in the background. I watch financial shows whenever possible, but I also watch the baseball games. I am not very interested in the game itself, but the analysts converse nonstop, so it is beneficial for my English. Each night at midnight I see a long advertisement for a machine called Steve Winslow's Juicinator that produces juice out of vegetables and fruits. By the third night I can remember and predict what Steve Winslow will say, such as: **(1)** "This juice has powerful, all-natural antioxidants"; **(2)** "It's made with high-quality, durable plastic that will outlast you"; **(3)** "It's not a blender; it's not a juicer; it's a Juicinator"; and **(4)** "If I didn't believe in it, I wouldn't put my name on it." On Wednesday night I buy the juicer, as I do not eat enough fruits and vegetables here, and because it is durable it will survive for many years and retain its value.

Late on Tuesday night my program reaches an average of +2.0 percentage points above market returns in tests, which means it is a positive investment risk. I stay up until Wednesday morning writing a short report on my program and explaining its benefits. It is challenging to write something in English that a native speaker will read, but most of it is mathematical and financial jargon terms, which I am more comfortable with, such as:

> The model can be interpreted probabilistically, so it can derive error bounds on estimates. Then it runs secondary simulations, with different possible values. Then it creates agents that model activities of major players in the market . . .

I notice I use many words that the baseball analysts frequently say, e.g., in this section: "error," "runs," "agents," and "players," which is logical, since baseball is partially what helped me conceive this idea and is also a system of independent players and actions and laws that people like Dan attempt to predict.

On Wednesday I wait until Jefferson is alone in the office kitchen and tell him about my program and show him my report and ask which superior I can give it to. He scans the pages for a few minutes.

"You've coded it pretty good, but it's a little Karim-esque," Jefferson says, "in that it's littered with grammatical errors." I want to tell him that I rarely make grammatical errors and that I merely have problems with idioms, and that his last sentence in fact contained a critical grammatical error, but he is helping me, so I nod. "If you like, I can clean up the writing for you and submit it to a higher-up I know in quants." I thank him and ask him to keep these data private.

"*This* data," he says. I merely nod again.

I return to my pod and try not to think about the potential success of my program, because it is unhealthy to speculate before it has even been accepted, but whenever I make an advance in my career I recall what my mother said to me once when she was in the hospital. It must have been a few months after I turned 12, because she was not yet attached to the machine that breathed for her and was still strong enough to talk for long periods of time. Also, they still permitted Zahira to visit her. At the end my parents decided Zahira shouldn't see her in that condition, so only my father and I went and she stayed with our aunt and uncle. After our visits, he always exited to their bedroom alone and closed the door, and I had to tell Zahira about the visit. The doctors advised me to lie to her and say that our mother merely had to go away for a long time, and although possibly that lie would have protected Zahira's feelings more, that is one area of life people should never lie about. In addition, she was very smart even then and understood what was happening.

But I remember Zahira was there, because she had to use the restroom, and my father left my mother's room with her to find a nurse. When the door closed behind them, my mother sat up in the bed. I thought she was going to ask me to retrieve her some water, as she frequently did. But she said, "Karim, if I ask you to promise me something, will you always honor it?"

I moved around in my chair and wished a nurse would return, but I said yes.

"When I—" she said. "I want you to take care of Zahira."

"I always take care of her," I said.

She shook her head. "I want you to be the one who takes care of her. *You*. Do you understand?"

I quickly looked at the closed door. "I understand," I said.

"And although you may not see why now, I also want you to look after your father," she said.

I said I understood again, but I didn't 100%. Then my father returned and we discussed something else.

Zahira is fortunate to grow up as a female now in Qatar instead of one or two decades ago, but if she lacks sufficient funds then it limits her options, and I will not be honoring my promise to my mother.

antioxidants = substances that restrict cancer; found in juice
higher-up = superior in a pyramidal hierarchy
juicer = device that produces juice
Karim-esque = representative of Karim
littered with = filled with

On Thursday I am nervous to ask Jefferson if he has heard from his contact in quants, and he does not mention it or email me about it. At the end of the day he and Dan discuss where to go that night.

"What's wrong with Haven?" Dan asks.

"The patrons are morons," Jefferson says. "And ugly, to boot."

Dan deposits one hand in his pocket and pets the back of his head with the other. "Fine, we'll go to Scorch." He detects me looking at them, which is impolite of me, but when they are conversing so loudly it is natural to pay attention. "We only have space for a couple of guys on the list. But we'll get you another time."

After they leave, Rebecca focuses on her monitor while she speaks to me. "You're not missing out on anything, by the way," she says. "They're hoping some vapid Alpha Phis will be impressed by the fact that they spent $400 for a bottle of vodka and two seats at a table in a room full of date-rapists."

I do not want to spend $400 on seats, but there are some areas of life I would like to observe in New York that are challenging to experience in Doha, e.g., alcohol and females. The few times I have gone with my coworkers and foreign businessmen to hotel nightclubs where they serve alcohol, I restrict myself to a maximum of one drink, although my coworkers consume more than that, and they dance with foreign females and sometimes leave with them. Three months ago a female banker from Jordan sat next to me as I ordered my drink. After we talked briefly about her work, she moved slightly closer to me and said, "I am staying in the hotel by myself for three nights."

Her face was highly symmetrical, and under her business suit her body had a pleasing shape, and she smelled like a garden. But she was two years younger than I was, and I could not stop considering that she was someone's daughter, or possibly sister, and I negated the temptation. To be polite I bought her drinks for the duration of the night, and before I left I told her I found her insights into the cultural contrasts between Jordan and Qatar intriguing, especially about how the two countries treat females (Jordan is more advanced, although I noted that Qatari females do possess some rights that are forbidden in many countries in the Middle East, e.g., driving).

My Doha coworkers never discuss these nights afterward, which is unlike Jefferson and Dan, who frequently enter the office in the morning and analyze their actions from the previous night as if it were a sports event. Typically Jefferson succeeds and Dan fails.

On Friday afternoon Jefferson still has not said anything to me about the program, and I cannot wait any longer and email him even though he is next to me. He replies:

> Sorry, I meant to shoot you an email before. They said they already have similar programs that outperform the market by 3-4%, so they're going to pass. Better luck next time?

I stare at the monitor until all the words become blended. I do not know why I thought I could write a program that is more advanced than what workers with MBAs and advanced computer science degrees and broader experience can produce. I am merely self-taught and without a true university education and have only one year of experience at Schrub. It was a waste of energy.

I also will now look foolish when Zahira asks me about the project.

On Saturday I do not know what to do with myself, as I do not feel like programming because I have no new ideas, and my ideas are inferior and unoriginal anyway. Therefore, I go to the office, because at least I can be productive there, as my work does not require any creativity and it is the solitary role I can be efficient in.

The WTC is peaceful when I enter. There is no receptionist, but a few coworkers whose names I do not know are in the office. So is Rebecca.

She explains she missed some work recently because she was out of town and is compensating by logging extra hours today.

"Where did you go?" I ask, but then I regret it because I do not want to be too investigative and sometimes people have private reasons.

She says she visited her brother David at a university I have not heard of in the state of Missouri. "It's his first year, and he's sort of having a rough time."

"Is that where you attended university?"

"That's what it says on my student loans," she says. "Well, technically, it doesn't actually say the name."

Tuition in Doha is comparatively inexpensive, and since I did not attend authentic university my education was even more discounted. "I am glad that Zahira will not be indebted," I say. Rebecca does not respond, so I ask, "Do your parents live in Missouri?"

She opens up a spreadsheet and begins entering data. "My mother lives in Wisconsin, a few hours away," she says. I do not ask where her father lives.

In the early afternoon Rebecca invites me to partner with her for a coffee break. The coffee in the office is free, but it is not high quality, so we leave the building and locate a nearby Starbucks.

We do not converse much in the elevator or as we walk to the Starbucks or on line for the coffee vendor, even though we have to brainstorm frequently about programming roadblocks when we labor. I am a strong communicator in team situations for problem solving, but I am not as expert in conversing about nonproblems, and I think Rebecca is also deficient in this area. Jefferson has mastery over it and modifies his conversation when he networks in the office. I can converse merely in one mode, which is a skill set I must enhance to grow as a business leader.

I am relieved when it is our turn with the female vendor with pink hair. Rebecca orders a complex coffee, and I order a regular coffee without milk. The vendor informs us of the cost, which makes me question if it is worth buying premium coffee over receiving subpar coffee for free. Rebecca opens her purse.

I remove my wallet. "It is my gift."

"Don't be silly," Rebecca says as she searches in the purse, which contains numerous objects and papers and even smaller purses.

"I am not being silly," I say. "I want to purchase this."

I hand the vendor a $50 bill, which is the only denomination I possess at the time, and Rebecca closes her purse and does not say anything.

We sit at a table as the song "Believe" by Cher plays. Its frequency is high in Doha as well.

Rebecca tells me this is her third year at Schrub, and it is her first job she acquired after college even though in university she studied history with minimal studies in economics and computer science.

"I'm competent, but I wasn't really born to number-crunch or code," Rebecca says.

"Would you prefer a job incorporating history rather than economics and computers?" I ask.

"I guess maybe teaching, someday."

"Why do you not pursue it now?"

She raises and lowers her shoulders and drinks her coffee and scans the room.

"You should pursue what you want to pursue," I say.

"Yeah, well, you can't always get what you want." She laughs, but to herself and quietly. "And if you try sometimes, you just might find you get fucked over even worse." Then she consumes a long drink and says she should get back to the office.

I follow her, and outside she retrieves a cigarette pack from her purse and smokes. We do not talk at all as we reenter the WTC. I think she is upset with me because I sounded like I believe I am better at my job since it is closer to my career goals. I disagree with her statement, however. When people start believing they cannot get what they want, they trash their original goals and settle for smaller ones.

We pass the coffeepot in the office, and Rebecca refills her cup from Starbucks, removes a small purse from her bigger purse and extracts one quarter, two dimes, and one nickel as if she is performing surgery and removing tumors, and deposits them in the vending machine for a bag of potato chips, and I understand she is not upset because of my previous hypothesis, but because she thinks I am wealthy, because (1) I said Zahira does not have loans without explaining it is because tuition is discounted in Qatar; (2) I paid for our coffee with a $50 bill; (3) I said she should do whatever job she wants without considering the salaries; and also possibly because (4) Qatar has a high GDP per capita.

I feel so humiliated that I do not know how to apologize to Rebecca for it, and we spend the rest of the day laboring with minimal conversation and leave independently.

On Sunday morning I again do not know what to do, and I do not want to reencounter Rebecca at the office. I consider calling relatives of my family's friends, but they will ask me about my job and I do not want to discuss it now.

I would like to go to a Broadway play or a classy restaurant, but I prefer to conserve money, and also I do not have anyone to partner with. So I take the subway to explore the neighborhoods downtown. In Chelsea I observe a few art galleries, although I do not enjoy the paintings in them as much as the ones in the Museum of Modern Art, probably because I do not understand them as well, and it is difficult to enjoy a system you are not competent in. In the early night I walk through Little Italy and then Chinatown.

It begins raining lightly, so I enter a restaurant and order vegetarian dumplings. As I wait for my food at a small square table next to the window, a Chinese family with one grandmother, two parents, and five children eats at a round table next to me. They slightly parallel the one quarter, two dimes, and one nickel Rebecca deposited in the vending machine. Their table is littered with steaming bowls and plates of noodles and vegetables and meats. They are all conversing with each other, and of course I cannot decipher what they are saying, but even if we spoke the same language I think I would not 100% decipher it, because frequently families have their own mode of speaking, e.g., my father usually does not understand what Zahira and I are saying.

Out the window the blue and red lights mirror on the wet black street. In a few hours Zahira and my father will eat their breakfast of bread with labneh, olives, and yogurt.

When the waiter deposits the dumplings on my table, I ask him to contain them so I can consume at home.

In my apartment I watch the other New York baseball team, the Mets, play against the Atlanta Braves in a playoff game. I permit myself to microwave and eat one dumpling every 1.5 innings as I study the game's internal logic. It enters overtime, and when I stretch my neck I see the Schrub monitor outside and a scrolling news item:

FRENCH EMBASSY BOMBED IN IRAN . . . NO CASUALTIES . . . SEVERAL INJURED . . .

I search other channels for additional data, but no one is discussing the bomb, not even the all-news channels. Finally I find a short report on the Internet that says a terrorist group in Iran "claimed responsibility." This phrase intrigues me, as I know only the phrase "take responsibility." I perform an Internet search: "terrorist" + "claimed responsibility" has six times more hits than "terrorist" + "took responsibility." Possibly that is because when a person commits an error but confesses to it for forgiveness, he "takes" responsibility. When he is boastful of his actions, he "claims" responsibility.

I walk around my living room as the Mets game continues. Everyone in the stadium is anxious about the game, which now seems to me foolish, although I understand why it impacts them. The Mets win with a home run, and at 11:30 p.m. I make a telephone call.

Zahira picks up on the first ring and says she has a few minutes to talk before she leaves for school. I tell her I merely called to say hello.

"What happened with your computer program?" she asks.

I look at my laptop that I have not even booted up today. "It is turbulent now in the stock market, so I decided it is not a strategic time to present a new program to my higher-ups."

"You sounded very optimistic about it before," she says.

"Yes, but sometimes the risks are greater than the possible rewards, and you must certify that a new idea is 100% foolproof before you launch it." She does not say anything. "Anyway, I am doing very well at Schrub overall and am making a great amount of money and friends."

"You have made friends at work?"

"Yes," I say.

"Have you socialized with anyone yet?"

"I recently had coffee with one coworker. And two others told me they will invite me next time they go to a nightclub."

She pauses. "That is good," she says. "But you should call our friends' relatives if you need to meet other people from the Middle East."

"I will, but I am satisfied with my current social network," I say.

I do not need to ask if she is making friends at university, because she emailed me that she has, and also she typically makes friends with ease. She has our mother's skill set for that.

She says she will put me on with my father before he leaves for work. "Take care, Zahira," I say.

I am uncertain if she hears me, because then my father is on the telephone. I ask him if he has heard the news about Iran yet. He has not, and I explain the situation and tell him that the news said a terrorist group in Iran has claimed responsibility. "You should not believe everything you hear on the news in the U.S.," he says.

"Why do you say that? Do you think they are lying about the attack?"

"No," he says. "But they call them a terrorist group. You do not know what this group stands for. They do not define themselves as terrorists. To them, the French government is a terrorist group."

"Yes, but the French government is not bombing civilians," I say.

"No, they have simply colonized other countries for centuries and oppress Algerians in their own country."

"Where are you getting these ideas from?" I ask.

"Just because I labor in a store does not mean I do not read, Karim."

"I did not say you do not read," I say. "I asked where you are getting these ideas."

"From newspapers that are not about money and computers and are not published in the U.S." Then he adds, "You should read one sometime."

The sounds of people celebrating and cars honking in the street because of the Mets victory rise all the way up to my apartment.

"I have to go to sleep for work tomorrow," I say.

We disconnect, and I consume my final dumpling, but its skin is now cold and has little flavor and I do not feel like microwaving it. The cars continue honking outside, and I open my window and lean my head out and shout for them to be quiet in Arabic, but of course it achieves nothing.

Alpha Phi = a social group for university females

claim responsibility = take responsibility for an event others view as a negative but that you are boastful of

date-rapist = a man who forces a female he knows into sexual activity

number-crunch = make intensive calculations

shoot an email = send an email, especially about business

to boot = in addition

vapid = non-stimulating

On Monday at the office I am even more quiet than average, which is nearly mute because on average I converse exclusively when someone first consults with me or if I have an urgent query.

During lunch, Dan reads *The New York Times* on the computer while he eats the Indian chicken tikka masala he orders daily and Jefferson scans baseball statistics.

"You hear about this French embassy bombing in Iran?" Dan asks. "*Times* says a splinter terrorist cell took responsibility and vows more attacks. This shit's not even front-page news, that's how common it is. Why don't they just incinerate their whole uncivilized backwater country and jack up gas prices even more?" He looks quickly at me. "No offense, Karim."

"I am not from Iran," I say.

"I know," he says. "I didn't mean anything by it." Then he asks Jefferson about the fantasy baseball production of a player named Yoshii. Jefferson owns all the Japanese players.

In a few minutes I receive an email:

Sender: Rebecca A. Goldman <r.goldman@schrubequities.com>
Recipient: Karim Issar <k.issar@schrubequities.com>
Date: Mon, 18 Oct 1999 12:26:18
Subject: Dan is a . . .

. . . jackass. (Not front-page news, either.)

After I research the word "jackass," I smile at her. She reciprocates, and I feel enhanced, as we have had restricted conversation since our coffee meeting.

And then I have another mental image of the stars at night.

I research today's crude oil futures ASAP. They have risen 77 cents. That is expected because of the news.

I use the search engine on *The New York Times* and input the phrase "Middle East." It lists all the articles from the last 14 days about the Middle East. Of course, it is not always about terrorist attacks or war, e.g., the articles typically discuss government leaders meeting or business negotiations or other events that are nonviolent. I note which days the phrase appears most frequently, and how many times it appears. Then I correlate those days to the crude oil futures prices of that day or the next day.

Although I am not making intensive calculations, I think I see a correlation between how frequently *The New York Times* discusses the Middle East and the fluctuations of oil futures.

I input the names of specific countries, e.g., Saudi Arabia, Iran, United Arab Emirates, Kuwait, Iraq, and Qatar, which only produces approximately 0.5 million barrels per day, but that is a great amount for its small size.

The correlations appear stronger.

Schrub has a subscription to a service that scans all the major U.S. newspapers. I log in and input the country names again for the last 14 days.

The correlations appear very strong.

"Karim, want to do me a major-league favor?" Jefferson asks.

Whenever he asks if I want to do him a major-league favor it means he wants me to repair a glitch that he has caused himself.

I close up the windows about oil prices. I should not be laboring independently on company time anyway.

The remainder of the day I cannot contain my stimulation. Before Dan and Jefferson leave, they converse about a nightclub they are going to that is providing free tequila to promote its launch. This time I am careless.

Then Rebecca leaves, and I am free to labor on my project.

I can now utilize spreadsheets and other programs to determine if the correlations are accurate, and broaden my newspaper search to 60 days for additional coverage.

1. First, I decide that not every expression of a country's name is equally integral, e.g., "Iran AND bomb" has more influence than "Qatar AND diplomatic talks."

2. So I begin by employing a boosting algorithm that weights specific words, which I perform by reverse-correlation, so that I see what days the oil prices moved most sharply and then determine what keywords ignited their movement. "Terrorism" and "terrorist" are heavily weighted, of course, and so are "war" and "attack" and "gunfire" and similar terms. Words like "unrest" and "protest" and "demonstration" are in another class, and words like "treaty" and "diplomatic talks" are also in a different class. Also integral is that some words are important exclusively in pairs or in longer phrases, e.g., "white" and "house" mean little independently, but "White House" is critical. Words have elastic meanings from their context.

   A. When a word or phrase proves that it has high predictive abilities, the algorithm boosts its weight.

   B. The names of the countries and cities that produce more oil and are more volatile also have different weights.

    C. More recent articles weigh more.

    D. Although logic predicts certain actions, such as a terrorist attack, *always* raise the price, this is not true, as it depends on a constellation of variables, and in a few instances an attack actually lowers prices.

3. But because the algorithm is automated and it analyzes *every* word in an article, it also selects many words that I think no one else would pay attention to, such as "bitter" and "weary" and "resigned," as in this sentence: "The Prime Minister, after a round of bitter questioning, appeared weary and resigned." I think these kinds of words can in fact be more important because:

    A. By the time a bombing has occurred, e.g., everyone knows about it and they can predict what will happen to oil prices and they act accordingly.

    B. But fewer people read about a politician appearing weary and resigned after receiving bitter questions.

    C. A few people do read it, however, and they begin acting in a predictable way; then a few more people follow their lead, and more and more, until it becomes as if everyone *did* read it, even though they did not.

4. I can aid the automated algorithm by examining articles manually, and as someone whose native language is not English, I must pay closer attention to the words to produce logic from them, and sometimes I observe things others do not about English.

5. Therefore, if I can collect enough data like this, I can gain a major advantage over others who are merely using obvious data that are front-page news.

Because this central idea is truly an analog to scanning un-observed partitions of a Pollock painting, I am able to piggy-back it onto my previous program. I also link it to the newspaper search engine. It is taxing (although it takes less time because of the previous program), but it is the class of labor I enjoy.

The nighttime janitor cleans as I program, and when I give her my trash bin, it is the solitary time I look away from my monitor.

In fact, only when I am nearly finished and my cursor is on the word "casualties" do I evaluate the big picture of what I am creating. When violence occurs, especially in the Middle East, my program will attempt to leverage it for financial gain. But this violence will happen with or without my program. Therefore, by making money, the program produces at least some positives from a very negative situation. It turns the violence into a zero-sum game, because the money and violence cancel each other out, instead of producing exclusively a negative game.

I decide to complete the program.

I finally stop near 3:30 a.m., and I notice I have been alone for several hours and I have not eaten dinner. I am not even that hungry, but I purchase an apple from a vending machine. Typically when I am programming like this at home, Zahira forces me to consume food because I forget.

My program is finally functional, although I do not know how accurate it is until it sifts historical data. I direct it to use data from the last six months and to make oil futures predictions on each day as if it were truly that day.

It will have to number-crunch overnight, so I leave my computer on but turn my monitor off and open a spreadsheet so others will not identify the true labor of the computer, and then I go home and wait until the morning to discover if my program is successful.

backwater = an unimportant or unsophisticated location

incinerate = burn down

jack up = inflate prices

jackass = stupid person; Dan

major-league favor = significant favor

I do not sleep the entire night. At 6:00 a.m. I get out of bed and decide to go to a mosque, as that is a profitable destination when my brain is overstimulated, and my program at work will not be ready until probably 8:30 a.m. The other mosques near my office and apartment are adequate, but it is time for me to visit the chief mosque in New York.

I take the subway to the Islamic Cultural Center on the Upper East Side. It is as attractive as I have read, with a dome and Turkish architecture that resembles the Hagia Sophia with sharper lines.

The prayer hall has tall glass windows and pure white walls and hanging cords creating a circle with lights attached to the end, like an inverted birthday cake with candles. There are no columns inside, and the dome is simple but elegant, and the patterns on the carpet have a complex repeating pattern. This is what I want my programming to have: mathematical precision that is also beautiful. As a parallel, Jackson Pollock's paintings are beautiful even though they are not precise, but by being so imprecise they are also in a way precise.

Half of the men are black, and in one corner men in robes read the Koran together. I consider partnering with them, but I want to be alone with my prayers now.

Once I begin praying I do forget about my program. It is as if saying words to Allah mutes all the calculations and ideas that are making noise inside my head and transports me to the spiritual world that is non-numbered, and performing the actions I have performed thousands of times reminds me of my body, which is also non-numbered, which is why I also enjoy racquetball.

After an hour I am recharged. On the subway to work I observe all the businessmen reading *The Wall Street Journal* who are trying to find ways to decipher the stock market. Maybe I have done so with oil futures.

Jefferson said Schrub's programs yield 3–4% above market returns for yearly returns. So I hope to gain 5% above market returns on oil futures based on historical data, with minimal risk. This will mean a minimal average daily return above market, approximately 0.02%, but it is like the way a child becomes taller: You do not observe daily growth.

My podmates are not in yet. My hands vibrate slightly as I approach my desk and power on my monitor.

I close the spreadsheet window above my program. There are many numbers on the monitor, and I still need to do some calculations to receive the final results.

For overnight predictions, which means the user trades immediately in the morning and trades again at the end of the workday, my program correctly predicts the converted price of oil futures on that day within a 12% error, e.g., if oil rises $1, then 68% of the time my program predicts that prices will rise between 88 cents and $1.12. On the historical data, this means its average daily profit on oil futures is 1.1%.

There must be an error, so I reenter the calculations.

It is again 1.1%.

I try to sit very still although I am vibrating even more. I will not say anything about this yet before I know it truly works. I cannot risk humiliating myself again.

Dan enters the pod, so I reopen the spreadsheet window in case he sees the program, although he will not understand what it is. He turns on his monitor. His computer has been downloading music overnight without paying for it. He does that frequently, which is not only illegal normally but is even more illegal to do at work. The current song is titled "Mashup—Livin' La Beasta Burden (Livin' La Vida Loca vs. Beast of Burden)."

An error range of 12% is impressive, but I must refine the program to gain even higher average returns and minimize risk. I cannot resist, and I start recoding a section.

"What are you slaving away at?" Rebecca asks.

I am so focused on my work that I did not hear her enter and I left the program observable. Rebecca might understand it more than Dan and Jefferson do.

I consider revealing my project to her. But there is no way to do it quietly without Dan and Jefferson hearing, and they would understand the idea when translated to English.

In addition I am afraid she will again think I am interested exclusively in money.

"It is only some number-crunching," I say, and close the windows.

Later in the day Rebecca strikes her hand on her keyboard. "Fucking machine," she says quietly.

"Are you having a technical issue?" I ask.

"Yes, I'm having a technical issue. How'd you guess, Karim?" she says. Then she adds, "Ignore me. It's not your fault. I'm just having a hard time dealing right now."

She explains that there is a virus in a spreadsheet she has been working on for several hours which prevents her from accessing it.

"I have some experience with viruses," I say.

First I quarantine the document in our pod's recycle bin, which is stored on a separate drive, so that it cannot impact any other important documents. It is a class of virus I am familiar with, so I approximately know how to proceed.

But as I fix it, I notice a document in the recycle bin: "market prediction.doc." It must be Jefferson's refined version of my first program proposal. I open it.

The document looks similar to what I gave Jefferson although with slightly enhanced language, but the end does not include my name, as I originally wrote. In fact, it does not include anyone's name.

I define two possible theories: (1) At Schrub New York it is considered unprofessional to include your name at the bottom of a proposal, and Jefferson told the higher-up (whose name I read is George Ray) that I was the programmer, or (2) Jefferson claimed responsibility for my program and pretended it was his.

I decide it is the first, as ultimately Jefferson could not claim responsibility because he would have to come to me for the program, unless he was skilled enough to decipher and recreate it from my proposal, but I do not think he possesses sufficient skills.

After several minutes I heal the virus and return it to Rebecca. Healing a virus is a delightful feeling, especially when you do it for someone else, because they previously thought their file was corrupt and lost but now it is healthy and accessible.

"It's funny how you only seem to lose data that you really need, and not, like, idiotic joke emails your mom forwards you," she says. "I owe you big-time."

"You do not owe me anything," I say. "We are coworkers, and coworkers are parallel to family members in that you do not incur debts."

She looks at me with a strange expression. Then she says, "Okay. You're a lifesaver, though. Thanks." She contacts my shoulder as she says this, and then she retracts her hand as if she touched a hot stove. This is the first time she has contacted me.

I want to tell her that I do not 100% agree with all rules of Islam, and that some of them are in fact impossible to fulfill while in a modern workplace, e.g., technically Rebecca and I are not permitted to be alone, and the only conversation we are allowed to have must be humorless (which is not difficult for me, because I am always humorless, but Rebecca enjoys producing jokes).

But I do not know how to explain this without making us both more uncomfortable, so I merely say, "You are welcome."

At home I refine my program until it attains 8% error range. On historical data, it averages daily profits of approximately 1.3%.

This does not sound like much, but over 20 business days 1.3% daily profits means that investing $1,000 in a futures contract on the first day, then using that new money to invest in another futures contract the next day, will yield by the end of the month $1,295. Of course, you are not guaranteed to make money each day, but this is a potential outcome: 29.5% monthly profits.

And Schrub can invest much more than $1,000.

I rewrite my proposal to incorporate the new data, which takes a few hours. It is still not perfect English. I am about to shoot Jefferson an email again for help, but I stop. What if he did try to take responsibility before? This new idea is more secretive to boot. I could ask Rebecca, but I do not think she has access to the right people in quants.

Therefore, I decide to contact George Ray myself, except I am still uncertain if the program works, and I may look foolish again. But now I see my first program was too safe and conventional, and even if my program does not function, it is an ambitious idea, and I would prefer to fail with a big-picture idea than succeed on a small scale.

I email him:

Sender: Karim Issar <k.issar@schrubequities.com>
Recipient: George B. Ray <g.ray@schrubequities.com>
Date: Tue, 19 Oct 1999 22:23:06
Subject: 2nd proposal
Mr. Ray, I understand the previous quants program I created that Jefferson Smithfield showed you as a favor for me was not robust enough to risk investment. I have a new program that I believe works more efficiently. It is yielding 1.30% daily profits in tests. My proposal is attached.

Then I begin the copyright process for my program with the Library of Congress.

I do not expect to hear from him for at least a few days, but one hour later I receive a reply:

You mean 0.13% daily profits?

I write:

No, it is 1.30%.

He replies once more:

Meet me in the conference room on 89 tomorrow at 8:30.

I reread that sentence five times. It is the happiest I have been so far in New York.

have a hard time dealing = have difficulty managing life
lifesaver = someone who helps another person in a significant mode
slave away at = labor diligently for

The layout of floor 89 is equivalent to 88, and the receptionist who wears makeup that looks like mud on her cheeks guides me to the conference room. Then she exits, and I sit alone in the room, which has dark blue walls and a projection monitor that is powered off and a long rectangular black table that feels like ice from the air-conditioning even though it is the middle of fall.

In a few minutes Mr. Ray enters. His hair is partially black and partially white and his skin is very pale. His fingernails have some dirt underneath and his armpits have small ovals of perspiration, but most people would not observe these things because he otherwise looks like an actor in an advertisement and his teeth are so white I can almost see myself mirrored in them, and I am also very aware of other people's hygiene, e.g., Dan requires shaving twice daily and Jefferson's ears contain wax. Rebecca veils the odor of cigarettes with perfume and gum, but she does not always succeed.

After he introduces himself, he holds up a printout and says, "Your proposal was a little vague on how accurate the program will be in the future."

I intentionally did not include these data because I wanted to explain it in person, in case he thought it was too risky, and I also did not want to send any specific information about the algorithms over email.

"It currently functions for historical data retrieving back six months. It utilizes a signal that was present in that time period. Signals can convert over time. Therefore, this algorithm will not work as efficiently in the future, although the programmer can continue modifying the algorithm," I say.

He scans the front page again. "I've read this three times over. These are absurd numbers—so absurd I can't believe it'll work. But if this program does even a quarter of what you say it will, we have something very special on our hands," he says.

"It is extremely difficult to 100% predict the future, but this is a new way that I do not believe anyone has thought of, and that is the critical idea, to do something no one else is doing so you have an advantage," I say.

"I want to get this going immediately, so I'll green-light you for a trial run the rest of the week," Mr. Ray says.

My muscles relax for the first time all morning. I hope three days is enough time to prove its merit and that I have enough liquidity to make significant gains, even though the percentage gain is all that is important. The futures contracts trade at a minimum of 1,000 barrels, and the current price is approximately $22 per barrel, so I will need at least approximately $22,000.

"Is $300,000 enough?" he asks.

I pretend to be calm, although it is difficult, because I smile instinctively when I receive optimal news. "Yes, that should be sufficient," I say.

We discuss how to set up a fund for me to use, which will use legal offshore accounts so that Schrub remains anonymous and does not create market disturbances. "By the way, what do you call your program?" he asks.

I had not considered this. Jackson Pollock did not name his paintings, but gave them numbers because he did not want people to have preformed thoughts before observing the painting. But my program is already about numbers, so it should have a title. I search my brain, and all I can think of is that my program capitalizes on oil prices, and it makes me think of the blended title of the song Dan was downloading.

"Capitoil," I say. But if I am not going to get public kudos for my program, I want others to remember that it is Karim-esque. "K-A-P-I-T-O-I-L."

"Kapitoil," Mr. Ray says. "Nice play on words."

I believe it is the first time I have played on words in English.

"Mr. Ray, may I request you do not reveal this to my pod-mates yet?" I ask before we leave.

"Yes. It's highly privileged information," he says. I do not say that that is not the primary reason I do not want him to reveal it.

In my pod I set Kapitoil to aggregate recent newspaper searches, and it predicts oil futures will rise 21 cents total by the end of the day. This is only a 0.95% change, but that is still a good amount, and it is more critical to show that the program works. I immediately enter an anonymous order for 5,000 barrels at the current price of $22.17.

For the first two hours the oil price rises slowly as Kapitoil predicted. I watch it, although I do not focus well on my work.

Then at 11:45 a.m. the price drops. I hope this is temporary turbulence, and monitor the prices more closely.

At lunch Dan and Jefferson make a wager for $200 that Dan cannot eat 12 donuts in five minutes. The rules are he may have one glass of milk and may not eject the donuts during the consumption, although he may afterward. He eats six ASAP, then slows down. He eats the tenth donut very slowly, and he has one minute to finish the final two.

"Dan, you don't have to do this," Rebecca says.

"Yeah, let's call it even," says Jefferson, who looks slightly nervous.

Dan shakes his head and eats his 11th donut. "30 seconds left," Jefferson says. Dan shifts back and holds his desk for stability. He eats half the donut, then looks at the remaining half. With 15 seconds left, he puts the donut in his mouth and intakes it. His throat broadens as if it is a snake consuming a bird. Then he runs to the restroom and remains there for 20 minutes.

I review my monitor. Oil futures are now lower than the original $22.17.

The price continues falling through the afternoon, and at the end of open outcry at 2:30 p.m. it is 23 cents below the original price. I am interested exclusively in short-term gains and do not want to invest more money in this contract, so I sell it to someone at $21.94 and lose $1,150 on the sale.

Mr. Ray emails me:

We'll try it out again tomorrow. These things don't always work right away. Am withdrawing 100K from your account.

Except I believed it would work right away, and now I am afraid I have already trashed my one opportunity here and I will never come up with an idea that works and I will be a nonentity in finance my whole life.

On the subway after work I do not feel like immediately returning home, so I transfer trains and ride uptown until I reach Central Park. It is already dark at 6:00 p.m. and getting colder. I enter the park and walk without knowing where I am directed, and find a bench on a wide pedestrian road underneath leaves that blend red and orange and yellow.

A female walks by pushing a stroller with a baby inside. She is Middle Eastern, possibly Iranian, and looks like my mother when she was younger, with the same nose I also have, thin with a small angle in the middle, which some people might evaluate as ugly on a female but I think is elegant on the correct face. I stand up, but she is already beyond me, so I walk behind her and to the side to observe her features.

She turns her head and looks back at me, then accelerates the stroller.

"Miss, please do not run away," I say as I also accelerate. "I notice that you look very similar—"

"Leave me alone," she says, and she turns the stroller to where other people are. I stop following her and turn back.

In my apartment, I retrieve from my top desk drawer a small photograph of my mother. I am approximately seven years old and sitting on her lap. Her eyes are bright holes against her dark burqa as she laughs.

It is my solitary photograph of her, and I wish I had additional ones, but by the time we knew we should take more, her body had lost much mass and her skin was gray and her hair was voided in partitions and the corners of her forehead angled in because she had no muscles. But she never complained about her health. The only subject she complained about was one time when I heard her crying on the telephone and telling my aunt that she would not get to see Zahira grow up. In some ways that is better, since Zahira was not old enough to 100% understand what was happening, but in most ways it was not, because now she says she has few memories of her, and memories are the only way for someone who is dead to continue approximately living.

And although I am glad I possess this photograph, it also

frustrates me, because I have no idea now what happened before it to make her laugh, or what happened after, and it captures an infinitely small moment out of her entire life, and although I have other memories of her, they are slowly being deleted, e.g., when I was young and had difficulty falling asleep she used to sing Beatles songs in English to me. I can remember with accuracy the sound of her cream of the cream voice, and if she had been born in the U.S., I predict she would have been a musician.

But I do not remember what her preferred song was that she frequently sang ultimately, just before she kissed my forehead. I have played nearly every song of theirs for years to launch my memory, but I am never certain which one it is. My father would not remember, and even if he did, we do not discuss her.

green-light = permit a project to continue
highly privileged information = private data
play on words = create a secondary or tertiary meaning via original
   usage of language

On Thursday Kapitoil predicts that prices will drop 15 cents, so I short a contract for 5,000 barrels. Before I make the transaction, I review Kapitoil's prediction and the data that support it, in case I can decipher why it has been erroneous. But I do not detect any glitches: It is using the most recent newspaper articles in the U.S. from this morning and should be accurate.

The prices drop at first, as the program predicted, but then they fluctuate during the day, and by the end of open outcry it is up 17 cents and we again lose money.

Mr. Ray emails me:

One more chance tomorrow, or we'll have to kill it.

I strike my desk hard, and Rebecca looks at me. "I am having a technical issue," I say.

Several minutes later, Jefferson disconnects his telephone. "Scored two tickets, mezzanine, game three of the World Series," he says. "Check the weather for the 26th."

Dan clicks on his computer. "Damn. 70% chance of rain."

Jefferson says, "Don't be so pessimistic, baby. That's your problem. October weather goes through volatile ch-ch-ch-changes," and he sings this last word as he intentionally stutters.

And then I have a positive short circuit about why my program is malfunctioning, or instead why it functions at first and then stops: because it is processing articles written the previous night and published in the morning. But by the afternoon it is obsolete news, which is why Kapitoil performs poorly then. The Internet is a constant source of data, like a spacious bin the entire world is depositing trash inside, and my program is calibrated so precisely that it must process the most recent data: the trash on *top*. The trash underneath is less valuable.

The solitary way to profit with it, I hypothesize, is to make transactions and run Kapitoil every hour, although this poses great risk for major losses.

"Karim, check us out on TV Tuesday night," Jefferson says.

I am frustrated that he is interrupting me when I am in the middle of an important thought, so I say, "I will, if you are not obstructed by the people sitting in front of you." He does not understand this is a reference to his height, and resumes working.

I shoot Mr. Ray my idea. He agrees it is high risk, but greenlights me to try this new hourly strategy tomorrow.

I receive an email from Rebecca at 5:45 p.m.:

Interested in seeing the movie "Three Kings" tonight? (Short notice, I know, but I figure you're busy next week trying to spot Jefferson on TV in vain--the camera only adds ten pounds, not ten inches.)

I know it is customary in the U.S. for a female to invite a man to socialize, but it still makes me uncomfortable. Although of course *I* would not have the confidence to invite *her* to socialize, so in some ways I am relieved. But then I have another source of confusion: I am uncertain if this is a romantic date or if it is just two friends partnering for a movie.

I reply that I would like to see the movie, which I have seen advertisements for although I do not know what it is about. She responds immediately that a theater nearby is playing it directly after work. I was hoping her writing would suggest whether she believes it is a date or friends partnering, but nothing in her email is a strong indicator, or possibly my skill at reading English is not advanced enough to analyze her words.

A few minutes after Jefferson and Dan leave, Rebecca asks if I want to go now. We get in the elevator, and it is similar to the time we went to coffee together and did not speak. She touches the material of her white shirt sleeve and gray pants as we descend.

"I've read really good things about this movie," she says finally.

"I have not."

"You heard it was bad?"

"No," I say. "I have not read anything about it."

She laughs, although when she laughs after I make a conversational error (she explains the error to me) it does not make me feel humiliated as it does when Dan laughs, and it becomes slightly easier to converse as we walk to the movie theater.

She tells the vendor we want two tickets, and I take out my credit card. She pushes it away.

"How about I'll get the tickets and you can get the popcorn and soda?" she says, and she pays before I have the opportunity to reject the idea.

The popcorn and soda is less than 50% of the ticket price, and I offer to pay Rebecca some money to compensate. "You can get me back another time," she says.

The movie is entertaining and intriguing. At four points during it I rotate my eyes to observe Rebecca. The monitor is mirrored on her glasses and behind them her eyes are very wide. Although I am a more experienced programmer, I am certain her ideas on the movie are more complex than mine.

But halfway through I worry that Rebecca invited me because it is about the Gulf War in Iraq and she thinks of me as merely a Middle Easterner, and so I do not try to discuss it with her when we exit the theater. The only person I see movies with is Zahira, and typically she launches her analysis of the movie immediately, so it is strange to be with someone else and for us both to be silent as we transition from the world of the movie to the real world outside.

"You feel like grabbing a bite?" she says as we exit into the cold air, and I say yes. We stop in a street near an Afghani restaurant, and I am afraid Rebecca again thinks I exclusively enjoy Middle Eastern things. "This place okay?" she asks.

Then I relax because she is pointing at a bar named Flannigan's.

It is the first American bar I have entered, and it is more casual than the hotel bars I have been to in Doha. We sit in a cushioned area, and a waitress with her brown hair tied up but some parts descending gives us menus. "Something to drink?" she asks.

"You want to split a—just two waters for now, please," Rebecca says.

The waitress leaves. "I have had alcohol, if that is why you did not want to order it. I do not want any now, but if you want to drink some, you should," I say.

"I don't really want to. It's sort of a reflex."

"Why?"

"You go out socially, you usually end up drinking," she says. "It makes things flow easier."

"If things do not flow easily without alcohol, why do you go out socially at all?"

"I don't know." She examines the reverse side of the menu. "Maybe I shouldn't."

We're mute for a few moments while we decide what to order. I crave the stir-fried vegetable dish, but it costs $12.95, and I already spent nearly that amount on the popcorn and soda.

The waitress asks Rebecca what she would like. "You go first, Karim," she says.

I order a veggie burger, which is still nutritious and halal and costs $7.95, and a Coke. "Anything else?" the waitress asks.

"No," I say. "You may book it."

Rebecca looks at me. "I'll have the same," she says. I ask if she's a vegetarian. "No, but I should eat healthier," she says, and I hypothesize she was prepared to order a meat dish but converted her order when I asked for the veggie burger, because she again was afraid to offend my religious beliefs.

"What kind of stuff have you been doing in New York?" Rebecca asks when our food arrives.

"I have gone to the Museum of Modern Art. I have explored Central Park and many neighborhoods."

"Do you know other people here?"

"My family's friends in Qatar provided me with the contact data of several people here," I say. Then I add ASAP, "I apologize for not asking you before. How was your trip to see your brother David?"

"Good. Except he's a little homesick," she says. "And sort of lonely."

I look down at my veggie burger for a few moments. "My sister Zahira is fortunate to live at home while attending university."

"Though it doesn't leave much room for growth," she says.

"But I guess it's different over there. Do you talk to her much?"

"No. The time difference is difficult. But when I am there, we talk constantly."

"She must miss you, then."

"Yes," I say. Suddenly the bar feels very dark and cold even though we are next to a heated pipe, and I wish the rock music was muted. "I think so." Then I ask Rebecca about her neighborhood called Fort Greene in Brooklyn, and we discuss that for a while and other parts of New York. But we have frequent interims of non-conversation, and although it is mute, I can feel the slight vibration of my voice recorder powering on and off in my pocket for only a few seconds, e.g.:

REBECCA: [voice recorder powers on] "Do you go to the movies a lot back home?"
KARIM: "Sometimes. But most of the movies that come to Qatar involve car accidents and explosions, which I do not like to observe. So I do not go frequently." [voice recorder powers off]

Then it remains off for another 30 seconds while we eat until I ask Rebecca a question. It would be enjoyable if the voice recorder remained on the entire duration, but that's difficult with someone you still do not know well. Or if it remained off the entire duration but neither person experienced discomfort.

Near the end of the meal I become anxious about when the bill arrives. I want to tell Rebecca that I am not wealthy, as she thinks I am, but if I do that she may believe I am innovating an excuse not to pay for the meal, and I do think it is my duty to pay. When the waitress comes, she points to my plate. "Are you still working on that?" she asks. I say no, although I am.

Rebecca is finished, and she takes out a cigarette and asks, "You mind if I . . ."

I say I do not mind, but I wish she did not, both because of the odor and because it is unhealthy for both of us, but people do not like being told their choices are unhealthy, especially if they already know it. It also surprises me that she is worried about drinking alcohol around me but still smokes.

Then I tell Rebecca I must excuse myself briefly. On the way to the restroom I locate our waitress. "Miss, may I pay by credit card now for the meal so you do not have to bring the check to our table?" I ask. She takes my card and swipes it. I add, "Please withhold from my friend this highly privileged information," and I give her a 30% gratuity to certify that she follows my request.

I return to the table and pretend to dry my hands on my pants. "I have positive news," I say to Rebecca. "When I was at the front of the bar, I learned we were automatically entered into a lottery, and we were the winners, so therefore our meal is free."

"You sure?" she asks.

"Yes. You will see. The waitress will not present us with a check."

The waitress arrives in a minute to retrieve our plates. "Thanks a lot, guys. Have a nice night," she says.

"Thank you, Karim," Rebecca says.

"You do not have to thank me. It was a random accident that we won."

"Thanks, anyway," she says. "Randomly and accidentally."

We walk to the Chambers St. subway station that we can both use, although I am going uptown and she is going to Brooklyn. My entrance is across the street from hers. She stands at the top of the stairs.

"This was fun. We both work a little too hard. You especially," she says. "Let's see if we can't do it more often."

"I would enjoy that," I say. "But let us see if we can do it more often."

She looks confused. "That's what I said."

"You said, 'Let us see if we *can't* do it more often.'"

She says, "That's an idiom. It means 'Let's see if we *can* do whatever.'"

"Why would you employ the negative when the intention is a positive?" I ask.

"Maybe to make it seem like you're not fully invested in it?" she says. "Not that I don't care. I don't know what I'm saying, I'm rambling." We pause for several seconds. "Well," she says, then puts out her hand, "have a good night," and she shakes my hand hard like we are at a business meeting and quickly descends the steps.

I enter my subway, and by then she is reading a book on a bench at a distant end of the station. Her forehead is very concentrated most of the time with a small compression in it and sometimes she smiles to herself at what she is reading and once she even laughs quietly to herself, which I have never done while reading, but that is because I read financial books, which are humorless. She does not notice me, and I keep observing her until her train arrives, and through the window I see the back of her head and the subway light mirroring the top of her hair like a silver crown until she disappears into the tunnel, and then I listen again on my voice recorder to her saying "Well . . . have a good night" multiple times to decipher it, because fre-

quently it is not the words themselves that matter but the way
they are said.

are you still working on that = are you still continuing to eat a meal

grab a bite = get something to eat

homesick = missing home so much as if it were an illness

invested in = care about

kill it = terminate services

let's see if we can't do = let's see if we can do

On Friday morning I greet Rebecca, and she tells me again that she had a good time last night. Dan enters, and she says, "Time to put our noses to the grindstone."

At 9:00 a.m. Kapitoil predicts the price of oil will rise 6 cents. I buy a contract. Kapitoil looks similar to other programs I am running, so my podmates do not know what I am doing.

At 10:00 a.m. the price of oil is up 4 cents. I sell the contract and we profit.

I immediately run Kapitoil again and put more weight on articles written in the last 90 minutes. It has a new prediction: down 3 cents. I short a contract.

At 11:30 oil is down 4 cents and we again profit.

I email Mr. Ray that we have made two consecutive profits on the hourly transactions. He green-lights me to continue until 5:15 p.m.

I make five more transactions during the day and profit on all of them. At closing time we have made 1.6% profit even though the ending price is only a few cents higher than the original price.

I decipher the reason it was malfunctioning. With the historical data, the program used newspaper articles written through the entire day and averaged them collectively to predict the closing price, but in practice I was using articles published in the morning. It was a foolish but understandable error: When you initially succeed without resistance, you sometimes overlook serious problems that may appear later. When people face challenges, however, they innovate more, e.g., in the way that the mother of a poorer family may produce a complete dinner out of minimal and inexpensive ingredients.

I can now revise the program's potential. Because the market can vacillate approximately 0.5% every hour, if Kapitoil operates at full efficiency, it can achieve up to 4.0% daily average profits during standard business hours. Over four weeks, assuming maximum vacillation and optimal predictive ability, this equals profits of 219%.

Mr. Ray emails me at 5:30 p.m.:

Nice work today. Finesse the program some more over the weekend, and let's do it again on Monday. I'll replace the 100K in your account.

Mr. Ray does not seem like the class of higher-up who frequently provides compliments, so for him to write "Nice work today" means very much to me. I almost forward his email to Zahira, but I do not want her to know about the program, both because (1) it may still not function and I do not want her to think I am a failure, as she considers me the smartest person she knows, even though I believe she is probably smarter than I am, which normally bothers me but not when it is Zahira, and (2) Kapitoil must remain highly privileged information.

After Dan and Jefferson leave, Rebecca puts on her blue wool hat and coat. "You up to anything fun this weekend?" she asks.

I will be refining Kapitoil to operate at full efficiency, but I cannot tell her that. I also do not want to lie 100%, so I say, "I will be laboring on some projects."

She crashes her hand against her head as if we are in the military. "At ease, then."

Over the weekend I finesse Kapitoil. I am focused, but several times on Saturday night I wonder what Rebecca is doing, e.g., is she at an event, is she with friends, or is she alone like I am.

finesse = labor on for enhancement
put one's nose to the grindstone = labor intensively

On Monday morning Kapitoil continues generating hourly profits. By noon, out of a possible 2.1% profit based on how much the oil futures have vacillated per hour, we have made a 1.7% profit, which is not full efficiency but is still robust.

Mr. Ray emails me:

Meet me in the conference room on 89 at 1:30.

Possibly he has reconsidered that Kapitoil might still be too risky. There are rumors that layoffs will soon occur, and maybe they do not have the money to continue high-risk programs like mine.

Or possibly they do not even have the money to retain me as an employee.

I omit lunch because my stomach is turbulent, as it frequently becomes when I am anxious, and do not run Kapitoil at noon, because I do not want it to lose money suddenly and give Mr. Ray more reason to kill it.

At 1:30 I knock on the door of the conference room. Mr. Ray says "Come in" from inside, and I open the door.

He is sitting, and at the head of the table is an older man. He has tan skin and black and white hair, and his nose slightly curves down like a vertical asymptote. His suit is gray and blue and his tie is dark red like blood that has dried.

It is Mr. Schrub.

"Karim," he says. He stands and extends to a few inches taller than I am. "Glad to meet you."

I am afraid to look into his eyes as we shake hands, so I look at his red tie. "It is my honor to meet you, Mr. Schrub."

Mr. Schrub puts out his arm to signal his permission to sit down opposite Mr. Ray.

"George tells me," he says, "that you can see the future."

I look at Mr. Ray for help, but he is not looking back at me. "The program has been successful so far at predicting pricing variance," I say.

"What's the 1,000-mile view on this thing?"

"I am unfamiliar with that term," I say.

"What are its long-term prospects?" he says.

"It is employing a market signal from news reports, and it should function for the duration of that signal's strength," I say, and I am no longer nervous because I am in the intersected world of programming and finance. "But if the signal converts a great amount, I will have to write a 100% new program, and that new program might not function as efficiently." Because I am uncertain if *he* is familiar with *these* terms, I translate them to a sports analog: "It is parallel to predicting the strategy of a racquetball opponent. If you compete against him for a long time, you can predict his strategies. But if you receive a new opponent, you have to adopt new tactics because your old predictions will be obsolete."

He smiles, possibly because he does understand the jargon terms and does not require the racquetball analog. "Is there a chance our competitors could catch on to what we're doing?"

"If we continue making anonymous desk transactions through offshore holdings and keep them frequent but minimal, then no one will know it is Schrub, and therefore our market entry will not cause fluctuations in the market," I say. "We can still make strong profits, as long as we practice restraint."

Mr. Schrub taps his fingers on the desk. It makes a loud sound in the large room. Then he says, "I'll level with you, Karim. We took a big hit in the fourth quarter. We bet the lion's share of our capital that the bubble would finally burst, but it didn't, and it burned us. Now we need to rebound, and from what George has told me, Kapitoil might be the way. So, as long as it keeps returning profits, we're going to plough a lot of money into your program."

I knew from released reports that Schrub suffered losses in the fourth quarter, but I assumed they had rebounded since then. If Mr. Schrub wants to plough money into my program after it has worked for just 1.5 days, then they must truly be in the red and not have other options.

Mr. Ray says, "You'll receive a raise and promotion."

"Therefore I would not be working on the Y2K project?" I ask.

"No. We want you working full-time on Kapitoil, doing everything you can to keep it humming."

"I do not think we should tell my coworkers about this," I say.

Mr. Ray says, "Absolutely. We can't let on what you're doing. We'll just say you're working on futures."

"Speaking of which, how is the program protected?" Mr. Schrub asks.

"I have formally copyrighted it in my name, although I am not patenting the software, as that would force us to disclose its contents to the public," I say. "And it is encrypted, so only I can enter into the code."

"Good. Let's keep it that way," he says. "I know you two are very busy, so I'll let you get back to your work," he adds, although of course he is much busier than we are, but it signifies control if you give permission for the other person to exit the conversation, e.g., Jefferson always ends personal calls by saying "I'll let you go."

He shakes my hand again, and his grip is strong but not too strong like some businessmen's grips are to prove they are powerful. "A pleasure meeting you, Karim. I'm sure we'll see each other again." He looks closely at my left eye, and this time I do not allow myself to look away, although my blood simultaneously seems to stop and accelerate in my veins.

Then he leaves, and Mr. Ray and I discuss technical issues and how to enable him to utilize the program as well, and he terminates by saying, "Why don't you finish up the Y2K work you've been doing over the next few days, and then I'll let your podmates know we're transferring you to another project next week."

This is positive news, as I was truly non-stimulated by the Y2K project, but I feel bad about abandoning my podmates, especially Rebecca. But Rebecca also seems careless about which project she works on and is not envious of others, so maybe she will be happy for me.

When I return to my pod, people are whispering to each other and scanning the room. Rebecca explains to me that Mr. Schrub was just in the building. "He only comes in a few times a year, so it's a big deal," she says. "I'm having trouble containing my excitement. It's like Christmas morning on floor 88." She stops smiling and returns to her work and adds, "Or something like that."

Near the end of the day, Jefferson and Dan discuss their plans to go to a nightclub. Jefferson asks me, "Karim, you want to come with?"

Although it is a Monday night and this is when I should be

finessing Kapitoil even more, this may be my solitary chance. I can feel Rebecca listening to me even though she is pretending to focus on her computer, and I want to suggest that she should attend as well, but it is not my place to do so. "I would be delighted to come with," I say.

At 6:30 p.m. they are ready to leave, and I say good-bye to Rebecca, who is staying late. Without looking up from coding, she says, "Have a blast, Karim."

We taxi to Jefferson's apartment near Rockefeller Center and Radio City Music Hall. It is the first taxi I have taken here, and the driver is African, although I am afraid to ask what country he is from, and I think of Barron, as the only two people who have driven me in a car here are black men. When we arrive I retrieve my wallet, but Dan says, "Don't sweat it," and he and Jefferson divide the cost.

Jefferson's building is classy, but not as classy as mine (e.g., he does not have a doorman), so I feel bad about not paying for the taxi. His apartment structure is similar to mine inside, although it is smaller and the furniture is less expensive. He has posters in frames on his wall of some of the movies he has on postcards in his pod, as well as a painting of an obsolete Japanese soldier with a sword on a horse. Over the television on the wall is a true silver sword that curves at the ends.

Jefferson has a record player but not a CD player, and he cautiously removes a record from its case and centers it on the player as if he is carrying an infant. I hear a saxophone. Dan says, "Can we please play some rap for once?"

"When we go to your place, we can listen to your commercialized, Top-40, disposable MTV garbage. And if you had any sense of history, you'd know nearly all rap derives from jazz,"

Jefferson says. "In this day and age, your ignorance of the oppression my brothers and I suffered at the hands of the white man is unconscionable and, frankly, straight-up racist. I'd think you'd sympathize, as a dirty Jew."

I look to see if Dan responds to the fact that Jefferson called him an ethnic insult and also that he called himself black, but he merely smiles and remains on the couch.

Then Jefferson powers on his DVD and television and inserts a movie and plays it mutely. It is in Japanese, and it is about another obsolete soldier in a dark blue uniform in an area of Japan he does not know who carries only a magical sword for protection.

Jefferson retrieves a takeout menu from his small kitchen area and withdraws three Sapporo beers from his refrigerator. He drops the menu on his coffee table, next to four separate stacks of *The New Yorker* and *The Economist* and *Architectural Digest* and *Gourmet* magazines.

"I'm gonna shit-shower-shave," he says before he exits the room. "Order the sushi boat for three, some Asahis, and get the sea urchin with quail eggs. Say it's for me, and they'll add this goma-shio sesame salt that doesn't condescend to gaijin palates."

I do not understand why he orders additional beer if we have more Sapporo here, but I remain mute and watch as the Japanese soldier travels independently on a country road through a snowstorm and fights a team of men who launch a surprise attack.

After Dan orders, he asks how I like my job. I do not want to indicate that I am soon advancing, so I say, "It is enjoyable."

He laughs. "Very diplomatic. You can admit it's beneath you—I won't rat you out."

I get up and examine the sword so he reroutes the conversation. "I wouldn't touch that," Dan says. "It's from the 18th century, and Jefferson has an aneurysm if anyone breathes on it." He puts his fingers over the buttons on the remote control without pressing any of them. "He can be kind of a cocksucker sometimes."

When the Japanese deliveryman with an earring in his left ear arrives, Dan and Jefferson do not let me pay for the food. I eat the sushi that is vegetarian, and it is flavorful, but too expensive if it's mostly rice. I also drink three beers total and Dan and Jefferson drink more as we watch the movie. We leave before we can finish it, which disappoints me, because the soldier's enemy has just stolen the magical sword from him and I am curious to see if he can recover it.

When I stand up my head feels filled with helium. Possibly it is because I just watched the Japanese soldier, but I also feel that I could defend myself against a team of attackers, and although of course I do not say it, that I am the cream of the cream programmer at Schrub and have won Mr. Schrub's confidence after just three weeks.

We taxi again, even though the address is on 20th St. and 5th Ave. and the subway is probably faster. "You're our guest, Karim. You should never have to touch your wallet," Jefferson says when I try to pay. "It's the Japanese way." He asks for a receipt and winks at me. "Besides, we'll expense it."

We walk to a cathedral on the corner of the street, and when we turn the corner, many young people are on line behind a velvet rope to enter it. My clothing is not as sexy as anyone else's and they will see that I do not belong here, and my body vibrates even though it is not very cold, but I am glad I am with Dan and especially Jefferson, who does look like he belongs, even though he is the shortest man on line. He bypasses the line and talks to the guard at the front, who is a very large black man in a green coat that looks like it is inflated with air, and points on a piece of paper the guard holds. In a minute he waves for us to join him.

Jefferson leads us inside the tall wood doors. It is a true former cathedral. I cannot see well and it is warm and smells like alcohol blended with perspiration and I do not know what song is playing, but it has a robust drumbeat that pains my ears. Next to the stained glass windows are paintings of Jesus Christ and the Virgin Mary, and attached to the wall in the back of the dance floor is a ten-foot cross with toggling lightbulbs around its edges.

Jefferson finds another man he knows approximately our age with blond hair spiked like an electrocardiogram. They both put out their right hands in a class of handshake and they touch the other person's back with their left hands as if they are hugging slightly.

The man extends his hand to me like he did with Jefferson, and I do the same handshake/hug. "I am Karim," I say. "Glad to meet you."

"Andy Tweedy," he says, although he is already looking at Jefferson. "What are you guys drinking?"

Jefferson says, "Screwdrivers."

Andy stops a waitress who wears a minimal skirt in a green and red pattern with long socks that reveal her upper legs and a white shirt with a collar that reveals her stomach. "Set them up with a VIP table and bottles for 'Nailed to the Cross,'" he says.

The waitress leads us through the main floor, which has bright blue lights and some people dancing, although not many yet. We ascend some steps, and many people observe us as we elevate above them. A muscular white guard in a priest's costume detaches another rope for us. I have never accessed a highly privileged place like this before, and now I am vibrating not because I am nervous but because I am so stimulated.

On the second floor she takes us to a small table that overviews the dance floor and has a cushioned red bench around it. Most of the other tables on this small second floor are also occupied, usually with several men and sometimes a few females also with the men.

Before the waitress leaves she smiles at Jefferson, because he is the most handsome of us and looks like the chief member of our cluster, except that his ears angle out like satellites. We sit down, and Dan rests his legs on the barrier over the dance floor. "Congrats, Karim. You're a Very Important Person now," Dan says.

And I do feel VI.

Jefferson stands up and scans the floor. "I fucking detest this place," he says. "Up to our ears in Maries and Joeys fresh off the LIRR."

The waitress returns with a tray that has one bottle of vodka inside a bucket of ice, a bottle of orange juice, and three glasses. She angles over to pour the vodka in our glasses and displays her breasts, which are very tan and three-dimensional in a way I have seen exclusively on television or in pictures.

Jefferson asks her for extra glasses, and after she leaves Dan mixes us drinks and says, "She can get it, Smithy. You're a machine."

"Not my type. You can take her."

"Out of my league."

"Don't talk that way, sweetheart. She's just pumped full of silicone and teeth whitener. And that's a self-fulfilling prophecy. Look at me. I'm a goddamn dwarf. But at the end of the day, it's all about confidence. People are waiting for someone else to lead them." Jefferson is also more confident in the office, and he makes a better impression on coworkers than Dan does, who often avoids looking people in the eye and shakes hands weakly and speaks quietly to anyone outside of our pod. "And so what if she rejects you? If you want to increase your success rate, double your failure rate." He looks closely at Dan and decelerates his words and points his index finger on each syllable. "If you believe it, you can achieve it. Put that on your wall in the fucking pod."

He raises his glass and says, "To Dan the ladies' man," and Dan says, "Don't mock me, I'm not in the mood," and Jefferson says, "I'm not mocking you. Women have wet dreams about rich guys your height," and then we all crash our glasses and drink, and Jefferson and Dan guzzle theirs rapidly, so I guzzle mine, and then Jefferson kisses Dan on the cheek and calls him a "handsome bastard." The drink is robust and difficult to swallow, but when I finish it Dan mixes me another one, which is easier to consume, and I again have a mental image of myself as the Japanese soldier.

They observe the dance floor and assign ratings to different females from 1 to 10. They say an overweight female is "the worst" and is "four 40s deep," and rate her a 1, which means 1–10 is a poor scale, because it assigns a point even when someone is "the worst" and there exists only a 9-point total range.

A friend joins the overweight female, and she is additionally overweight, and Dan says she's "even nastier" and also assigns

her a 1, even though if she is in fact inferior, then she should receive less than 1 (or the first female's rating should retroactively
rise slightly). This is why the Y2K bug is happening: Humans
usually do not anticipate what comes next after what initially
seems to be the limit, so they programmed their computers to
function up to the year 1999 and not 2000. Even Jefferson and
Dan, who are resolving this problem nonstop, did not consider
the maximum-limit issue in this context. But possibly it is because they have been drinking alcohol, and also they are not the
most considerate people.

Then Jefferson stands at the railing and points to an Asian female on the floor he has just rated a 9.3. She looks and he holds
up the vodka bottle. She shakes her head, but he takes the bottle
downstairs with him and refills her glass and the glasses of her two
friends who are also Asian. After they talk for a few minutes he
leads them upstairs. He introduces them to Dan, who he says is
a vice president at Schrub. He puts his arm around me. "And this
is Karim. He's from an oil family in Qatar, and is here on vacation."

The female sitting next to me is named Angela Park. Her
arms are thin and elongated like pencils and she wears purple
makeup above her eyes. She says she is in public relations for a
fashion company. "It must be great not to have to work for a living," she says.

I wish Jefferson did not say this, because now I have to maintain the lie, which I only do because not lying would damage his
reputation. "It is relaxing," I say.

Angela receives a call on her cellular, and I whisper to Jefferson, "Why did you say I am from an oil family?"

"Play along. This is a golden opportunity," he whispers. He
adds, "Besides, truth is relative."

Angela ends her telephone call and asks me questions about my family. I provide the basic details, such as the names of my father and sister and uncle, but when she asks what they do, I say, "If I told you I would have to kill you," which I heard on a comedy television show the previous night, even though I didn't find the threat of murder amusing, but the audience did.

She laughs and places her hand on my leg. I feel myself rising.

"It's strange how you're from Qatar, and my family's originally from Korea, and now we're meeting in New York," she says. "That's so random."

"Americans frequently misuse the word 'random,'" I say. "Merely because an incident is unlikely does not mean it is random. I believe that if we were able to analyze every variable of the current situation, which is of course impossible, we could determine that our meeting was in fact predetermined. Therefore, when people say something is 'so random,' they should truly say that it is 'so destined.'"

She smiles but does not respond to my observation. Instead, she says, "I feel badly that we're not talking to the others."

"Is your tactile sense operating inefficiently?"

"What do you mean?" she asks.

"You used the adverbial form of 'I feel bad' to express a negative emotion and said 'I feel badly,' which means your sense of touch is performing poorly."

Again she smiles and says nothing. I certify that that is the last time I will note anything about usage or grammar to an American.

Jefferson is kissing his female and Dan is whispering in the ear of his female. So I whisper in Angela's ear, "I am not used to being around someone as beautiful as you."

"Really?" she asks.

"Yes," I say. "If someone told me a week ago that I would be sitting with someone like you at a place like this, I would not have believed them."

Angela smiles and removes her hand from my leg. "You're sweet," she says, and she looks at her friends. "I have to go to the ladies' room." She leaves the VIP area and goes downstairs, and I wait for her to return. Dan is still talking to his female, and although she does not appear as interested in him as Jefferson's female is in Jefferson, I look straight ahead so that I am not infringing upon their privacy.

In ten minutes she has still not returned, and then Dan's female receives a call on her cellular, and she taps her other friend and says something to her that I cannot hear, and then they stand up with Dan and Jefferson and go downstairs. They all dance together very closely, and Angela joins them and dances with them as well, and although I am of course not very invested in Angela, I still feel foolish for what I told her and my chest feels like someone has punched me in it and left his fist there.

I want to leave, but someone has to protect the vodka and orange juice, as there is still approximately 25% of it left, so I wait another 15 minutes at the table. When another song begins and they still do not return, I go downstairs.

I do not have Jefferson's or Dan's telephone numbers, but I do not want to disturb them now, and I especially do not want Angela to see me again, so I escape through the dance floor, which is highly bottlenecked and difficult to divide, and exit past the guard outside and the people on line, which is now quadruple the original length, and walk to the N train and wait a long time for it, then take it home, and pray and record my journal until

I feel normal again, and before I finish, without attempting, I load an image in my brain of Rebecca, who is probably sleeping right now.

1,000-mile view = future outlook

at the end of the day = in conclusion

aneurysm = expansion of a blood vessel that often results in sudden death

big hit = major loss/major success (in baseball as well)

come with = come with (but the object of the preposition is not necessary)

don't sweat it = be careless about a problem

gaijin = Japanese term for non-Japanese person

golden opportunity = opportunity with great profit potential, monetary or nonmonetary

have a blast = enjoy yourself

hum = function well

level with = be transparent with

lion's share = majority

LIRR = Long Island Rail Road

Maries and Joeys = nicknames for the class of people who take the LIRR

out of one's league = a romantic higher-up

plough money = invest money

rat out = reveal highly privileged information

she can get it = a female has romantic interest in you

shit-shower-shave = consecutive actions a man performs before a nightclub

VIP = Very Important Person

I wake up exhausted and spend more time in the shower than normal, and I arrive at work a few minutes late when everyone else is present. When I enter the pod and sit down, Dan says, "What's up, player?" and extends his fist horizontally to me without looking, as he often does with Jefferson.

"Good morning," I say, and I roll my chair forward to him and contact our fists and then roll backward to my desk, except one wheel is misaligned and I have to pause and readjust before resuming.

Kapitoil performs well and we slowly increase our investments, although we are careful not to create market fluctuations. At noon I receive an email:

> Mr. Issar,
> This is the secretary for Derek Schrub. Mr. Schrub would like to know if you are free to play racquetball at 3 p.m. today (he has already spoken to George Ray). Clothing and equipment will be provided.

I try to contain my stimulation in front of my podmates by clapping my hands together softly under the desk, as this presents a golden opportunity to become acquainted with Mr. Schrub. In addition, now I know why Mr. Schrub smiled at the racquetball analog.

When I am ready to leave, I put Kapitoil on automatic trades and pick up my briefcase. "Where are you going?" Dan asks.

"I am meeting with another Schrub team member," I say, which is true. "I want to discuss the Doha operations and the cost-cutting measures my supervisor there, Mr. Sayed, took.

E.g., we saved 7% in telephone costs by metering employees' personal calls, and 12% in productivity costs by blocking various email websites. Mr. Sayed, whose first name is Sadik, which means 'full of truth'—"

Dan plugs in his earphones.

I take the subway uptown to 59th St. and walk east along the border of Central Park to his apartment. There is a doorman outside who is white and has whiter hair. I tell him I am there to see Mr. Schrub. "I work at Schrub Equities," I say, which is now strange to say because I am saying it at Mr. Schrub's residence and not his business.

"ID," the doorman says, with an accent that I believe is Irish. He looks at my Schrub ID, calls on a telephone inside, and directs me to take the elevator up to the athletic complex on floor 13.

Instead of wood and brass and gold like inside my lobby, this one does not appear as quality, which initially surprises me. There is white marble with pink veins like the sky at sunset, and the walls and ceilings have frames of regular plaster. The classier buildings do not have to attempt so hard to look classy, just as Mr. Schrub does not have to shake hands with too much force.

I receive clothing and equipment from the reception desk and change, then go to the court and wait several minutes, but Mr. Schrub does not appear. I am glad I am about to play racquetball so I have an excuse for perspiring. To reroute my brain I challenge myself with a problem: How many racquetballs can fit inside a racquetball court?

1. The court is 20 feet wide and 20 feet high and 40 feet long, so there are 16,000 cubic feet of space for the ball to pass through. In inches, this is $(16,000)(12^3)$.

A. I estimate the diameter of a racquetball ball is approximately 2.5 inches. If I create a box that fits 2 balls by 2 balls by 2 balls for 8 balls total, then the box is 5 inches in each direction, or $5^3 = 125$ cubic inches.

B. Therefore, $(16,000)(12^3)/125 =$ number of boxes, or approximately 220,000 boxes = 1.76 million balls.

2. But boxes are an inefficient method of storage because they waste the space between the balls. So if I have a method of wasting zero space and packing the court 100% with racquetballs, I would use this equation:

A. $(16,000)(12^3)/$the volume of a sphere. The volume of a sphere is $(4/3)(\pi r^3)$, or in this case $(4/3)(\pi)(1.25^3)$, or approximately 8.3 repeating cubic inches.

B. Therefore, $(16,000)(12^3)/8.3$ repeating = approximately 3.5 million balls.

3. So, by packing them in boxes we can fit in approximately only half as many balls as we could in an ideal scenario in which the balls waste no space between them. But the ideal cannot exist, because then they would not truly be balls anymore.

4. The compromise between the box scenario and the ideal scenario is what supermarkets do with spherical fruits, which is a best-practice method of stacking them in pyramids, and this is another reason I value pyramids. In fact, this pattern is also the way some crystals align themselves under pressure, which is why diamonds are so sharp, because high pressure forces carbon atoms to align in the most compressed pattern possible: a regular, repeating structure. Most people think diamonds are beautiful because they mirror light, but I prefer

to think of them this way, which is also one of the ways I think of Zahira and her name, because her brain's connections are so sharp.

But I do not have time to evaluate the supermarket approach because the door opens behind me and Mr. Schrub appears. He is wearing white shorts and a white shirt with a collar that are parallel to mine, except his look higher quality.

We hit to each other, and I strike slowly at first, because I am uncertain how skilled he is and do not want to look like I am showing off, although I also do not want to look like I am a poor player. But he is better than I anticipated, so I hit harder, and after a few minutes we launch a game.

He lets me serve first. I know from the warm-up that I can defeat him if I want to, but I decide to win the first game, then lose the second game, then lose the last game in a close match. Typically this outcome pleases competitors I should lose to in Doha, and I think the same will happen with Mr. Schrub. I am not truly invested in the outcome of a match, but I merely enjoy playing it, although it is more fun when I can play my hardest and challenge my own limits.

I win the first game 15–9, but I intentionally let him score a few points. I am not a skilled liar with words, but it is easier with actions. He smiles and says, "Good game."

When the score is 13–10 in my favor for the second game, I plan to lose the point on my serve so that I am not in danger of serving again on match point, but I accidentally win it when Mr. Schrub can't return a ball I hit. "Avoidable hinder," I call on myself.

"Nonsense," Mr. Schrub says.

"I obstructed your path," I say. "It is your serve."

He waves his racquet like he is negating the idea. "Your point, fair and square. I'm just slow and old."

Now I am nervous again, because if I win another point on my serve I will defeat him. But if I hit a very poor serve or shot, he might detect that I am trying to lose. So I decide I have to aim precisely and miss a shot by only a few inches.

I serve, and we rally for a few shots and Mr. Schrub continues hitting hard. I am surprised he does not play more cautiously, as people often do if they are afraid of losing. But that is how you must be in business as well: Reject fear and take calculated risks. On my fourth shot I swing very hard and aim at the base of the wall, but I aim to hit the floor just before the wall so Mr. Schrub wins the point, and it is almost as if, before I strike it, I can observe the ray that links my racquet and the ball to my target.

Fortunately my mathematical brain makes me very skilled at racquetball.

He takes the ball for his serve and does not say anything, and I let him win the next five points, although I make it appear close. "Good game," he says again, although this time he does not smile. "Tiebreaker to 11."

I take an early lead but allow him to reduce the margin of deficit. When it is 8–8, Mr. Schrub says, "Looks like your program's better than your backhand," which is not very good sportsmanship, but I smile slightly and let him win the point when I hit a weak forehand that he smashes.

Before he serves, he says, "You can't win with a pussy-willow shot like that." I win the point, and then win a point on my serve to make it 9–9. Then I let him win two points in a row so that he serves for the match at 10–9.

"I can't believe you're about to lose to a guy two and a half times your age," he says. I was able to ignore his previous insult, but I dislike when anyone predicts that I am going to fail at something. In addition, he would be 2.5 times my age only if he were one year older.

He serves, and I win the point with a strong backhand that he cannot return.

I make it 10–10, and now I have match point, although I still plan to lose this point and let him win on his serve. "C'mon, Karim," he says. "You gonna choke now? You wanna run home to Mommy?"

I squeeze the racquet hard, which slightly pains my hand. "Is that it? You're a mama's boy?" he says.

He returns my serve, and I play a strong point and he mirrors my skill, but soon he makes an error and hits a floating shot, and I leverage the situation by jumping up and swinging my hardest on a smash and even yelling, which I never do.

Mr. Schrub watches the ball go past him. He smiles the widest this time and shakes my hand. "Thank God," he says. "For a second there I was afraid you were actually going to let me win."

I do not know what to say. "It's okay, Karim," he says, and puts his hand on my shoulder. "I've had plenty of people lose on purpose to me. I'll take an honest, hard-fought loss over a fraudulent win any day. I can tell you're a real player. A competitor."

He invites me to recuperate with him in the sauna. We relax in the hydrated heat and do not say anything for a few minutes except when Mr. Schrub makes sounds because his body pains him. "Ah, I'm mature," he says. "That's what my wife calls me—a 'mature man.' I don't know how many more years I have in me to do this."

At first I think he is talking about racquetball, but then I realize he means work. It surprises me, because he is only 64, and many people in business work at least a decade more than that, but also he could have easily retired a long time ago, so the solitary reason to continue working is because the challenges still motivate him, as they do for me.

"What are your plans, Karim?" he asks.

"I am planning to return to the office after this," I say.

He laughs. "That's not what I meant. But on that note, what are you doing tomorrow night?"

"I have no plans except to work on Kapitoil," I say.

"I'd like you to take the night off and be my guest in my luxury suite at the ball game. Game four, the Yanks could win it all."

I tell him I am delighted to attend and ask what subway line I should take. He makes a face as if he tastes something bad. "Too crowded. I'll send a driver to pick you up from the office. He'll take care of everything."

I almost say, "But the subway is fast, cheap, and entertaining; a car is none of those," but I practice restraint.

We then consult about Kapitoil, and he asks insightful questions about the algorithms. When we are finished, Mr. Schrub walks me to the elevator. "Anytime you want a rematch, Karim, let me know," he says, although of course I would never invite him to play. He winks and shakes my hand. "As long as you don't let me off the hook."

As I walk to the subway I call Zahira. It is after midnight in Doha, but she will be up studying, and I know my father will be asleep.

After she tells me that she received a perfect score on her biology test and I praise her, although I certify to praise her for studying hard and not merely for being intelligent, I say, "Zahira, I just played racquetball with Mr. Schrub."

She becomes very stimulated, because although Mr. Schrub does not interest her the same way, I have told her much about him. "I am also going to a baseball game with him tomorrow, and it is because of the success of my new program," I say.

"You wrote another program?" she asks. "I thought you said this was a bad time to try out new programs."

"It is the same program as before," I say. "I reconsidered and decided to show it to my higher-up." She does not say anything, and I add, "I also went to a classy nightclub with my coworkers the previous night. I apologize if I email less frequently now because I am too busy with work and networking."

"I know you are," she says. "I tell all my friends about you. And I also remember what you always told me."

"That if you work hard, you can achieve anything?" I ask.

She speaks very clearly: "That being a success at work does not equal being a success at life."

I am a block away from the subway entrance. "I am about to lose our connection in the subway," I say. "I will email you later."

In the subway I think about how Mr. Schrub said I was a competitor. I am glad I deposited my voice recorder in my shorts pocket so that I can listen to it again.

player = someone who succeeds in the field of business, athletics, or females

pussy-willow = weak

On Wednesday morning I check my work email from home. Everyone in the office receives an email stating there have been several layoffs and that the selected employees have already been informed. I accelerate to work.

Rebecca, Jefferson, and Dan are in the pod, which relaxes me, but when Dan sees me, he puts his head in his hands.

"Did you hear the news?" he says.

"You have been laid off?" I ask.

"Yes." He covers his eyes with his hands and vibrates as if he is crying. "And I've got prostate cancer."

Rebecca says, "Don't be an asshole, Dan," and I see he is vibrating from laughing. "He doesn't have cancer."

"Sorry." Dan wipes his left eye. "There were less layoffs than expected. And none of us are laid off."

"Yes, there were fewer layoffs than expected," Rebecca says. "And none of us is laid off."

Rebecca has optimal grammar.

"Neither of those subjects is something about which you should make jokes," I say to Dan.

I also have strong grammar skills.

That afternoon I receive my paycheck. It is three times the normal value. I email Mr. Ray about the error and ask if I should contact Human Resources. He writes back:

The paycheck is correct. We want to compensate you accordingly for the profits Kapitoil continues to bring in. Enjoy the bonus--you deserve it.

I cannot believe this is the true amount of my salary. It's about as much as I made in three months in Doha, or as much as my father makes in half a year at his store. But Mr. Ray is correct: I do merit it, because I have accumulated even greater profits for Schrub and its shareholders. Although some people lost their jobs, it's probably because they're not producing profits for the company. And if Kapitoil continues to perform high-end, possibly we can rehire those former employees or new ones.

I find it difficult to work the rest of the day as I think about tonight. I still know very little about baseball compared to Dan and Jefferson. However, I have been reading about the mathematics behind baseball called sabermetrics, and I spend another hour in the afternoon researching the players on the Yankees and the Atlanta Braves. Today one of the Yankees' stars, named Paul O'Neill, found out that his father died, although he's still going to play.

I have to leave work earlier than usual so the driver has time to navigate the traffic to Yankee Stadium. Fortunately Dan and Jefferson depart earlier than I do, so I do not have to explain why I am going, but when I retrieve my briefcase Rebecca says she will walk out with me.

"Kind of early for you to be heading out, isn't it?" she asks as we wait for the elevator.

"As you said, I especially work a little too hard."

We step into the elevator, and her eyebrows squeeze together, which I find not sexy but still pleasant to observe. "When did I say that?"

"After we saw the movie *Three Kings*, outside the Chambers St. subway station, when you were at the top of the stairs."

"You have a pretty good memory," says Rebecca.

"For certain subjects," I say.

Another female from the office runs to the elevator, and I press the button to reopen the doors. We zoom downstairs and watch the elevator monitor's weather forecast. It's difficult to have a conversation in the elevator when there is a third party.

Rebecca updates me on the progress on the Y2K project as we exit through the lobby. "It's going well," she says, "but there's still a lot of freaking out across the industry about what might happen."

Fear and panic cause severe market vacillation, and Y2K will present a golden opportunity for major earnings with Kapitoil.

Because I'm concentrating on Kapitoil and do not respond, Rebecca says, "I hope I'm not wasting my fascinating cocktail-party chitchat on you."

"I am sorry," I say. "I was thinking of another subject. It will not happen again."

"I'm teasing." She punches my shoulder with minor force. "Lighten up. That's your next goal."

I take out a pen, stop walking, and write on my other hand so that Rebecca can see: "GOALS: (1) LIGHTEN UP." "I will make efforts to meet that goal," I tell Rebecca. "Thank you for suggesting it."

Her facial expression is very confused. I wait a few seconds, then say, "I am teasing as well," and punch her shoulder, although I contact the metal on the strap of her bag, which hurts but I pretend it is painless.

She lets out a strong breath and laughs. "Maybe I need to lighten up, too. It's been a long day—I wouldn't mind unwinding."

Outside, black cars wait next to the sidewalk in a line as if for a funeral, and I see mine, with a sign that displays "13" in the window.

"Which way are you heading?" Rebecca asks.

"Oh, I forgot a disk in my office," I say, although I pronounce "Oh" with too much volume.

"Want me to wait?"

"No, that is unnecessary. In fact, I have some more work to do."

"Burning the midnight oil, are we?" she says. "See you around."

She walks toward the subway and I return to the building. There is probably a better means of negotiating the situation, but it is hard to strategize the right thing to do when you have to act quickly.

I wait inside the building until Rebecca disappears, then knock on the dark front window of car 13. The doors unlock and produce a sound like a bullet firing.

The face of the driver surprises me. "Do you remember me?" I ask.

Barron turns his head a quarter of the way. He still has a mustache. "Sorry, I drive a lot of people."

"It was on October 3rd," I say. In some ways it feels longer and in other ways it doesn't feel that long. "From John F. Kennedy Airport. My name is Karim Issar."

"I go to JFK all the time. Yankee Stadium, right?"

"Yes." I don't say anything for a minute, as I don't want to make him feel uncomfortable that he can't remember me. Although I am truly the one who should feel uncomfortable, because it means I'm not that memorable, which I already know, e.g., I don't talk loudly or dress with unique fashion or have an appearance others consider very sexy.

Then Barron depresses the gas pedal harder as we pass a

yellow light, and after we safely cross, I say, "Do you remember I asked you how many gallons of gas your car guzzles?"

He is quiet at the next red light for a few seconds, then says, "Oh, yeah—I remember you." He turns his head all the way back this time. "What's happening?"

"I am going to the Yankees game."

"You must be doing pretty well for yourself if I'm driving you to the World Series."

"I did not pay for the ticket myself," I say.

His eyes observe me in his mirror. "My bad."

We drive for several minutes and reach FDR Drive. The picture of Barron's daughter is still underneath his sun-protector.

"How old is your daughter?" I ask.

"She just turned seven," he says. "Sorry—six. They grow up quick here."

Zahira also grew up quickly, but for different reasons. In other ways of course she's still a child, e.g., she has never had alcohol or a boyfriend, because I will not let that happen to her until she's truly an adult.

The traffic becomes denser, so I don't distract Barron anymore by talking. The car reroutes off the highway and onto the streets, and the buildings aren't like the buildings in Manhattan, which are either modern or historic. These are obsolete and they all look the same, like ugly red rectangles, and although my family's apartment building in Doha isn't luxurious, it is superior to the apartments in this section of Manhattan and the Bronx and its architecture is unique from the other buildings. Everyone on the street is black or Latin American. I haven't seen anyone in my building who is, minus the doormen and one black couple.

We approach Yankee Stadium, which is a massive white building whose shape is a hybrid of a circle and a triangle, and Barron stops and gives me a business card with his number on it and his full name: BARRON WRIGHT. "Call just before the game's over, and I'll tell you where to meet me," he says.

"What are you going to do during the game?" I ask.

"Get some dinner around here, listen to the game in the car. Not worth driving all the way to Queens and back."

I don't like the image of Barron eating a discounted dinner and waiting inside the car for the whole game, but I merely say, "Thank you for driving me." He nods but angles his head out his window at the other cars so he won't cause a crash.

I pick up my ticket, and when I enter the stadium I see signs up several escalators for the mezzanine where Jefferson and Dan sat and where a large crowd walks, and for a second I want to tell Jefferson to search for me on television in the luxury suite before I remind myself that not everyone is as fortunate as I am to receive this golden opportunity.

The luxury suite is in a room off a hallway. Inside are several men in suits and a few females in dresses and fur coats. I expected other guests, but not so many. The females drink glasses of wine and the men drink bottles of Budweiser beer, and some of them eat off paper plates. A black man in a tuxedo stands behind silver trays of food on a table and serves sushi, and a Latin American man also in a tuxedo pours wine at a wooden bar. A large painting hangs on the wall of a Yankees player wearing number 7 and his signature, although I can't decipher it and his last name isn't on his uniform, as none of the Yankees' are, possibly because they are like the residents of Mr. Schrub's building and don't have to call attention to themselves. The strongest programming code does the same thing: It is not always sexy, but it functions efficiently and without flaws.

I don't see Mr. Schrub, and no one introduces himself to me, so I stand near the door. I'm hungry, but I don't know if I'm allowed to request food or if it requires previous payment. I take a free game program and read about the teams for ten minutes, and finally I decide I'm a guest of Mr. Schrub's and should chit-chat with the others, so I approach a small cluster of men and say "Excuse me" to the oldest one with white hair and steel glasses, because it is usually appropriate to initially address the senior member of a group.

He turns his head and says, "Oh, thank you," then hands me his empty Budweiser bottle and paper plate.

I quickly return to the door and trash the bottle and plate and continue looking into the bin as if there is something of interest inside. Possibly he made an error just because my clothing is not high quality and looks like a waiter's outfit, even though the waiters all wear tuxedoes. But whatever the reason is, suddenly I want to leave.

Then someone says the game is beginning, and everyone exits the room through a glass door into the outdoor area, where there are 20 seats that look like the business seats in an airplane, and I know I have to stay.

It isn't truly outside, however, since we have a small roof over us and lamps that produce heat. There is even a television here, although I don't know why someone would watch the game on television when we have the chief seats in the stadium, but some of the people near me utilize it.

No one scores for the first two innings, and the game is more boring than it is on television, because on television the analysts explain the mathematical variations of the game and you have access to numerous statistics, which is the only part of the game I truly enjoy. So occasionally I do look over at the television for the displayed statistics.

Then everyone turns around because Mr. Schrub finally arrives. He's dressed in his business clothing but he also wears a Yankees hat. He talks with another man approximately his age and they quickly bypass me in the last row and I don't think he even sees me. Mr. Schrub then shakes the hands of the other men and kisses the females on the cheek before he sits in the front row with two other men.

There's one voided seat in the front row, but I don't want to interrupt Mr. Schrub and his friends and it would be boastful of me to believe that I merit a seat next to them. So I remain where I am and try to watch the game, but truly I'm watching Mr. Schrub, who records something on a piece of paper after each batter.

After Atlanta terminates, Mr. Schrub turns around. "Karim!" he says. "What are you doing in the nosebleeds?"

I'm humiliated, and I put my finger under my nose, but it is bloodless. Some of the people around me laugh.

"No, it's—never mind," he says, and signals for me to come closer.

I walk down the steps and feel all of Mr. Schrub's friends observing me as if they are a wall of security cameras. He pats the seat next to him like it is a dog, and I sit down. Then he quietly explains the meaning of the term "nosebleeds," and I also laugh now, because it is a clever application of language.

Mr. Schrub asks if I know much about baseball. I tell him I am trying to learn.

The Yankees hit efficiently and soon have players on second

and third base with one out. One of Mr. Schrub's friends, who must blend something into his gray hair because it looks like silver, says, "Cox has to have Smoltz walk Williams here to pitch to Martinez and set up the double play."

Mr. Schrub says, "It's a given, with one out."

I access the statistics of the players they are discussing and note that:

1. The Yankees player Bernie Williams does not perform well against right-handed pitchers;

2. but Tino Martinez does, and the Braves pitcher John Smoltz is right-handed.

3. In addition, I previously memorized a sabermetrics table of how many runs are expected to score in 24 different game situations dependent on the number of outs and how many players are on base;

    A. and in the current situation a team is expected to score 1.371 runs;

    B. but if the Braves walk Williams and load the bases with one out, the Yankees are expected to score 1.546 runs.

4. Therefore, even though it appears to be the safe move, Mr. Schrub and his friend are advising a statistically unsound maneuver. Their strategy is understandable, however, as my line of thinking is unconventional, because it employs tangential statistics most observers ignore.

Mr. Schrub explains the situation, even though I already understand it. "See how it makes sense, even though in the short term it looks worse?"

"Possibly it is an error," I say, although I intended to remain mute, but when I see an error in logic I find it difficult not to correct it.

"What do you mean?" Mr. Schrub asks.

"He's confusing fielding errors," his friend says. "See, they're walking Williams. Cowards!" Then he makes a sound like a cow to express his frustration.

Now that I've already said a little, I decide I should express the complete idea, so I explain it to Mr. Schrub.

"Hmm" is all he says.

Tino Martinez hits a ball to the first baseman. It angles off his foot and two runs score for the Yankees. Then another Yankees player singles and Williams scores, which was possible only because the Braves walked him.

When the inning is over, Mr. Schrub introduces me to his friend and adds, "Karim's one of our brightest young minds downtown. And I don't count a single error in that statement."

Those words will go in my archive of important recordings.

Mr. Schrub also teaches me how to "score" the game, which is why he was recording notes on a specialized paper. It is similar to tracking the stock market with various indices, and I learn quickly.

In the fourth inning Mr. Schrub says to me, "I could use some real ball-game food—none of this sushi crap. What do you say to a couple of dogs?"

I know "dogs" are not real canines, but I'm uncertain what they are, so I nod. He turns and waves from his seat to the black man in the tuxedo inside.

"Can you scrounge up two hot dogs?" Mr. Schrub asks as he pays the man $20, and now I recognize the term from street vendors.

The man leaves, and later he returns with two sausages in elongated bread inside a paper box. "Keep the change," Mr. Schrub says as he transfers one of the sausages to me.

I look at the red cylinder of meat in my hands. Of course I can't eat it, but I also don't want to offend Mr. Schrub and his gift.

I bring the hot dog closer to inspect it. The scent is like something burning flavorfully, and my stomach wants me to consume it, and my tongue wants me to taste it, and even my eyes find it delicious, and maybe Allah will be careless of a solitary offense.

But I can't do it.

Then Mr. Schrub says, "My God, what was I thinking?" He takes the hot dog from me. "I'm sorry, Karim. I can't believe I forgot."

He gives me a napkin so I can clean my hands. "I've got an idea," he says, and he waves to the black man again. He hands him another $20 bill. "A bag of Cracker Jack," he says. "Actually, make it two."

He puts his own hot dog in the box and sets it on the concrete. "This probably isn't the healthiest option anyway," he says. "Who knows where this meat came from."

The Cracker Jack is like sweet rocks that divide easily when I bite and I'm pleased I'm not offending anyone, although at the end I wish I didn't eat it so rapidly.

For the rest of the game Mr. Schrub introduces me to some of his other friends, who are all more friendly to me than the man with mirroring hair. When we are alone again, Mr. Schrub whispers to me, "Nice people, but most of them could give a damn about who's out on the field."

The Yankees win, as I predicted, as they have the best and most expensive team. The players crash into each other and all the fans dance and Mr. Schrub and some of his male friends hug and clap and cheer. Then the friend with the silver hair says, "We have to sign a bigger bat in left field next year." He and Mr. Schrub consult about other ways to enhance the team. In some ways they're not enjoying their team's success right now, but that's also why Mr. Schrub is so successful: He's never satisfied with mere achievement and is always thinking outside the box.

The Yankees player Paul O'Neill, who did not perform well in the game, covers his face as he walks off the field because he is crying.

Mr. Schrub is also watching Paul O'Neill, and as the other men around us talk he appears to be unfocused, but then someone asks him something and he resumes talking.

While the Yankees players and manager and their employer make speeches on the grass about how they took every game in singular quantities and labored at over the 100% efficiency threshold, which is illogical but no one corrects them, Mr. Schrub says we should defeat the traffic and invites me to ride home in his car.

Mr. Schrub's car is an actual limo. His driver, who is white, which surprises me, because every salaried driver I've seen in New York is not white, opens the door for us. Mr. Schrub says, "How was the seat, Patrick? Good view?"

"Very good, Mr. Schrub," he says.

Mr. Schrub and I sit on opposite sides, and I'm the one riding backward, which I've never done in a car. It feels like I'm disappearing from the baseball game and the crowd, which is positive, because I was feeling bottlenecked and the bottoms of my shoes have much food and gum attached to them. Even guests in the luxury suite deposit their trash on the ground.

Mr. Schrub asks if I enjoyed the game. "I did. Thank you for inviting me, Mr. Schrub." Then I add, "I apologize for not thanking you before."

He smiles. "You're very polite, aren't you?" I don't know how to respond to this without in fact sounding impolite, so I only reciprocate a smile. "I wish my sons were like that. I tried my hardest to raise them without a sense of entitlement, but . . ."

"It is difficult to raise children under any circumstances," I say.

"I suppose," he says. "Maybe it's my fault. No one could accuse me of spending too much time at home while they grew up. Looks like your parents did a good job, though."

"It was difficult for them as well."

"How so?"

I don't want to stimulate pity from him, or from anyone, but I think maybe telling him this will make him feel enhanced about his own family, so I say, "My mother died when I was younger, so my father raised my sister and me independently."

His mouth opens a fraction, and it looks like he's trying to make words but can't. Finally he looks out the window and says, "I'm very sorry to hear that, Karim."

"It is not your fault," I say, which is how I always respond.

We are quiet for a few minutes as the lights on the side of the highway flash periodically. We arrive at his home first and he directs Patrick to take me home. I decide not to tell anyone else here about my mother, although I don't know anyone else who might want to know about it.

When I get home, I remember I never called Barron, and when I call his telephone I don't access him, so I record an apology.

But I keep thinking about making him wait for three hours for no reason, when he could have gone home to his family and eaten a real dinner. I dial another number.

Zahira picks up and says she only has a few minutes before she leaves for university. She asks what I have been doing lately. For some reason I do not tell her about the baseball game, and instead I ask her about her classes. Then she says, "I want to talk, but I have to go, Karim."

"Wait," I say.

"What?"

The toggling lights of Times Square mirror on my blank television. "You do not remember the song mother used to sing to us before sleep, do you?" I ask.

"No. You have asked me this before."

"It was a Beatles song."

"How could I remember it?" she says. "I was four years old."

"I thought possibly you might," I say, although our father trashed all the Beatles records after she died, which would make it even more difficult for Zahira to remember.

"Why are you asking about this now?" she asks.

On the street people are celebrating and cars are honking again even louder than when the Mets won their game. "I don't know," I say. "I was thinking about it."

She says, "It's not good to always think about these things."

"I don't always," I say.

"I don't have time to discuss this now," she says. "You can call me tonight."

We disconnect. I don't remind her that I can't call tonight because our time zones are so divided.

burn the midnight oil = work late into the night

chitchat = conversation used in a social environment to fill up silence

freaking out = panic

lighten up = relax

my bad = it is my fault/error

nosebleeds = inexpensive seats that render the sitter vulnerable to nosebleeds

score = record statistical events for a baseball game

scrounge up = search for and retrieve

When I arrive at my pod, my computer is missing from my desk. Only Dan is present. "Is this a joke?" I ask him.

He denies responsibility. I log in to Rebecca's computer. Maybe I offended Mr. Schrub last night and I am no longer working in the pod.

There is an email from Mr. Ray asking me to meet him on his floor. Now I am truly fearful.

When I find him, he tells me to come with and leads me downstairs again. We walk past the kitchen and into another hallway where some of the senior employees have private offices. He swipes his ID card on the reader of a door and opens it.

It is a spacious room, with a blue carpet on the entire floor and two leather chairs on our side of a black wood desk and a chair with netting on the other side. The entire wall also has windows with a view of the Statue of Liberty. The computer has two adjacent monitors: One is a standard horizontal monitor and one is vertical for enhanced observation when programming.

And in the middle of the desk is a name bar:

KARIM ISSAR

Before Mr. Ray leaves, he touches one of the leather chairs and says to himself, "Nicer than my office."

I spend a few minutes sitting in my chair and reclining against the strong netting and observing out the window. Then I swipe my ID card several times and watch the light convert from red to green. Finally I remember they are not paying me all this money and providing me with such a luxurious office merely to recreate.

Rebecca knocks on my door after lunch.

"So you're no longer in the tech ghetto," she says as she scans my office. "What nefarious schemes are you masterminding in here?"

"I am working on futures," I say.

Then we do not say anything for a few seconds, and she says, "Don't be a stranger," and leaves.

In the afternoon I start thinking that if I have a private office, I should look like I work in one. I email Jefferson for advice on where to purchase clothing. I don't want to ask Rebecca, because she might not know where good men's clothing is, and also it's not in her class of interests. Her clothing looks nice on her but it's not very expensive. And Dan's clothing looks expensive but is not attractive and never fits him well, e.g., he always reminds me of what I looked like in my first suit I bought for work at age 18.

After work I visit the first store on Jefferson's list, Barneys. I've been inside stores like this in Doha, but of course the items are always too expensive for me. I examine an attractive dark blue suit. A female in a black dress as restricting as a tie walks over and says, "That's a gorgeous suit. Do you want to try it on?"

I try it on in a dressing room and observe myself in the mirror. It fits my body like suits do in advertisements, and the color is pleasing, and I do look sexier than normal in it. Then I see the price tag. It's greater than my former weekly salary. This is my most major purchasing decision ever, and after I consider the cons, I evaluate the pros:

1. Previously, if I had to purchase a new suit, I would have spent a large percentage of my weekly salary, so why should I not do that now?

2. I am working extremely long hours; if I do not get to enjoy at least some of the financial compensation, I will not be motivated to continue working so much, because the output is less than the input.

3. Quality clothing will help me in future business transactions.

4. My purchase will stimulate the economy.

5. I will still have much money left over for Zahira.

I tell the female I will buy it, and a Greek man who smells like mints and soap takes my measurements so they can tailor it and deliver it later. At the counter, the dollar value appears in green digits on the cash register and she swipes my credit card, and my heart spikes and charges my entire body and I feel like when I drank alcohol with Jefferson and Dan.

Then she says, "Did you want to get some shirts and ties to go with that?"

She is correct, as I should not wear a new suit with old shirts and ties. She helps me select some shirts and recommends buying five so I can wear a new one each day.

Two of the shirts are white and look like each other, so I decide to take only one. I examine them for differences in quality, but I truly cannot distinguish them, as they both feel soft and durable and are attractive. The tag on one reads "Made in Italy" and the other reads "Made in Philippines." I discard the second shirt.

I buy the five shirts and five ties and am again electrified when she swipes my credit card. Then after I leave Barneys, I consider that I can't wear the same suit daily even if my shirts and ties are different, and I go into the nearby Saks Fifth Avenue store. I also can't buy another suit that is less gorgeous than my

Barneys suit, so I find one that costs nearly the same amount, and then buy three others of equal quality.

"May I tailor the others and bring one of these home with me now?" I ask the salesman as I point to one that is gray with blue stripes that already fits me well.

I am now carrying several heavy bags, and it is fortunate that I do push-ups and have inflated triceps. I set them down outside on the sidewalk to signal for a taxi, but it is rush hour. While I wait, I withdraw all the store receipts from my wallet and add them.

In 90 minutes I have spent two weeks of my new salary. My stomach becomes dizzy. I consider returning one or two of the suits, but I have made my decision and I should not reverse it, and it would be humiliating to return it immediately because the employees would know it was because I overspent.

A taxi stops for me, but I pick up my bags and shake my head at the driver and walk west. After a few blocks my arms slightly pain me.

When I reach 7th Ave. it starts raining, and everyone runs to the buildings for protection. The rain contacts the ground like bubbles on the surface of a new glass of Coke. Someone says it will continue all night.

I have just two blocks remaining, and there is even a nearby empty taxi that no one else is taking yet because they are either hoping the rain will stop or they have umbrellas, but I certify that my shopping bags are shielded from the water and walk.

My hair and current suit quickly become hydrated. Although sometimes I enjoy walking in the rain in Doha under the gray and black sky and feeling as if I am alone in the world but strong from my independence, now it is uncomfortable and my forehead coldly burns from the wind and the walk seems to take an infinite amount of time.

After I dry off at home, I wear a new shirt and tie and the gray suit with blue stripes and evaluate myself in the mirror.

It was worth it. I truly look like a cream of the cream American businessman.

I cook rice and vegetables for dinner while still wearing my suit and guarantee to myself I will not spend any more money on clothing while I am here.

digs = living area

don't be a stranger = remain in contact with others

ghetto = undesirable neighborhood

mastermind = innovate as leader

nefarious = immoral

Zahira emails me a humorous newspaper story while I am at work about a thief who fell asleep during a bank robbery. I say, "Rebecca, this is humorous—" before I remember I'm alone in my office. I forward her the email and a few minutes later she replies that it's funny, but our exchange is not equivalent when communicating via email.

In the afternoon Dan knocks on my door and enters before I can respond. "Karim the Dream, looking *hot*. I'd do you. New threads?" I thank him for the compliment, although I don't mention that I asked for help from Jefferson. "That an Aeron chair?"

"I am uncertain," I say, although I know it's an expensive chair and is more comfortable than the chairs in the normal pods, but I don't want to appear boastful about my chair, especially because I know Dan likes to spend money on seats.

"Hey, sorry about that joke the other day," he says. "Just trying to burn off the stress about the layoffs. Put it in perspective, you know?"

"Some people already have sufficient perspective," I say.

He touches the name bar on my desk and rotates it 30 degrees before letting go. "Anyway, Jefferson and I wanted to let you know about this Halloween party on Saturday. Some dotcom dude's town house in Chelsea. You in?"

I've never celebrated Halloween in Doha, but it would be enjoyable to see what it is like in the U.S. In addition I haven't been to a party at someone's home yet here. Even though I didn't have a very profitable experience at Cathedral, I tell Dan I'd like to go, and he says he will provide a costume for me when we "pre-game" at his apartment.

After he leaves, I rotate the name bar back to its original position and shoot Rebecca an invitation. She replies:

Thanks, but I'll pass. Dot-com asshole's party + Dan/Jefferson = my personal Halloween horror movie.

I'm disappointed, but I like how Rebecca expressed her lack of interest with an equation, although to be clearer she should not have used a slash sign between Dan's and Jefferson's names because it looks like a division sign.

Before I leave my apartment Saturday night for Dan's apartment, I receive a telephone call, which is rare for me if it's not Zahira. It is Rebecca.

"What is happening?" I ask.

"I don't know," Rebecca says. "What are you up to?"

"I am leaving for Dan's apartment to pre-game."

"Pre-game?"

"It is the term for consuming alcohol in an apartment before a party."

"I know, I just didn't think . . ." She has a very pleasant voice to hear on the telephone. I predict she is a good singer to boot. "Well, I was kind of thinking about going out tonight, and I was wondering if—"

"Would you like to pre-game with us?" I ask.

"I don't know about pre-gaming, but maybe I could meet you guys after?"

"I will ask Dan right now."

"Wait," she says. "You don't have to do that."

"It is careless," I say. She is about to interrupt again, but I tell her I will call her back.

Dan says "Go for it" when I ask him, and I provide Rebecca with the address.

On the subway to Dan's apartment on 22nd St. and 6th Ave., the females mostly wear minimal materials for costumes. One veils her face and body with a sheet like a ghost, except it doesn't cover her legs and a hole reveals a large partition of her breasts where they are bisected.

Dan greets me at his apartment door in a President Clinton mask and a cigar in the corner of his mouth. Rap music plays on his stereo. I ask who the musician is.

"That's Tupac. You like?" To be polite, I tell him I do, although I cannot usually understand the lyrics to rap. "I'll burn you a CD," he says.

"You do not have to do that," I say, but what I really want to say is that it's not ethical to copy music.

"It's nothing," he says. As he begins the burning process on his laptop, he says to Jefferson, "At least some people here have musical taste."

Jefferson is reading a magazine on the couch. He wears the costume of the Japanese soldier in the movie: blue material like a bathrobe with shoulder armor. His hair is in a knot at the top of his head and he has an artificial sword at his waist. It is strange to see that outfit on a white person, although possibly some people would find it strange to see, e.g., a racquetball outfit on someone like me.

Dan offers me a drink, and I ask what he has. "Let's see," he says as he looks in his refrigerator. "We've got OJ, purple stuff, soda, Sunny Delight." Jefferson laughs, although it is the class of laughter that does not utilize the lungs. I tell him I will have the same drink he has, and he retrieves a beer.

Two shelves like skyscrapers of CDs are near the stereo. From the plastic cases and the plastic materials in the CDs, I try to calculate how much petroleum they all contain, but it is of course impossible without knowing the precise material breakdown.

A shelf littered with books is next to the CDs. The lion's share are finance books, but there is one large book on art. Possibly Dan has more interests than I previously estimated. Sometimes small details tell you more about someone than the big picture does, in the same way, e.g., that the infinity of real numbers between 0 and 1 is actually greater in cardinality than the infinity of all integers.

Dan also takes out two small sheets of paper and hands one to Jefferson. "Got this weekend's point spreads. Fill it out now and we can drop it off with my doorman on our way out." He rotates to me. "Want to bet on football?"

He explains to me the concept of the point spread, which is similar to strike prices with options. I ask Dan for advice on which teams to pick, but he says, "With the spread, it's basically random—just go with your gut," which is poor strategy, because a knowledgeable expert would find a way to calculate better odds, so I bet only $5.

"Ready for your costume, high roller?" he asks as he takes my money. He gives me a plastic bag. Inside is a wrench. Despite my skills with computers, I am inefficient with the repair of physical objects. My father is much better in this department. He tried to teach me many times when I was young, but I was never good at it and he always became frustrated, so finally he stopped.

"Do I say I am a wrench or a tool?" I ask.

Dan's laughter always sounds like he exclusively understands what is humorous about a situation. "Whatever you want. But I suggest saying you're a mechanic."

When Dan is in the restroom, Jefferson says, "A 'tool' is someone who gets used by others." He lowers his volume. "Dan's a good kid, but a little immature. And with a narrow worldview." He shakes his head. "Sometimes I think he's just in this for the money."

To reroute the subject, I tell him I like his costume and ask if he has visited Japan. "I did my junior year abroad in Tokyo," he says. "And I backpacked through Southeast Asia in '97, just when the financial crisis hit."

We discuss the Asian Financial Crisis in more depth. Jefferson has a broad knowledge base and I learn some new facts, e.g., because Japan was the world's largest holder of currency reserves at the time, the yen remained stable, but after the crisis, when Japanese manufacturers couldn't compete with cheaper rival countries, the GDP real growth rate in fact fell into recession in 1998.

"They've bounced back, though. One thing those people know, it's how to safely weaken their currency and create a current account surplus." Then he says, "And produce fine women who think all white guys are goddamn Vikings. Even the runts." I believe this is a joke but I am not 100% certain, and therefore I produce the same laugh without lungs he used before, but he is serious and returns to reading *Wired*.

When Dan comes back, we drink more beers and watch a movie about a man with long hair who likes to bowl, and Dan and Jefferson state much of the conversation simultaneously with the actors. Before we leave, Dan gives me the burned CD and writes on it: "To: Karim the Dream, FROM: DAN." I still feel nefarious about accepting it, but it's a gift and Dan is trying to be more friendly, and possibly that compensates for the theft.

When we exit the building, Dan waits until no one else is around, then whispers to his doorman and transfers our three pieces of paper and some money to him.

Many men pass us in clusters as we walk south on 7th Ave. Although it's cold, their costumes are low on material and emphasize their muscles. "You have a lot of gays in your country?" Jefferson asks.

"No," I say. "Homosexuals can be imprisoned for five years and whipped."

"Do they even consider that a punishment?" Dan asks.

"Don't be a homophobe," Jefferson says. "You're not in redneck country."

The party is in an apartment building that just one person lives in. We take an elevator up three floors, and before the doors open we can hear the music and people talking and feel the temperature rise.

The elevator doors open directly to a large room bottlenecked with men like the ones we saw on the street.

"What the hell, Dan?" Jefferson says.

"I swear to God I didn't think it would be like this," Dan says.

"'Just because it's a Halloween party in Chelsea doesn't mean it's gay,'" Jefferson says in a voice imitating what Dan must have said to him previously.

"Look at it from the other side," Dan says. "The women here are probably desperate."

Jefferson rubs his eyebrows like he does at the end of the workday. Small pieces of dead white skin fall. "I can't believe we turned down the party at Pagan for this. All because you didn't want to pay a $75 cover, you cheap-ass Jew."

The elevator doors merge as we remain contained. "Well, it's too late now, and the only other big party we know about is on the Upper East Side, and cabs are scarce tonight," Dan says as he presses the "Door Open" button. "Let's try it out for a few minutes." Jefferson tells Dan that he owes him, and I follow them into the party.

Dan produces drinks for us at a table, but because they're disputing with each other I don't request a healthy beverage like orange or cranberry juice, so he makes me a Coke and vodka.

We stand near the drinks and observe the party. There are a few females, and some of them link their eyes with Jefferson's.

"See?" Dan says. "It's just a matter of finding the untapped market. We should've been doing this years ago."

As I consume my second drink, someone contacts my shoulder. Rebecca stands behind me in a coat. A white dress of satin material descends under it to a few inches above her knees. It is the first time I've seen her wear a dress. She opens her coat slightly and I see Post-its on the material that display "OEDI-PUS COMPLEX," "SUPEREGO," and "ID." She also reveals her upper arms and shoulders, which are pale and shaped like lightbulbs.

"It's a Freudian slip." She closes her coat. "It's idiotic and a cliché, but I didn't have anything else. What are you?"

I hold up my wrench. "I am a mechanic."

Then she says hello to Dan and Jefferson. Before I can ask how she is enjoying work, Dan says, "You guys want to play pool?" and he points to a black billiards table.

Rebecca says, "I don't really play, but—"

"Perfect," Dan says. "Cutthroat's better than two on two."

He defines the rules, the central one of which is to pocket your competitors' balls while protecting your own. Dan says, "What do you say we put a little money on this, just to make it interesting?"

Jefferson doesn't want to at first, but Dan says, "Money won is twice as sweet as money earned," and they agree to betting $20 each, which I don't want to do either, as I know I'll lose, but they also provided me with alcohol earlier and invited me to this party, so it's parallel to owing them $20.

Rebecca watches us play, and Dan and Jefferson begin by pocketing some balls of each other and ignoring mine, which is logical because I'm an unthreatening novice.

On my first turn to strike the white ball, I miss 100%. Dan says to Rebecca, "You want to get behind him and show him how it's done?" Rebecca doesn't say anything, but Jefferson stands next to me and demonstrates proper technique. They allow me to strike again, and I hit the white ball but it doesn't contact anything else.

I watch Dan and Jefferson shoot and practice my striking motion. Dan strikes like a puncher, fast and with quick oscillations, and Jefferson does one long withdrawal and launch like he is shooting a bow and arrow. When it's my turn, I aim like a sniper at the ball and produce solid contact, and it knocks in one of Jefferson's balls.

But now I'm in poor position to make another shot, and I realize that a smart pool player has a 1,000-mile view of not only (1) where the ball he is striking will go, but also (2) where the white ball will end up after, similar to how a chess player must think several turns ahead. This is why computer chess programs are now better than the best human players (and why a strategic and accurate robotic pool player would beat the best human player, because pool also denies the accident), because they can make infinite predictions that humans cannot, and this is why I believe Kapitoil is superior to human financial analysts. Although it is true that chess programs are *not* robust at endgame strategies, because there are too many variables that humans can in fact filter more efficiently. Therefore, chess programs have maximal databases of all possible endgame strategies and positions. They follow these databases mechanically and don't utilize their conventional artificial intelligence.

I miss my shot, and two females ask Jefferson if they can have the next game. The one who asks is thin and has blonde hair and wears false cat ears and has drawn whiskers on her cheeks, and her friend is heavier and in the clothing of a waitress from the English Middle Ages that provides her breasts with high visibility.

While Dan shoots, two men dance in the middle of the floor dressed as a policeman and the singer Madonna. They kiss, and then the man in the Madonna costume deposits his hand inside the front of the policeman's pants. Although part of me wants to keep watching, it also disgusts me, not only because it is two men, which bothers me (but I am in the U.S. now and specifically in New York and that is the custom here), but because they aren't respecting the privacy of others or even themselves.

Dan pockets the remainder of Jefferson's balls and loudly informs Jefferson that he sucks. Jefferson doesn't listen, however, as he's conversing with the cat. Then Dan deposits all of my balls in the table pockets except the last one, which is a difficult shot that he misses.

On my turn I take more time observing the table before I shoot and deciphering the optimal ball to hit. I link my stick between Dan's number 6 and the pocket, as I've seen Dan and Jefferson do, and aim at where the stick bisected the number 6 ball, and strike slowly and deposit it. I am also now in position to get another one, but this time I miss, and I leave my last ball vulnerable.

Dan has an easy shot, and he lines up and retracts and extends his stick several times, then he looks at me from the corner of his eye quickly as if he is certifying that I'm watching, and shoots. It misses, very slightly, and the white ball rolls into a strong position for me. He says, "Can't believe I missed that," and shakes his head, and now I know he missed on purpose, because when people are truly upset with themselves for making an error they are either more angry or mute.

I pocket Dan's number 9 ball, which leaves his last one. Now it is easier to focus, because (1) there are fewer variables (fewer balls), and (2) there is less need for prediction (I don't have to worry about placing the white ball after this). I strike the ball cleanly and Dan's number 7 ball rolls into the pocket.

Dan puts the three $20 bills in my hand and holds it above our heads and says I am the winner and still undefeated, even though I have never played before so of course I am still undefeated, but I don't feel triumphant, as it was a fraudulent win and Dan intentionally lost to me because I am now a higher-up.

Then Jefferson invites the two females to play against him and Dan, and I find Rebecca, who stands behind the two females. She compliments my pool skills.

"You could perform as well if you tried," I say. "It is merely a combination of geometry-based strategy and hand-eye coordination."

She smiles and says, "You certainly have a distinctive way of seeing the world."

I smile as well, but it is forced, because while I do enjoy the use of numbers and logic, her comment suggests that it's all I have to offer others and that, parallel to Dan, I have a narrow worldview.

Possibly Rebecca recognizes I'm offended because when I ask how the pod is, she says, "It's something to listen to Dan and Jefferson's repressed flirtations without any other witnesses. A truly unique experience." I want to tell her that I would like to have other witnesses in my office as well, but I don't want the risk of her asking what I'm working on or to appear ungrateful for receiving a private office. Then she adds, "Except you can't say something is 'truly' unique. It's either unique or it's not. Like pregnancy." I had not previously considered this idea. Placing an adverb before "unique" is similar to multiplying a number by zero: It will remain zero no matter what the modifier is.

I consult with her about the Y2K project, but she instead asks how my sister is. I tell her Zahira has developed an interest in biology and is performing well in school. "But I wish she displayed more interest in economics," I say. Rebecca asks why. "It is an interesting field and one that she would excel at."

"Maybe it's more important for her to find out what she's interested in and what she excels at," Rebecca says.

I do not reply, but it is a valid point, and possibly Zahira is not truly stimulated by my conversations and emails about finance and programming.

Rebecca lights a cigarette and accidentally exhales smoke in my face. "Oh, fuck, I'm so sorry," she says as she waves her hands to push it away, although once smoke has touched you it has already inflicted its odor and damage.

But I say, "You do not need to apologize to me. You should apologize to your own body."

"Thanks, Mom," she says. "I was in the mood for a lecture about something I only get reminded of 50 times a day."

"Then why do you not stop smoking?" I ask.

"Stop smoking," she says as if she is considering the idea for the first time. "Why didn't I think of that? I should just quit—it's so easy to do!"

I look directly at her and say, "That is an attitude of defeat. Your body is more powerful than cigarettes, and your brain is more powerful than your body, and you can overpower them if you truly want to."

Her eyes move slightly as they stay with mine. She deposits her cigarette inside her beer bottle. "Sounds a little Tony Robbins, but what the hell, nothing else has worked," she says. She looks at the long line for the restroom. "Save my spot?" I tell her I will, although I don't think anyone will occupy her spot to talk to me.

But soon a man in a costume with wings on his back that mirror light bumps into me. "Excuse me," he says, and from his voice I decipher he is a homosexual.

"It is not a problem," I say.

"Let me make it up to you," he says. "What are you drinking?" I tell him Coke and vodka, and he says, "My kind of guy."

I hope Rebecca returns before he does, but he's back quickly. "One vodka and Coke for Mr.?" he asks.

"Karim Issar," I say, and I shake his hand with great force.

"Easy, tiger," he says. "I need that. Jamie Spalding."

He asks where I'm from and what I do and how long I've been in New York, and I answer each question in a calm and quiet voice, which is simple because my normal voice is not very stimulated and is a facet I'm working on, as businesspeople respond to enthusiasm and energy.

When I tell him that I don't mind working long hours, and in fact I prefer them because sometimes I'm uncertain what to do with myself when I don't have a project, he laughs very hard, even though nothing in my statement is humorous. Then he touches my chest and says, "Do you consider dancing a project?"

I must remind myself that I am a guest at this party and in this country. "No, I do not," I say. "But I have to rejoin my friends now." Before I depart I shake his hand even though I don't truly want to.

At the pool table, Jefferson introduces me to the cat (Melissa) and the English Middle Ages waitress (Bonnie). He says, "Karim works with us at Schrub. The boss fucking *loves* him—he took him to the World Series the other night." I don't know how he knows this, and I wish he didn't know it. Then he whispers in my ear, "Bonnie's been asking about you. Talk to her."

I don't believe him, and I also think he wants me to talk to her so that he and Dan can possess Melissa exclusively for themselves, and it frustrates me that Jefferson always secures the optimal female, but Rebecca is still waiting for the restroom and I do not want to be alone or have Jamie converse with me again, so I engage Bonnie. She is studying for a master's degree in sociology at a university in New York, and although she is friendly and intelligent and I do not think females who are slightly overweight are unattractive, as Jefferson and Dan do, I keep looking over at Melissa and partially listening to her, even though what she is saying is vapid (she is discussing where she bought her costume and how the idea launched from a television show), but Jefferson and Dan pretend to be very stimulated.

Dan continues refilling my drink and I become dizzier but I don't want to appear like a boring socializer so I continue drinking, and then Dan and Jefferson pour us all small amounts of tequila and we consume them as a group project. The liquid produces flames in my throat and my eyes hydrate and when I open them everyone has a compressed face. At one point Dan says quietly to me "Karim," and because he uses only one syllable I can tell he is also drunk. "I know I can be a dick. I can't help it. It's not personal. I'm just that way sometimes." When I say it is okay, he squeezes my shoulder and says, "No, really. I'm a bastard. I can't stand myself most of the time." I tell him he is a better person than he credits himself, and I think I see a tear in one of his eyes before he deletes it with his fingers but it may be a result of the alcohol, and he hugs me with force and makes me drink another small glass of tequila with him.

The remainder I don't remember with clarity. I know that soon Melissa began talking to me, possibly because I was pretending not to pay attention to her, and people act according to a supply-and-demand equilibrium like prices do, and then she was touching my arm frequently and laughing at my jokes that I knew weren't very humorous and licking her lips just below a small birthmark that looked like a decimal point, and she asked to hold my wrench and then pocketed it in my pants, and we all drank more tequila, and soon we were all dancing in the middle of the room and Melissa was dancing with her back to me but adjacent to my waist and her neck had the most delicious smell of vanilla and felt like silk sheets against my cheek, and when I turned around at one point I saw Rebecca standing in our former spot, and we looked at each other briefly although she was blurry but I could see she was smoking a cigarette again.

Melissa went to get another drink, and Rebecca came up to me and said, "Sorry to interrupt. Maybe I'll see you on Monday, if you make it in," and left. Sometimes I wish my voice recorder didn't record everything.

Then Melissa returned and kissed me and tasted simultaneously like a soft dessert and alcohol.

Dan and Jefferson were both dancing with Bonnie dividing them, and she was alternating in kissing both of them, and then I saw Dan bend down with his President Clinton mask off and kiss Jefferson with his tongue and Jefferson permitted it for many seconds before he pushed Dan away and called him a fucking fag.

Melissa licked the inside of my ear and whispered, "Do you want to get out of here?" and I said yes and licked her ear but instead contacted her hair with my tongue.

In the elevator we kissed more as we descended, and she also put her hand inside my pocket and said she was looking for my wrench and laughed, because it was the pocket without the wrench. When we exited the building it was much colder than before and my body was vibrating from the temperature and the alcohol. She said we could go to her apartment in the East Village. We waited for several minutes but couldn't receive a taxi because they were in such high demand. Then a white man driving a bicycle with an attached carriage came down the street. Melissa stood in the street and waved her hand, and when he stopped she entered the carriage.

I couldn't believe the man was going to transport us with his legs all the way across Manhattan. But Melissa said, "What are you waiting for?" and I got in.

The man pedaled to her address. He looked like he was my age and wore a wool hat for the cold, but soon he perspired from the work. Melissa continued kissing and touching me. I looked at the driver's legs periodically and tried not to pay attention to people on the street observing us.

When we arrived at Melissa's apartment, I gave her my wallet because I couldn't focus on the numbers on the bills. She paid and returned it to me and exited the carriage, and I gave him another bill whose denomination I couldn't read.

Her apartment was on the fourth floor, and I was breathless at the top because I have had little challenging exercise in New York. Her bedroom and kitchen were in the same room. "I guess it's not quite what you're used to?" she said.

In fact, it was similar to what I was used to in Doha. "It is sufficient accommodations," I said, although I did not pronounce the words clearly.

She took my hand and led me to the bed, and soon we discarded all our clothing. She said she liked my body and that my skin had "such beautiful coloring." I said I liked how smooth hers was (although one small section of her left leg was not because of a shaving error) and how soft her hair was, and we spent a long time touching each other's skin and faces and hair and I forgot all about Kapitoil and work and being a foreigner and everything else, and all I thought about was how luxurious my body felt next to Melissa's and that I had won the cream of the cream female at the party.

Finally she opened a drawer next to her bed and removed a

condom. I had a moment of clear thought in which I truly understood what I was about to do and what it would mean and how
I might feel after it, and my initial reaction was to tell her that I
needed to go home, but then she exhaled warm air on my neck
and my body defeated my brain and the thought deleted and I
asked her to place it on me.

I don't remember all the details. I wasn't as nervous as I always predicted I would be, probably because of the alcohol, but
when I had difficulty releasing her bra she slightly laughed and
made me feel like a novice. I don't believe I was very skilled, because I didn't truly know what actions to take, and at one point I
remembered what I had done to Rebecca and I temporarily lost
the desire to continue.

But it was still mostly pleasurable, and I spent much time
touching her left breast and observing how it felt like nothing
else on my body and nothing else I had ever remembered touching, and the pleasure reached its peak at the end, when it was
as if my system crashed but in a delightful way, and for several
seconds all my thoughts were voided, which never happens to
me. After we finished, we rested on our backs without contacting and she said, "I came really hard, twice."

She fell asleep quickly, but I didn't, because my body no longer had power over my brain and my thoughts were becoming
clearer and the effects of the alcohol weren't as robust. I placed
myself under the blanket, but Melissa's body was facing up on
top of it. There was no method to place her under without waking her. But she seemed like she would be careless if I saw her
without clothes.

And then I truly started to think about what I had done. I
wondered what my mother would say. Possibly she would under-

stand, because she was modern, but she might also say that I was rejecting not only Muslim values but also personal values, e.g., I didn't know or even respect Melissa very much and the main reason I was with her was because she was sexy and I wanted to prove that I could obtain her so that I would also feel sexy, which was never something I was invested in before.

Although we had done an act that was the opposite of violence, in some ways I understood how a person might feel after committing murder. In my brain I kept hearing my voice repeat the word "aasef," but I simultaneously knew that apologizing achieved nothing, which only increased the volume of my interior voice in a cycle.

I remained awake because of these thoughts and also because I was not used to sleeping next to anyone, especially not someone I met just a few hours before. In some ways that part presented more highly privileged information about another person than intercourse itself. At 5:00 a.m. my mouth felt like chicken bones and sand were blended inside it, and I removed myself from the bed slowly and fell down when my weak legs contacted the ground.

I drank cold water from the sink faucet in her restroom for a full minute. I had never valued water as much. Her sink was covered with long blonde hairs that were black on one end and white toothpaste remainder like lines of writing in the sky from airplanes. When I lifted the toilet seat, I almost ejected when I saw how dirty it was on the reverse side, so I closed it and used the toilet while sitting down. It was difficult to believe such a dirty restroom could produce such a clean body.

I considered leaving my email address with her, but I knew we didn't have many intersected subjects of interest and another meeting would not be profitable. So instead I wrote on a piece of paper: "TO: MELISSA—Thank you for an enjoyable night. FROM: Karim."

It was dark and cold outside and I was still partially drunk. A taxi drove down the street and I raised my hand, but when it stopped I told the driver, "My bad—please resume." He cursed at me in his language and left. I walked north and west, and with every step I wanted to eject, but I told myself I merited walking home. Bags of trash sat along all the sidewalks like palm trees in Doha and the smell made me feel even unhealthier, so when it was possible I walked in the dividing islands of the streets to avoid the smell and other people. In one hour I was at my apartment, where finally I did eject everything I drank the previous night in my restroom, and I then drank water until I felt I had consumed an equal quantity to the alcohol, and showered for a long time and washed myself well but was too exhausted to pray.

high roller = gambler with significant funds at his disposal

mechanic = worker who repairs machines

pocket = deposit an object inside a pocket

pre-game = drink alcohol in the apartment before external parties to
    reduce panicked feelings

redneck = negative term for someone who lives in the southern U.S.

repressed = emotions that a person attempts to restrict

tool = someone who is leveraged by others

NOVEMBER

When I woke up after Halloween, I was still ill. I hydrated on my couch and watched American football on television, which was less stimulating than baseball even though there was more continuous action, and I also failed to cover the point spread in one of the three games I bet on and lost my $5.

I considered calling Rebecca, but I was uncertain what to express.

After two hours of not moving from the couch, I forced myself to take the subway to the mosque on the Upper East Side.

There were again many people inside. I performed wudu, and felt especially refreshed after rinsing my mouth and inhaling and ejecting the water into and out of my nose. Wudu is like defragmenting a bottlenecked hard drive: You do not realize how enhanced you will feel until you do it.

I found an area in which to pray. When I stood to leave, an older man with dark skin and long eyelashes wearing a white robe walked over. "As-Salāmu ʿAlaykum," he said.

"Wa ʿAlaykum As-Salam," I said. It felt strange to speak Arabic to someone in New York.

"This is your first time here?" he asked.

I didn't want to admit that I had been there before but had never talked to anyone in nearly a month in New York. "I recently transferred here for work at Schrub Equities," I said.

"Ah, you are a banker." He rubbed his fingers together and smiled. "You are making money, yes?"

"Yes," I said. "I donate Zakat to schools in Qatar."

"Are you from Doha?" he asked. I told him I was. "Then you should meet Fawaz." He waved his hand at another man his age also in a white robe. Fawaz had one golden tooth, and told me that he was an Egyptian who previously lived in Doha but hadn't been back in over a decade. He had lived near my family's neighborhood, and we discussed the infrastructure changes there in the past ten years, e.g., construction for what will be the largest shopping mall in the Middle East.

Fawaz wrote his address and telephone number on a piece of paper. "My family is having a dinner with others from the mosque on Friday," he said. "Your presence would honor us."

"It would honor me as well," I said.

After I left I felt enhanced in all ways, so I decided to visit the Metropolitan Museum of Art, and walked south on 5th Ave. past the wealthy apartments bordering Central Park. Mr. Schrub probably knows many of their residents. One goal I had hoped to achieve here which I haven't yet is meeting more businesspeople and networking partners to build social capital. But whenever I meet someone, I have difficulty thinking primarily of that person as part of a future network.

The museum entrance was similar to a palace and made the Qatar National Museum seem like a small store. I was seven when I first went. I do not remember the actual visit, but only what happened before it. There was an exhibition on Qatari traditional clothing and how it is produced. Even though clothing is not my preferred subject now and it was not then either, my mother talked about it for several days in a way that stimulated my interest.

The day arrived, and we were about to leave when my father, who was reading a newspaper at the kitchen table as he often does, asked where we were going.

"I told you before," she said. "I am taking Karim to the museum."

"You are pregnant. You should be resting at home."

"I can manage a museum," she said. "And Karim is very interested in seeing the exhibition."

He put down his newspaper. "What is the exhibition?"

"Traditional Qatari clothing."

My father turned to me. I was even worse then about reciprocating visual contact, and I looked at my shoes. "Clothing." He laughed. "My son is interested in clothing."

I wished she had at least said it was about how the clothing was produced. But my mother just shook her head and took me to the door. "Do not forget to show him the jewelry and perfumes as well," my father said as we left.

When we got outside she said, "Do not ever let anyone make you feel inferior for what interests you." I tried to remember this advice whenever my classmates made fun of me for being interested in computers before technology became popular.

In the Metropolitan Museum I decided to observe exclusively the European paintings, as the museum was so vast that I had to specialize, and that area is also a major knowledge gap to address if I am to become as well-rounded as Mr. Schrub.

I spent a long time studying the paintings of Paul Cezanne, who focused on objects and sometimes nature. But he also painted men and females bathing. At first I stood far away from the painting so no one would witness me looking closely at it, but then I listened to a museum leader lecturing to a cluster of tourists.

"Cezanne was noted for his discomfort with female models," she said. "He compensated by concocting imaginary tableaus in sylvan environments, and that visionary quality is what lends the bathing paintings a sense of the mythic. Note the characteristic diagonal, parallel brushstrokes that weld the bathers to the landscape while simultaneously asserting their division . . ."

I stopped listening, because although I appreciate receiving some data to help decipher a problem, it's always more enjoyable for me to utilize my own intellect. After the tourists left, I moved closer to inspect the brushstrokes. The leader was correct, and I examined them for several minutes and was careless when other visitors came nearby. It's beneficial for my programming to remind myself that major projects ultimately derive from discrete miniature components.

For the rest of the paintings I selected just a few that intrigued me, and similarly magnified them, even when they were of bathing females. After two hours I was taxed and walked home for exercise.

I rerouted through Times Square, as I had not been there in several weeks. While I waited at a corner, a man nearby with an advertisement on a board surrounding his body said, "Naked girls! No cover! $10 lap dance specials all night!" A mother was adjacent to me with her young daughter, and she covered her daughters' ears by pretending to hug her.

I wanted to call Zahira when I came home, but it was too late in Doha. On Monday morning I called as I ate my labneh and pita, but my father answered. "Is Zahira at university now?" I asked him.

"It's pleasant to hear from you as well," he said.

I asked him how his business was progressing.

"Not well," he said. "That's why I'm home early. No one entered the shop today. I told Qasim I will have to let him go."

"But he has worked for you for four years," I said. "And without him, you will have to spend extra hours stocking and cleaning the store."

"I cannot afford his salary. If I must work harder, then that is what I will do."

"You should update your computer inventory system," I said. His computer is obsolete and not connected to the Internet. "For instance, you do not currently use it to search for different suppliers, which could help you find lower prices and—"

"I am satisfied with my current arrangement," he said.

It was frustrating, because I had several ideas for how a new computer could benefit his business, but I knew he wouldn't listen. So I discarded the idea and told him he should advertise his shop in the newspapers, as I've advised him to do for years, because his shop does provide a valuable and unique service of searching for items that are difficult to locate. "You must spend money to make money," I said.

"Advertising inflates prices without enhancing the product," he said.

"Yes, but with greater profits from advertising, the manufacturer or supplier can then work on enhancing the product." It's an argument we've had frequently and we always state the same ideas, and I was able to discuss it while I tied up my full kitchen trash bag to deposit in the hallway incinerator.

"A new department store recently opened nearby," he said. "Nearly everything I have they also have, plus additional products. And now there is an advertisement on our street for it that depicts a white female coloring her lips."

Outside my window were many advertisements depicting females doing much more than that. "That is the means by which consumers respond," I said. "It's normal."

"It's immoral. And if we permit foreign companies to advertise like that here, soon Qatari companies will advertise similarly."

"Showing females' bodies is not necessarily immoral," I said. I was about to tell him about the Cezanne paintings, but he interrupted.

"Is that what you think after one month as an American banker?" His voice was sharp like a right angle on the words "American banker." "Have you completely adopted American values?"

I didn't know why he had to note that I was an American *banker*, as I was a banker before, and he never previously criticized me for my profession. "I have not completely adopted American values. But after spending time here and seeing more of the world than merely Doha, I see that not all of them are harmful."

"If you think that, then you are already brainwashed," he said.

If there is one thing I dislike, it's someone telling me that I am not in control of my own thoughts. "I would rather be brainwashed than not have a brain at all," I said. "You are jealous because you don't have the skills to succeed in a field like mine."

After a period of muteness, he said, "I will tell Zahira to call you," and disconnected.

The piece of paper on which Fawaz had written his address and telephone number was on my kitchen table. His address in Queens was in Arabic letters. I found an opening in the kitchen trash bag and put the paper inside, and in the hallway I threw it down the incinerator and shut the small door with force and went to work.

While I was in a restroom partition in the afternoon, I heard Jefferson and Dan use the urinals. Under the door I saw their feet at opposite ends of the row. Dan said, "My friend Tim's coming in this weekend. Want to go to Gentlemen Only with us?"

"Yeah," Jefferson said. "This time I'm getting the champagne room."

"Didn't you hear? There's no sex in the champagne room," Dan said.

They sang those words multiple times, and then Jefferson said, "Fuck that, if I'm shelling out 200 bucks, I'm getting a hand job," and Dan said, "I hear that," and they both left without depressing the flush handles or washing their hands.

I didn't see Rebecca the next two days, which relieved me, as I still didn't know what to say. Then I finally innovated something. The brain frequently works in the background on another problem when it is solving something else.

Sender: Karim Issar <k.issar@schrubequities.com>
Recipient: Rebecca A. Goldman <r.goldman@schrubequities
.com>
Date: Tue, 2 Nov 1999 21:14:38
Subject: I am a . . .

. . . tool.

I waited for her to reply, and when she didn't I grew panicked that she no longer wanted to be my friend at all. But on Wednesday morning she wrote:

You don't owe me any apology/explanation. If you want to, though, you can come to a party my roommate and I are throwing on Friday. Details below.

I told her I would attend, but she didn't write back then or the remainder of the week, and I didn't see her in the coffee room.

Zahira emailed that she didn't have time to call me but that she had received a 97 on another biology exam. She didn't mention anything about our father.

sylvan = related to forests
tableau = picture

Rebecca's building didn't have an elevator. A female with short very blonde hair like a boy's with plastic clips in it answered the door. She held a drink and wore a black dress that was the class of dress on old movie stars.

"Hellooo," she said as if she were singing a note. I didn't hear anyone else inside.

I tried to look into the room, but I didn't see anyone. "Is this the apartment of Rebecca Goldman?"

"It is. You're Karim, I take it?"

The solitary way she could know my name was if Rebecca had talked to her about me, which would be positive, but only if she gave me kudos. "Is this the night of the party?" I asked.

"It is indeed the night of the party. You're a little early, hot stuff."

In fact I wasn't early, because the invitation stated the party started at 10:00 p.m. and it was 10:04 p.m., but I didn't correct her. She told me her name was Jessica, and waved for me to follow her inside and danced as she walked to the sounds of a fast song that I didn't recognize, then yelled for Rebecca.

Rebecca entered in jeans and an informal shirt, which I had never seen her wear before.

"This is for your guests," I said, and offered her a container of ma'amoul I had baked and juice I had poured into a two-liter bottle of Coke. "And for you, of course."

"Thank you." She put the container on the table with the other food and held the juice. "I hope Jessica didn't scare you off."

"No, she is not scary," I said.

"Can I fix you a drink?" Jessica asked. "I make a mean mojito."

Before I could respond, Rebecca said, "Hey, don't start stealing away my guests." She directed me to give my coat to Jessica and to come into the kitchen, where there were several bottles of liquor and also nonalcoholic beverages. She handed me a red plastic cup. "Have whatever you like. Or your juice." I had told her about the juice previously at work and urged her to have it because it is high in antioxidants. She tried it once and said she disliked the flavor. I told her most things people dislike are in fact healthy for them.

I didn't want to repeat what happened the previous weekend. But I also didn't want Rebecca to think I was someone who never experienced fun. So I said, "I would like one beer, if you have any."

She took a bottle out of the refrigerator and opened it rapidly with a bottle opener. When she transferred it to me, our fingers briefly contacted.

"I haven't seen you around the office much lately," she said.

"I have been working overtime."

"Right, on your little Manhattan project."

Then neither of us said anything, and I was nervous because we were alone in the kitchen and the only sounds derived from the stereo. I was glad when the doorbell rang.

The guests were a man with a black beard he continuously petted and a female who wore glasses with thick frames shaped like the eyes of a cat. Rebecca hugged them and offered them some food on the table, and the female said, "Is that ma'amoul?" Rebecca asked me to confirm it, and I said yes.

"Where'd you buy it?" the female asked. "I can't find it anywhere." She picked one up and put it in her mouth.

"I—" I said, then I stopped myself and waited for her to

eat it, as I didn't want her to convert her judgment because she knew its origin.

"This is so good," she said. "John, try one. It's a cookie stuffed with dates."

"I baked them myself," I said. "But I wanted to wait for you to eat it before I confessed."

Everyone laughed, although I didn't intend for it to be a joke. The female wiped off her hand and held it out. "I'm Eleanor, and this is my partner, John."

"You have a business together?" I asked.

"A business?" Then she laughed again. "Oh, no, I meant we're domestic partners."

"I understand," I said. "My name is Karim. Rebecca and I are international work partners."

I waited for the others to laugh at my joke, but no one did, and in fact no one said anything and it was tense until Eleanor asked where I came from. I told her, and she said she was an artist and had studied Middle Eastern art and she wanted to go there someday. John asked me questions about Qatar because he was a journalist and knew that we just had our first elections since our independence in 1971. I was happy to discuss politics, as I hadn't truly done that yet in New York. Rebecca is interested in the topic but she is always nervous when discussing it with me, so our conversations don't have much breadth.

After an hour of conversing with them the room had become full, but I wasn't anxious. A few more people joined our conversation and at one point I saw that Rebecca was watching us from across the room, but she turned her eyes away when I detected her.

Then Jessica requested that we all dance, and although I'm not a sexy dancer despite my athletic skills, it was enjoyable and we continued for a long time to songs I hadn't heard of because they weren't of the class that reaches Qatar. Rebecca joined us halfway through and we danced near each other several times, but every time she came close it was like we were magnets with similar poles, and she moved away. She left after a period of time and talked with a few men who had thin beards and glasses like hers and wore unconventional materials that blended in with everyone else's, unlike my suit, and I kept watching her even though I attempted not to. I didn't want to join her cluster because I was the only one who didn't wear glasses, and I would stand out like a syntax error in a program, even though my eyes were not defective and theirs were.

I also didn't understand what they were discussing, e.g., one of the men, who was not shaved and had long black hair tied with a green rubber band in the rear, said in a very deep voice, "I didn't say I *disliked* the Archdukes of Hazzard; I said they were *derivative* of so many late-'70s New York punk bands that I'd rather just listen to the original singers. Which, incidentally, would be a good punk band name—the Original Singers." And Rebecca said, "James, you're such an elitist, and an obscurantist," and he said, "Using the words 'elitist' and 'obscurantist' is a performative sentence which renders the speaker an elitist and obscurantist, as well. Read your Austin," and she said, "You suck—perform that sentence," but she smiled and lightly struck him on the shoulder.

Jessica left to talk with Rebecca and her friends, and she returned to our circle and asked, "Anyone for weed?"

Everyone else said yes. "You want to have some fun, Karim?" Jessica said.

I said loudly, "Yes, I would like to have some fun."

She said "All right," and we all followed her to Rebecca in the corner. Rebecca watched me closely. She whispered, "You know what this is, right?"

"I am not a child," I said. "I know about marijuana."

"Okay, sorry," she said.

Jessica retrieved from a closet a tall red plastic cylinder that had a metal smoking pipe attached to it. She took it to the kitchen, and when she returned the cylinder was partially filled with water. One of the men removed a clear bag with marijuana in it. He inserted his fingers into the bag to pinch a small quantity, as if his hand were a machine that picked up dirt, and carefully deposited it in the pipe.

I observed him closely so that when it was my turn I would not humiliate myself. He covered a small hole in the cylinder with his index finger while he moved an activated lighter over the marijuana, then he inhaled from the cylinder and simultaneously removed his index finger. The smoke passed through the water, and I hypothesized that it made it less carcinogenic and softer for the lungs, which made me less nervous about inhaling it, as I have never even used a hookah.

Then he contained his breath for over ten seconds before he exhaled the smoke like a factory chimney. After he finished he said, "That's a totally groovy bong, dude," in an intentionally false and high voice, and everyone else laughed with him although I didn't know why, and I decided I should not make any more jokes in the U.S. because I still didn't understand the logic of humor here.

He shifted the bong clockwise to the next person. I was next, and while the female next to me inhaled, Rebecca looked at me again as if she were afraid for me.

When I received the bong, I inflamed the marijuana for a long time and inhaled strongly. The water inside made a quiet bubbling sound that was pleasing and then the marijuana smoke reached my lungs, and it burned and produced tears in my eyes, but I closed them and continued inhaling at the same pace as if I were a machine that could proceed infinitely. When I was finally done, Jessica said, "Damn, Karim knows how to par-*tay!*" and I still contained my breath for even longer than the previous two people. By the time I exhaled there were just a few clouds of smoke, so I had absorbed the lion's share of it and was using the product efficiently.

I felt slightly imbalanced, but I was not truly inebriated yet. They passed the bong around the circle, and the originator asked if we were up for another round. A few people, including Rebecca, said they had inhaled a sufficient amount, but Jessica said she wanted more and asked if I did, and I said, "If you have enough remaining I would like more," not only because I wanted to see what the true sensation was like but also to show Rebecca that I knew how to party.

I watched the first man produce another cloud of smoke. I thought about how it was previously the marijuana plant, which came in a larger shipment that was probably sold by a drug dealer with a small income who bought it in a much larger shipment from a drug dealer with a larger income and so on, and was transported into this country by a drug dealer with an even larger income, and originally derived from marijuana plants in the ground, but that it was picked by someone with a very small income. It is always a valuable exercise to evaluate how a product arrives at its consumer, because it shows how many middlemen there are and whose labor helps determine the market price.

When the smoke contacted my lungs on the next round, it didn't burn at all, and my body instantly felt lighter, as if someone had rotated a dial and reduced the gravity in the room.

After I handed the bong to Jessica I thought about how:

1. The party was not stimulating the economy, because most of what the guests consumed for entertainment at the party minus the alcohol was either essentially "free" (all the food was homemade, although the raw materials were purchased elsewhere) or not purchased from a store (the marijuana) or was previously purchased and reused (e.g., the music);

    A. but then it also meant the guests were not paying for middlemen or advertising;

    B. and ultimately they were creating a "product" (a social event providing entertainment) from almost nothing via creativity and cooperation;

        i. which is impossible in the physical world in which matter cannot be created or destroyed;

            1. but this is how human emotions and intangible products differ from objects;

                a. and the most powerful material/emotion that you truly derive from nothing is love, which does not require a source and has no limit;

                    i. e.g., I have infinitely loved Zahira since the first time I saw her and will always feel that way.

As I concluded this thought, I observed Rebecca more closely than I would normally, especially the small area between her lips and her nose and the soft angles of the two vertical lines there, and I almost became imbalanced, but I put my hand on the wall and remained vertical. I could hear the blood zooming in my ears like water boiling in a teapot, and I licked my dry lips.

I craved water but I couldn't go to the kitchen because I didn't want anyone to see me in that condition. I went down a hallway to the restroom on the other side of the apartment.

The restroom was locked, so I leaned against the wall. It hurt my back and I plummeted slowly until I was sitting. That was uncomfortable also, and then I noticed an open door to another room. Multiple coats covered the bed in a pile like a bowl of colorful herbs, and I considered that if coats were allowed to be on the bed then I could be as well.

The room had only a small lamp on for minimal light. A picture of Rebecca's brother was on the table by the bed and next to a black-and-white picture of a young female with long straight hair who looked like Rebecca. Three framed paintings hung on her walls of men's faces in colors such as orange and blue and green that looked like the inverted true colors.

A bottle of prescription pills was next to her pictures. I rotated it to read the label:

Rebecca Goldman
Zoloft
Take daily with food (150mg)

I rotated it back and reviewed the paintings. The men looked like aliens, and their faces were very angry and sad simultaneously, and my heart accelerated and my skin perspired at what felt like an infinite number of points. I sat on the bed where there weren't any coats and reclined and closed my eyes because the ceiling looked like it was spinning. Then I grew very panicked, because I knew I did not have complete control over my thoughts anymore, and I didn't want to be at the party anymore and I regretted inhaling marijuana smoke only to impress Rebecca.

I tried to regulate my breathing but I was inhaling shallowly, and then a voice said "Here," and a cold wet cloth was on my forehead and absorbing the perspiration, and when I opened my eyes Rebecca was leaning over me. She said, "You've been gone almost half an hour," even though it seemed like only a few minutes.

"I am not feeling well," I said.

She continued petting my forehead. "Just stay still."

We stayed like that for a few minutes and my breathing deepened. "Do you think some slow music will help?" she asked, and I nodded.

I closed my eyes and focused on the words of the singer on the stereo she said was named Leonard Cohen, and it helped reroute my brain from panicking. The line "Your hair upon the pillow like a sleepy golden storm" especially helped because I had to mentally link the two images, and it was a logical connection I had never previously considered, and after he sang that I opened my eyes and Rebecca's hair was now hanging down on the pillow like falling black water and covering everything else around my face like a cylinder and all I could see was her face looking down at me, and my body felt more stabilized.

"Who produced these paintings?" I asked.

"My brother," she said. "He's studied art since he was little."

"Zahira is artistic as well." I didn't know what else to say in that position. "But my father discouraged her from taking classes like that when she was young."

"That's a shame," she said. "Girls can do whatever they want here." She removed the cloth from my forehead. Then she lowered her head and her hair touched my face like feathers. Her eyes fluctuated quickly from my eyes to my chest, and her warm breath moved over me, and my heart accelerated again.

I said, "Rebecca," because the silence felt like shallow breaths again, and she didn't answer, so I said her name again and she said, "God, it's been a while," and I wasn't certain what she was referring to but I had an idea, so I said, "Then possibly—"

Before I could finish my sentence, which was going to be "Then possibly we should first discuss this situation from other angles," she sat up and said, "I'm sorry, I'm sorry, this is a mistake." She kept saying the word "mistake" to herself as she stood up and moved away from the bed.

I said I was feeling enhanced and should go home, even though I was perspiring again, and tried to find my coat. The pile was large, and Rebecca stood there while I searched. She said, "You must think I'm a real shithead," which almost made me laugh after I had analyzed the word, but because I didn't know how to respond I looked around while I continued feeling through the pile and saw her blue wool hat on her desk.

I said, "That is a nice hat," and she said, "My mother knitted it for me," and suddenly I became very sad thinking about her mother producing a hat for her, even though there is of course nothing truly sad about it for her, but I could feel pressure behind my eyes, so I refocused on the pile and finally found my coat at the bottom and said I would see her on Monday and walked out while holding it, and I exited the party without saying good-bye to anyone and took a taxi home.

bong = device for inhaling marijuana

Manhattan project = term for atomic bomb project (not necessarily a project in Manhattan)

obscurantist = a person who withholds data from others

par-tay = different pronunciation for "party"

performative = a statement that also produces an action

On Tuesday I was making some trades in my office when some-one knocked on the door. The person knocked very softly as if waking a child, and I didn't hear it the first time, because it was raining loudly outside.

"What's up?" Rebecca asked when she entered, which I didn't know how to answer, because (1) she was the one to search for me, and (2) I never know how to respond to that question, since (a) people don't truly want to know exactly what you are doing at the moment and (b) I couldn't tell Rebecca even if she did want to know.

So I said "Nothing," which makes people think you are bor-ing, but I had no other ideas and I was slightly nervous.

"You're allowed to decorate here," she said.

"I do not own many objects."

"Still, a picture or something. Some personality." She was now standing across from me at the desk even though there were two empty chairs there. The sky outside was the color of smoke, which made the interior seem even less decorated. "It's pretty dead."

"Maybe you can lend me one of your brother's paintings," I said, and immediately I regretted it.

"Yeah," she said. "I wanted to talk to you about that. Not about the paintings." She picked up a pen on my desk and moved it in her fingers like a conductor of a symphony holds a baton. "So, the other night, I was pretty drunk and all, and I think I may have done or nearly done certain things that could be con-sidered somewhat inappropriate by some given the context of our professional relationship."

It was difficult for me to follow the meaning of her sentence but I could understand it from her expression and how she focused on the pen.

"So, basically I'm saying that I wanted to make sure you didn't get the wrong impression or anything." She looked at me for the first time since she had entered the room. "Still friends?"

The rain had stopped, and in fact the sun was now out, but I wished it was still raining. It felt as if someone had turned up the gravity inside my chest, the opposite of feeling high, and without looking at her I slowly said, "Still friends." I understand on a logical level how all real-world systems have finite resources and can partially satisfy only some consumers, and therefore the desires of two parties are sometimes incompatible. But it is still difficult to understand on a nonlogical level.

I heard her put the pen on my desk. "Great. Well, that's all I wanted to say." Then, to be polite, she asked me how work was proceeding, and I again responded like a robot, and she left, and I looked at the sunlight pouring into my dead office until I decided to concentrate on my work.

dead = lacking decoration or personality

The next two days I worked very late and was home only to sleep. My apartment had many luxuries but I was the solitary person using them, and that can grow boring, e.g., many times I was listening to the radio on the stereo and wished I could play the song for Zahira, but when I remembered she wasn't there, I didn't want to listen anymore.

Kapitoil was humming at near-optimal efficiency. We were restricting our daily investment so we would not cause market turmoil, and Mr. Ray didn't state any specific projections, but I calculated that if we continued at this rate for the next year, Schrub's quants revenues would increase approximately 30% over the previous year.

Then on Thursday morning I received an email from Mr. Schrub's secretary. I was so stimulated when I saw her name in my inbox that I spilled my cranberry-blueberry juice on my desk and it left a small red puddle. She wrote:

> Mr. Issar,
> Mr. Schrub would like to invite you to his estate in Greenwich, Connecticut, this coming weekend. Car service will pick you up at the office at 5 p.m. on Friday and deliver you to Downtown Manhattan Heliport, where you will meet Mr. Schrub and proceed by helicopter to Greenwich. A car will return you to your residence on Sunday afternoon. Please let me know at your earliest convenience if these terms are acceptable.

I almost called Zahira to tell her the news, but it was too expensive to connect to Qatar during the workday. And I couldn't tell anyone in the office because it would produce envy and they would question why Mr. Schrub was requesting my company, so I told my mother in Arabic so no one would understand me if they heard. I don't truly believe she is observing me, but it's nice sometimes to pretend she is.

I replied that the terms were acceptable, and she responded with further data about the car service. I asked:

Is it possible for me to arrange my own car service?

She wrote that it was. I removed Barron's business card from my wallet. It was easy to find because it was the only one I had received in New York so far.

When I made my reservation with Barron he didn't mention if he remembered me, but maybe that was because he was very busy and couldn't talk for long.

At noon on Friday I saw Rebecca in the kitchen. She was emptying packets of false sugar into her coffee. "Hey," she said.

"Hello," I said.

"Any weekend plans?" she asked.

"I have a busy weekend planned with friends," I said, which was at least partially true. "What about you?"

She stirred the coffee with a plastic straw without looking at me. "Nothing special," she said. "Have a good one." She walked past me and out the door. I should have said that I was instead going to try to compensate this weekend for work I had neglected. But maybe it's better I didn't. When people lie they often have to lie again to cover the first lie, and they continue for many iterations in a chain.

Barron was on time, and as I got into the car I said, "It is my pleasure to meet you again, Mr. Wright."

"You, too," he said, and although I know that people reciprocate that to be polite, it sounded more authentic with his voice. "Heliport, right?"

"Yes. It will be my first time on a helicopter." I added ASAP, "When you took me to the Yankees game, I forgot to call you after the game. My employer drove me home."

"That's cool. People forget all the time. I still get paid."

"No, it is not cool," I said. "It was my bad."

He turned his head and looked at me even though he was still driving. "Okay," he finally said. "Nice suit, by the way. Fits you right."

Barron turned down the sun-protector, and again I saw the picture of his daughter taped to it. I asked how she was progressing. He said she was excelling in school and he thought she would soon be smarter than he was. I told him I thought the same thing about my sister. "Although for now I want her to think I am more intelligent, so that she continues to try to impress me in school."

He laughed and said, "You're all right. You've got a unique sense of humor. It's subtle, but you've got one."

"Thank you," I said. "I will work to make my sense of humor less subtle." This was possibly the reason no one else found me humorous. Then I said, "It must be enjoyable to spend time with your family after a week of work."

Barron scratched the back of his head. His haircut was close to his skull, but many white hairs blended with the black ones. "It is. Sometimes it's not. But mostly it is." His eyes angled at me in the mirror. "You have any family here?"

I looked out the window, because suddenly it felt like tears were under the surface of my eyes and waiting to appear like perspiration on a Coke can. "No," I said. I remained in that position to avoid Barron and because we were now near the East River and I always enjoy observing the water. My father used to teach me swimming at Al Wakrah beach on Saturdays. He was a powerful swimmer, and I learned quickly, although I was never as strong in the water as he was. He didn't take Zahira, and of course my mother never went although I derived my broad shoulders from her and I believe she would have been efficient in the water as well. We stopped going when she became ill.

We arrived in a few minutes at the heliport, which had a landing pad in the shape of an L on top of the river, a large building behind the small parking lot for cars, and spaces for 12 helicopters, although just five were currently there. I thanked Barron. "Call me when you need a ride to the White House," he said, and I laughed and complimented him by saying he had a non-subtle sense of humor.

In a few minutes Mr. Schrub's limo entered the parking lot. The driver, Patrick, exited and opened the rear door for Mr. Schrub. He nodded at Patrick while he held a briefcase in one hand and talked on a cellular, and Patrick returned to the car and waited.

When Mr. Schrub was next to me, he said on the cellular, "John, I'm going to have to go—I'm with an employee," which was both stimulating, because I always enjoy when anyone mentions that I'm a Schrub employee, especially Mr. Schrub himself, but also disappointing, because he didn't refer to me by name. He closed the cellular and put down his briefcase and shook my hand. "Glad you could make it, Karim. I hope the late invite wasn't a problem?"

I told him it wasn't and that I was grateful for the opportunity to see more of the U.S. "Greenwich isn't exactly how the other half lives. But it's a good place for getting to know someone—it's not always so easy in the city," he said. I was glad he stated his reason for inviting me, because I didn't know if we were going to discuss business over the weekend, but then I got nervous because it meant I would have to discuss myself, and my background and opinions are not nearly as original as Mr. Schrub's.

Then he met with the pilot, who wore a blue uniform with gold buttons and a cap and had a thick black mustache, and they discussed some issues about the flight that I couldn't hear, and Mr. Schrub informed me we were ready.

The helicopter was much larger than I anticipated. It looked like a minivan with a skinny nose, an elongated tail, and blades on top. The rear had six leather seats opposite each other the color of yogurt, and in the front were two seats for the pilot and a copilot, although when I saw there wasn't one, Mr. Schrub said, "Don't worry—if Mike passes out, I know how to land."

Mr. Schrub and I faced each other, next to the windows, and linked our seat belts. After Mike toggled many switches and talked on the radio system, there was a sound like a powerful windstorm and the helicopter vibrated and it was like we were a vegetable pulled out of the dirt and finally we smoothly partnered with the air.

The sun was down now and the water below us was black, and I visualized that we were like the Schrub hawk, only the helicopter was not carrying the S and E, but Mr. Schrub himself and me, and for a second I also visualized a potential day Schrub Equities would have the name Schrub Issar.

I became very fearful as we flew higher and I didn't look

out the window anymore, because a helicopter doesn't feel as stable as an airplane. Mr. Schrub could detect I was nervous and said, "I've flown this route hundreds of times, Karim. It's perfectly safe." When we were high enough, the helicopter moved north and I let myself look out the window. The overview was more beautiful than it was on the airplane, because we were at sufficient altitude to get the big picture of the city but also close enough to see details like cars and people moving through streets like liquid through channels, and it's always preferable to have a macro and micro perspective simultaneously. E.g., when I'm on the street, New York seems so large, but now in the air I was reminded of how minimal Manhattan truly is, unless you consider the third dimension of height.

"Take a look, Karim," he said. We were traveling over downtown now. "That city is ripe with possibility. It's made for young men like you."

Below us the cars advanced in traffic like lines of ants. "I have never had problems with working hard," I said.

"It's not always just about working hard," he said. He looked like he was about to say something else, but stopped and removed his laptop from his briefcase and said he had to do some work, and told me I could use the portable DVD player and whatever movie was inside that his sons had been watching. He also mentioned that his sons might be joining us this weekend, and I said I was looking forward to meeting them. "I'm more looking forward to having them meet you," he said.

We bypassed the ultraviolet lights of Times Square and the Schrub logo and my building and the angular skyscrapers in midtown and then the quiet trees of Central Park and the shorter buildings uptown like young children at the knees of their midtown parents, then Harlem and its blocks of iterating apartments and the George Washington Bridge's white lights like points on a parabola, and then we flew east along the coast and the ground below wasn't as bright anymore, and the last unique object I could make out was a large ship exhaling black smoke into the air that Mr. Schrub said was littered with garbage and was probably heading to a landfill in Connecticut, and when I couldn't see anything anymore I powered on the DVD player and the movie *Armageddon*, which I had heard of in Doha.

Soon we were above large houses with long slanted driveways like snakes and empty swimming pools and fields. We zoomed toward a concrete square with lights around its perimeter far behind one of the houses that was shaped like a large U, but then approximately 200 feet above the ground we decelerated and landed very gently, as if we were tucking a child into bed.

The helicopter powered off and the blades stopped, and Mike helped Mr. Schrub exit. I jumped down without aid, which was foolish because I slightly hurt my ankle. Mr. Schrub asked Mike to take my luggage inside after he checked over the helicopter and to leave it with someone named Irma. Then we walked off the concrete and onto a path of small stones on a grass field and toward the house.

His house was not as big as some of the other houses I saw from the air. Its walls were white stone and it had a white roof which in a few areas was conical. In the rear, white columns extended from a wooden floor and formed a shelter, and we bypassed an empty swimming pool and a tennis court. It was like a larger version of Mr. Schrub's apartment building: very luxurious but not boastful.

Mr. Schrub promised that I would get a full tour later but that for now he was hungry. When we approached the rear of his house, a black man in a blue uniform was sitting on a chair. "Hello, Thomas. This is Karim Issar," said Mr. Schrub, and I shook hands with him. "He has full clearance this weekend."

Thomas opened a heavy black door for us and we entered the house. The room had as much space as a hall for concerts, with a crystal-and-gold object with false candles attached to the high ceiling, a staircase with a gold railing, dark wood furniture I could see my face in, and a large carpet with a pattern like an expensive tie.

Mr. Schrub led me into the kitchen, which was the size of my living room, and a man who looked Eastern European was sitting at the marble counter in the middle and reading a magazine. His name was Andre, and Mr. Schrub told me I could ask him to fix me anything I wanted. While he waited for me to decide, Mr. Schrub said he was in the mood for a steak and potatoes and salad. I was craving lamb kofta, but if I ordered it I would have to ask if the lamb was halal, which it probably wasn't, and it would take a long time to prepare and possibly Andre didn't have all the ingredients, so I ordered a salad.

"That's all you want?" Mr. Schrub asked. I said I had eaten a filling lunch and was not very hungry.

Andre told Mr. Schrub that Mrs. Schrub was dressing for dinner and would be down soon. "I'm afraid it'll be a casual affair tonight—just the three of us," Mr. Schrub said. "The boys will be joining us tomorrow." Then he told me I could wash myself in the restroom in my bedroom, and the maid Irma showed me where it was upstairs. My luggage was already present and the bedroom was larger than the bedroom in my apartment even though it was for guests. When I was finishing, someone knocked on my door. It was Mrs. Schrub, and I recognized her from pictures on the Internet of the Schrubs at social events. They looked as if they could be siblings, because they were both very tall (although she is approximately ten years younger), except that she had short blonde hair. She wore a pearl necklace and a long gray dress and high heels. I was glad I was in one of my nice suits.

She shook my hand. "You must be Karim," she said.

"You are definitely Mrs. Schrub," I said.

She smiled and looked as if she didn't know what to say for a moment, then told me to call her Helena and offered to tour the house with me before dinner. She displayed many rooms to me, and after seeing all the expensive furniture in them, they looked similar to me, but possibly that's because I don't have mastery in interior decoration, e.g., in the same way that Mrs. Schrub couldn't observe differences between C++ and JavaScript. But Mrs. Schrub informed me she had decorated the house herself and described the objects in detail, e.g., a "Louis the 13th armoire" in the master bedroom she had acquired from an antique dealer in Vermont, so I said each room was beautiful, which was true, except I was also afraid to touch anything in the rooms, and if you're afraid or unable to touch or utilize something it makes it less beautiful to me, and although the rooms were littered with decorations, in some ways they still seemed dead.

Then it was time for dinner, and we moved to the dining room, where we sat at one end of a rectangular wooden table that had 16 seats. Mr. Schrub said he hoped I wasn't too bored during the tour, and I quickly said that Mrs. Schrub was an informative guide and I especially liked the armoire. Mr. Schrub laughed and said, "Helena, do you think Karim really cares about the *armoire*?"

"Not everyone is allergic to interior decoration. And Karim has a good eye for design," she said, which was friendly but false, unless you consider theoretical design.

Andre served our dinners, and Mrs. Schrub had exclusively the salad. She apologized that we couldn't use vegetables from their garden because of the weather. Mr. Schrub said, "Andre, would you bring up the '93 Burgundy?"

After he left through a door in the dining room, Mrs. Schrub said, "Derek."

His eyes linked with hers, and I looked at my plate to let them communicate in privacy, and then Mr. Schrub said, "Karim, do you like wine? Or would you prefer something else?"

I said, "I do not normally drink wine, but I would enjoy some tonight."

Mrs. Schrub quickly asked me where I grew up, and I told her about Doha. She also asked about my family, which I valued, as the only other people who have truly inquired about them here were Rebecca and slightly Barron. Then she asked if I was "experiencing any difficulty acclimating" to life in the U.S. as "a citizen from an Arab country."

I took a few moments to strategize an answer, as I didn't want them to think I was ungrateful for being here or make them uncomfortable around me. So I said, "Americans are hospitable, although sometimes they do not know as much as they should know about the rest of the world considering how powerful they are."

"I agree." Mrs. Schrub put her fork down. "I very much support the Palestinians."

Mr. Schrub smiled to himself as he cut his steak. "The lion's share of people from my country agree with you," I said.

Mr. Schrub laughed loudly and turned to his wife. "You support the Palestinians? That would be like someone from Qatar saying to you, 'Just so you're aware, I deeply support the IRA.'"

"I simply wanted Karim to know that not all Americans are willfully ignorant about foreign affairs," she said, and I wished I hadn't responded to her statement.

"You hear that, Karim?" Mr. Schrub said. "Not all of us regurgitate our opinions from TV news. Some of us do it from NPR."

Mrs. Schrub looked down at her salad and Mr. Schrub leaned over to her. "Honey, I'm just joking." He kissed her cheek. "Still love me?"

"If I have to," she said. For a few seconds I had a mental image of Rebecca's hair creating a tunnel over my head, but then I forced myself to focus on the Schrubs.

Andre returned with a bottle of wine. He showed it to Mr. Schrub, who nodded, and then utilized a corkscrew made of black rubber that depressed itself into the cork and removed it with ease. Its efficiency and reduction of human error and labor was impressive.

Andre poured a small amount of wine into Mr. Schrub's glass. Mr. Schrub made a circular motion with the glass on his personal white tablecloth and the wine centripetally orbited around the interior. He inhaled the scent of the wine, then tasted it and gargled as if it were mouthwash. He said "Very good," and Andre poured him a full glass and the same amount for Mrs. Schrub and me. He also poured water for us, which made me feel like when the doormen at my building perform a service (opening a door) that I prefer to do independently.

Mrs. Schrub didn't drink her portion yet, so I wasn't sure if it was rude merely to drink the wine without copying Mr. Schrub's routine. I made the circular motion with my wineglass, but some of the wine spilled over the edge and stained my white tablecloth.

"I am very sorry," I said, because it's good to acknowledge your error in front of your employer before he does.

"That's all right—it's just cotton, we can throw it out," said Mrs. Schrub. "Andre, would you fetch Karim a new mat?"

Mr. Schrub later said the wine had "too many apple notes for a red," although I enjoyed it much more than beer and especially liquor, but I was careful not to have more than one glass. Mrs. Schrub had just one glass as well, but Mr. Schrub consumed the rest of the bottle. When we finished eating, Andre said the dessert would be ready soon, and Mr. Schrub asked him to bring up a dessert wine, then said he would retrieve it himself and invited me to see his wine cellar.

He led me through the door Andre went through and downstairs to a steel door. Mr. Schrub checked an instrument panel outside the door and said, "You want it at 55 degrees and 65% relative humidity."

He opened the steel door and we entered a room whose light powered on automatically to a low level so it looked like the production of many candles. Horizontal bottles of red wine occupied hundreds of slots on each wall. The different colors of their upper covers made a beautiful random pattern like a Jackson Pollock painting. Mr. Schrub went to a corner and selected a bottle immediately. He quickly told me about the different brands of wine and which ones he preferred (red wine more than white wine because it is more complex, and I predict I would agree with him for that reason).

Before we left he said, "Here, I'll show you my baby." He walked to a vault in a corner of the room I had not observed before. I looked away as he deciphered the combination and retrieved the bottle protected inside.

"1945 Bordeaux." He turned the bottle in his hands as if he enjoyed the feel of it as much as the potential taste. "Arguably the vintage of the century for Bordeaux." He held it out to me with both hands. "Want to see it?"

He handed it to me, but I was very nervous, like I was when my parents took Zahira home from the hospital for the first time and they let me hold her and I was afraid I would drop her because she was so small. I kept thinking that if I ever dropped her she would be ruined forever, like it would be if I dropped the wine, which is foolish because humans are mostly strong and repairable, but in some ways they aren't.

"When are you going to drink it?" I asked.

He shook his head and took the bottle back. "I'll never drink this." He observed it again for several seconds with a smile on his face as he held it near his chest, then replaced it in the vault.

I had baked baklava as a gift and brought it down for dessert, and we also had delicious sorbet and raspberries and wine, and Mr. Schrub consumed two glasses of dessert wine even though his wife and I only drank one glass each. Mr. Schrub yawned and said he was exhausted and he had planned a big day for us tomorrow, and asked if I minded if we all retired early for the night.

Mrs. Schrub said that she was very glad to have met me after she had heard so much about me, and I tried not to smile but I couldn't restrict myself, and I said I had heard a great amount about her as well, although of course Mr. Schrub hadn't told me anything, but I had read about her and the multiple charitable organizations she is on the board of.

My bedroom had a wooden bookshelf of a blond color with dozens of books. Many were about finance, and I initially selected one titled *Emerging Asian Markets*, as that is an area I have interest in. I was prepared to start, but then I saw that the bookshelf contained a few nonfinancial books.

This was an opportunity to broaden my worldview, as I don't typically read literature. Although it was very long, I picked the one that had the most intriguing title because its arrangement of words was illogical: *The Grapes of Wrath*.

I read the first few pages, and the language was simple for me to access, and the story incorporated me, and then I noticed I had been reading for three hours without stopping, which is rare for me to do with anything nonfinancial.

It was slightly after midnight. I wondered what Rebecca was doing. She had said she was doing nothing special, but maybe she was lying as well. I hoped she was home alone and not with any of the men from her party. I continued thinking about this scenario, and I couldn't fall asleep, and I told myself to reroute my thoughts but that made me think about it more, and finally I called Rebecca's home telephone number that she had listed in the email for her party. It rang several times, and each time it rang I was more certain that she was out with someone else, but on the fifth ring Rebecca picked up.

"Hello?" she said, and her voice sounded scratched.

I didn't say anything. "Hello?" she said again. "David, is that you?" My chest shifted until I remembered that David was her brother.

When I still didn't respond, she said, "Whoever the fuck wakes me up in the middle of the night should at least have the courtesy to identify yourself," and disconnected.

I closed my cellular and exhaled.

I woke in the morning feeling fatigued, because although the bed was very soft, in fact the softest bed I had ever slept on, it was almost *too* soft and I never felt comfortable, in the same way that some foods are too sweet to enjoy.

When I went downstairs, Mr. and Mrs. Schrub were already eating breakfast. "We didn't want to wake you," Mrs. Schrub said. "Derek is up at 5:30 every morning to go for his walk, but the rest of us mortals need a little more sleep."

They were reading their own copies of *The New York Times* and eating bacon and eggs, but Andre made me a flavorful vegetarian version of it with tofu and false eggs. Even though it was a substitute I believe it probably tasted superior to the authentic version. When we finished, we heard the front door open. Mrs. Schrub said it was the boys and that I should come and meet them. Mr. Schrub stayed to read an article.

I knew their names were Wilson and Jeromy, and they were putting down their luggage by the front door. A black sport utility vehicle was parked outside on the semicircular driveway.

Mr. Schrub's sons were both tall, even taller than he is, although they were also slightly overweight, especially in their faces, as if someone had inflated them, Wilson's more than Jeromy's, and Jeromy's neck had red bumps all over from shaving. Mrs. Schrub introduced me to them, and they both shook my hand and said they were glad to meet me. Then Wilson said he was starving and Mrs. Schrub told him Andre would fix them something, and we all returned to the kitchen.

Mr. Schrub and his sons said hello to each other. Jeromy ordered French toast from Andre and Wilson ordered steak with eggs. "Bloody and runny, please," he said.

"I was thinking of taking a hike around the Audubon Center today. Who's up for it?" Mr. Schrub asked. I waited for his sons to answer, but when they didn't, I said I was.

"Good," he said. "Guys? It's a beautiful day."

His sons were reading the newspaper now. Wilson had the National section and Jeromy had the Sports section. "I'd love to, Dad, if I could find the time," Wilson said, and he smiled very slightly to himself while he continued reading.

"Me, too," said Jeromy. "I've been getting literally raped at school."

"Jeromy," Mrs. Schrub said. "First of all, getting 'literally raped' would mean you're actually getting raped. Second, it's not the most polite language."

"Sorry," he said. "Figuratively speaking, I've been getting sexually harassed."

"Then it'll literally just be me and Karim," Mr. Schrub said. "Or is it 'Karim and I'?" he asked his wife, and pinched her waist. The proper grammar was in fact "Karim and I," and in addition to "me and Karim" being incorrect, it is considered impolite to state "me and [other person]" instead of "[other person] and me," but I remained quiet.

Irma provided me with hiking clothing and sneakers, and after I changed Mr. Schrub and I went outside to the driveway, where a dark green sport utility vehicle was already parked. Mr. Schrub drove and I sat next to him, and because we were so high off the ground in the car, it felt as if he were the pilot of a plane and I were his copilot.

The Audubon Center had multiple walking trails, and we took one that Mr. Schrub said was his preferred route. Of course I had been in Central Park many times, but there you are always seeing people and it doesn't feel like you are truly solitary in nature. We saw very few others, and the only sounds I heard were birds and the wind on the leaves colored like fire and the branches breaking under our feet. Mr. Schrub didn't talk frequently except to identify the names of the trees I didn't know, such as American sycamore, and plants with original names, such as honey-bells and eastern skunk cabbage.

We arrived at an open field, and Mr. Schrub handed me a pair of binoculars he had brought. "This is one of the best sites in the country to spot hawks," he said as he looked through his own pair. He pointed to a tree a few hundred meters away. "Look! That's a red-shouldered. They're rare, now." He exhaled loudly and said, "Moronic hunters."

It took me longer to find it, because I wasn't acclimated to searching for birds in trees. The hawk had red and brown horizontal stripes over its chest and shoulder and black and white on its wings and tail. Mr. Schrub told me facts about the bird, e.g., it locates prey from a tree branch, then dives quickly and retrieves its target and eats it on the branch again, and facts about hawks in general, e.g., their eyes are eight times more powerful than a human's. "Gorgeous creature, isn't he? You have to be a robot if that doesn't bowl you over," he said.

Maybe this was why Mr. Schrub gave his company the logo of a hawk, which was something I had always wondered and had never read about.

Then the hawk flew off its branch and zoomed down to the field. I couldn't track it with the binoculars because it was too fast, so I observed with my eyes. It plummeted to the ground and fluctuated its wings but without flying. "Use the binoculars again, and look at its talons," Mr. Schrub told me.

The hawk's talons contained a gray object. "What is that?" I asked.

"Lunch," Mr. Schrub said. "And dinner. Squirrel."

The hawk made noises that sounded like "kee yar," and Mr. Schrub joked that it was trying to call my country's name.

Through my binoculars I saw the hawk rip into the squirrel's body with its claws and beak. "Watch him go. It'll devour the whole thing right now," Mr. Schrub said.

I turned my eyes to Mr. Schrub, who was smiling as he watched. I reviewed through the binoculars. The hawk was now eating the squirrel, whose fur was bloody. I shifted the binoculars slightly to the left so it would appear I was still observing it, but instead I focused on an area of grass.

"He's hardly going to be able to fly after this," said Mr. Schrub. "See how engorged his chest is?"

I said yes. After five minutes, Mr. Schrub said we should go back into the trail and watch more birds. They weren't hawks, and none of them hunted animals, so I was able to magnify them.

As Mr. Schrub watched a downy woodpecker through his binoculars, he said, "I could never seem to get Jeromy or Wilson too interested in birding."

"It can be difficult to make someone else interested in what you are interested in," I said. "They have to have some initial interest independent of you."

"Maybe so," he said, and he put down the binoculars. "But you'd like to think a father and his sons would have some intersection. As far as I can tell, the only thing that drives them is having a good time."

"If you drew a Venn diagram of my interests and my father's interests, the intersection would also be minimal," I said.

"Well, you don't choose your parents. And, despite your best efforts, you don't really choose your kids, either." The woodpecker began contacting the tree with his beak. "Take a closer look," he said, and he put his arm around my shoulders as I used the binoculars. I was glad the binoculars covered my face and Mr. Schrub was focused on the woodpecker, because my smile was possibly the broadest it has ever been.

When we returned to the house Mr. Schrub said he had to do some work in his study. Sounds ejected from the living room, where his sons were playing a video game and yelling. "I'm afraid that doesn't sound too enticing?" he asked.

I said, "No, I would like to try to get to know them more."

He looked pleased. "Thanks, Karim," he said.

Although I'm a skilled computer worker and have optimal hand-eye coordination from racquetball, I'm poor at video games, as we were never allowed to have them, and the solitary way to become adept at any system is by practice. In addition, certain personality types excel at video games, and mine isn't one of them.

It was a shooting game, and the television was bisected so Jeromy and Wilson could each see out of the eyes of his own character as they hunted each other. "My hunger for human flesh is insatiable," Wilson said as his character ran through a dark tunnel. "My thirst for blood, unquenchable."

"Bring it on, fat boy," Jeromy said. "How were the birds, Karim?"

"It was educational and interesting," I said. "I have not been in a true forest before, and I have never seen a hawk in person."

"He does love those fucking hawks," Wilson said, and I observed his eyes rapidly shift to Jeromy's side of the television and then return.

"Yeah," Jeromy said, and his face and voice looked and sounded like he was going to cry. "More than he loves his own family."

Wilson crashed Jeromy with his elbow, and they both laughed. "Come on, play, you ADD-riddled piece of shit," he said.

Wilson soon shot Jeromy and his character exploded and fell and blood leaked out of his body. "Defeated," Wilson said. "Conquered, subjugated, dominated, enslaved, made my bitch."

"You cheat. You always look at my guy's POV."

"I'm trying to understand your point of view better—to empathize with you," Wilson said. "Karim, you want to try?"

I said yes. "I'll coach him," Jeromy said. "Let's beat this arrogant spoiled brat."

Jeromy instructed me on how to operate the controller, and soon I became efficient. Wilson's character and my character were both in the same maze, and because it was a newly created maze, Wilson didn't have a special advantage over me in finding weapons and power bonuses. In fact, because my spatial intelligence is robust, I quickly deciphered where these things were in the maze, and I could tell he was having difficulty because he was cursing to himself.

Then I saw Wilson's character far ahead with his back to me, but because I knew he cheated and would rotate if he saw that I was observing him on my side of the television, I rotated *my* character 180 degrees and ran in reverse so that Wilson didn't know I was near him.

Then, when I knew I was very close to him, I turned around again, and Wilson's character's back was directly in my targeting cross. Jeromy contacted my shoulder lightly with his hand to signal me to shoot.

But I didn't.

Wilson's character quickly rotated and shot me. My side of the television turned red like closed eyelids after looking at the sun.

"You had him," Jeromy said.

"No one ever has me, ha ha ha," Wilson said, and he put Jeromy's head inside his angled arm and depressed his fist over the top of his head.

"I am sorry," I said as I looked at the red half of the monitor and Jeromy pushed Wilson off and called him a motherfucker. "I will go upstairs now and allow you two to play." They said goodbye to me and restarted the game.

I resumed *The Grapes of Wrath*, which I enjoyed for two reasons: (1) It taught me about U.S. history during the Great Depression through a stimulating story (e.g., there was no minimum wage in the time period of the novel, which causes problems for the workers on the free market), and (2) I liked partnering with the main character, Tom Joad. He attempts to provide for his family and has strong values, and he has an intriguing way of speaking to boot.

Then Irma knocked quietly on my door and told me dinner was ready. In fact it wasn't dinner yet, but Andre carried a tray with a bottle of wine and crackers and several cheeses into the living room. Wilson and Jeromy wore higher-quality clothing now, and I felt foolish in my hiking clothing, but it was too late to change.

When Andre deposited the tray on a small table, Wilson reached for the knife and cut multiple large cubes of cheese for his plate and ate ASAP without crackers. Jeromy ate more slowly and with crackers.

"Save some room for dinner, boys," Mrs. Schrub said.

Mr. Schrub watched them mutely and looked as if he were truly watching something in his brain. "Maybe we'll have the '94 Burgundy tonight," he finally said.

"We had that last night," Mrs. Schrub said.

"We had the '93."

"Dear," she said as she put her hand on his leg, "I think you may be having a senior moment."

"Do you want me to go down and bring up the inventory?"

Mrs. Schrub smiled and petted his head. "I don't think that's necessary."

"You think I'm wrong, don't you?" Mr. Schrub said. "That's it, I'm getting it."

"Derek!" she said. "Do you *always* have to be right?"

I remembered also that it was the '93 and that he was right, and I also dislike it when someone thinks my memory has a glitch, so I said, "I think I can prove that Mr. Schrub is correct."

Everyone looked at me. "I use a voice recorder to learn English." I showed it to them. "If you give me a few minutes, I will locate the part when Mr. Schrub asked for the wine."

They all observed me as I set the voice recorder on rewind and listened at different points on low volume so only I could hear. It was high pressure with everyone watching me, but I felt confident that I remembered. Then I put it on the table and played it for everyone to hear Mr. Schrub's voice: "Andre, would you bring up the '93 Burgundy?"

"Much appreciated, Karim," Mr. Schrub said, and he picked up the voice recorder and inspected it before returning it to the table. He turned to his wife. "Do you have anything you would like to add?"

"I think it's very admirable that Karim is so industrious about improving his English." She kissed Mr. Schrub on the cheek. "We could all learn from his example of trying to better himself."

Mr. Schrub looked at his sons. "Indeed," he said.

I turned my face away from them all, especially Wilson and Jeromy, but a corner of my mouth curved up despite my attempts at restriction.

Then Andre told us dinner was ready, and Mrs. Schrub said they had a special treat for me. The dinner table had two lines of silver trays like expensive buttons on a coat, and when Andre opened them I saw kebabs, hummus and baba ghanoush, tabouleh, a lentil salad, and other Middle Eastern dishes.

It reminded me of when Rebecca invited me to see *Three Kings*. However, I was a guest, and once I saw it I did desire authentic Middle Eastern food, and I briefly felt my eyes hydrate like they did in the car with Barron, so I thanked them and quickly estimated the cost of all the food to reroute my thoughts.

The food was delicious. During the meal Wilson and Jeromy ate mostly the meat and didn't try the lentil salad or the baba ghanoush. Mrs. Schrub asked them questions about their progress at Princeton. I didn't ask anything, even though I wanted to know what a cream of the cream U.S. university was like, e.g., how the research facilities were and what class of visiting lecturers they host and if they could access the professors easily. That last subject is the area I especially wish I had in Doha.

Mr. Schrub asked about infrastructural development in Qatar, and I talked as intelligently as possible without appearing to be boastful, as I deciphered that Jeromy and Wilson weren't interested and Mrs. Schrub was interested only to be polite.

As we finished the main course, Wilson and Jeromy argued over the last kebab. Jeromy said he had "called dibs" on it first, and Wilson said he had. When Jeromy pulled the kebab away from his brother, he crashed his elbow into mine, and it made me spill my spoon of cucumber soup. It landed on my shirt, which was my second eating accident with the Schrubs, although this time it wasn't my fault and it stained my own material.

Mr. Schrub yelled at his sons for fighting, and when Jeromy saw my shirt, he said, "Shit, I'm sorry, man." Wilson didn't say anything.

Mrs. Schrub directed me to the nearest restroom to clean my shirt. "Actually, that one's having plumbing trouble. You can use the one in Derek's office."

I left the dining room and walked down a long hallway to Mr. Schrub's office and rotated the brass handle. I stepped onto a thick red carpet. In front of me was a dark wooden desk, and behind it a spacious window displayed a yard and the forest, and the walls contained bookshelves with hundreds of books. It looked simultaneously like an ideal and intimidating place to work.

I cleaned my shirt in the office's restroom, and when I exited I noticed the trash bin next to the desk had a paper shredder on top of it and fully contained shredded paper. This was in some ways how Mr. Schrub presented himself to me: He gave indications of who he was but he shredded the data so I could not fully decipher him. There was much more about him that I was curious to learn, but I could not gain access. He said that this weekend would enable us to get to know each other more, but nearly all he had talked about so far was birds, and he worked nonstop. I had observed his relationships with his family, but I still did not know what he was truly like.

And I considered that I am most truly like myself when I am working and in my office, and this was where Mr. Schrub was so frequently, and without 100% thinking through my actions, I took out my voice recorder and went to a bookshelf near the door and deposited it on a shelf at my height behind a thick book titled *Democracy Through Prosperity*.

I let my hand go. The voice recorder was hidden, and it would now record the hidden Mr. Schrub.

I exited the office and returned to the dining room. Without my voice recorder I felt naked, as I do when, e.g., I am away from computers for several days, but this was a different class of naked.

Only when I sat down did I consider what I had done. In addition to possibly being illegal, it was unethical. I had disobeyed Mr. Schrub's trust, and if he found out, then I merited being fired and ejected to Qatar early. And it was not even intelligent: The only data it would record would be telephone conversations, which are *not* when people are truly themselves. My foot started vibrating on the floor and I felt dizzy, parallel to when I had smoked marijuana. I couldn't believe I had acted so foolishly.

I had to return to his office for the voice recorder, but I

couldn't go right away again, and it was too risky to enter his office if others were around. And of course I couldn't leave it there, because if he found it later he would know it was mine. The solitary possible time would be that night when everyone was asleep.

Mrs. Schrub cleared her throat, and Jeromy apologized to me again for the accident, and this time Wilson apologized as well. He said something like, "Even though it was more Jeromy's fault, since I called the kebab first."

"Karim, can you settle this and check your recorder to see who called it?" Jeromy asked.

My stomach rotated. I waited to see if their parents would ask them to stop the fight, but they didn't say anything. "Yeah, the tape won't lie," Wilson said.

I said, "I just put it away in my luggage upstairs and deleted today's material. I did not want to make any of you uncomfortable about being recorded."

They stopped discussing the accident, although I kept thinking about the voice recorder. It was like the window Raghid broke, although much worse: That truly was an accident that my friends didn't take responsibility for, but this was a disloyal action that I didn't take responsibility for, and in addition I further lied about it.

Wilson and Jeromy said they were going to a movie about a fighting organization after dinner. Mrs. Schrub said, "Why don't you boys take Karim along?"

Wilson and Jeromy visually contacted. Jeromy was friendly, but Wilson was difficult for me to be near. Frequently that was the case here with sets of two people. I said, "Thank you, but I am taxed from the hike and prefer to stay home and read."

After they left, Mr. Schrub said there was no reason we couldn't watch our own movie, and he showed me his archive of DVDs and VHS tapes. He said he had bought everything on a recent list of the 100 best American movies of all time, and asked if there were any I had not seen yet that I wanted to. I said I had not seen any of them yet and if they were evaluated as the best movies of all time then I wanted to see all of them.

He said we could start with one from the top ten. I recognized most of the titles. Although I was interested in seeing it at some point, I didn't want to watch *Lawrence of Arabia* with them. I picked *The Wizard of Oz*, as I knew it was the movie least related to real life and wouldn't cause any problems for us.

Andre brought us popcorn and Coke and Mr. Schrub invited him to watch. The story was intriguing, and Mr. Schrub explained many political and economic analogs for the 1890s, e.g., the yellow brick is the gold standard and the tin man equals industrial workers. I think I liked the tin man the most, but not because of what he represented. Finally Mrs. Schrub told him to stop talking, although it always interests me when an artistic work has a one-to-one correlation of meaning with other systems.

When it was over, Mr. Schrub went to his office to do some work before bed. I read *The Grapes of Wrath* in the living room, and Mrs. Schrub joined me later to read her own book, whose title I didn't know, and when she saw what I was reading she said, "I just adored that book when I read it in high school."

I felt foolish that she read a book in high school that I was reading now, but I said, "I am adoring it as well."

"I devoured Steinbeck in those days," she said. "All those '30s writers. Odets, and West . . ."

She looked around the living room at all the wooden and mirroring furniture and moved one finger over the light pink couch she was sitting on, and then said, "We're not in Kansas anymore, huh? Though I suppose we all end up very different people from who we were at 16."

I nodded again, because even though I was a skilled mathematician in high school, I never predicted at 16 that I would be working for Schrub Equities in New York and actually be a guest in the home of Derek Schrub.

And although I did aim to have as impressive a position as I do now, at that age I wasn't thinking as much about making money.

We discussed the novel, and she told me more about the Great Depression and also about the charities she aided in New York. I lost count of how many she worked for and don't remember all the names, but many of them helped the poor in the U.S. and outside the U.S., and she said the organizations she was most invested in supported females in developing countries.

I talked about Zahira and how I hoped to give her the opportunity to come to the U.S. at some point. Mrs. Schrub said, "That's wonderful to hear. I wish more young men thought the way you do," which was nice, but made me feel uncomfortable again because of the potential comparison to her sons.

Then we both read mutely for over an hour, and Mr. Schrub remained in his office, and because I periodically looked up to see if he was still there, Mrs. Schrub said, "I'm sorry Derek's been holed up in there all weekend. You've gotten a pretty good idea of what we deal with."

"I understand he must work frequently," I said. "I am not offended by it."

She closed her book. "Well, it's past my bedtime," she said. "Maybe the boys will be home soon and you can play some video games together. And if you get hungry, make yourself at home in the fridge."

I thanked her again for hosting me and for dinner, even though I truly wanted to thank Andre for that.

I resumed reading downstairs, as I hoped Mr. Schrub would soon go upstairs, but he continued burning the midnight oil in his office. I was about to go to my room, with the plan to return in the middle of the night, when the door to his office opened and I heard Mr. Schrub say, "Karim, would you come here for a moment?"

My heart shifted position: He had seen the voice recorder. I didn't know what to say. I couldn't lie that I left it out and someone else must have put it in his office, because I had said that I put it in my luggage. It would be even more dishonest to blame someone else to boot. I would have to take responsibility and accept my punishment.

Mr. Schrub was already sitting in his chair, but he was facing the window. Only his desk lamp was on. We sat for several seconds in the partial darkness.

I was about to apologize when Mr. Schrub said, "Karim, I'm sorry."

Even though it's virtually silent because it's digital, I was still afraid we might hear the voice recorder power on. His back was still turned, and I didn't know if he meant he was sorry that I had been disloyal, so I asked, "What are you sorry about?"

He rotated back to me. His eyes were the color of red wine blended with water. "When you told me your mother died, after the Yankees game, I wasn't very responsive."

"You do not need to be responsive about that. It is not your problem," I said.

"I know," he said. "Still. My father died when I was a kid. How old did you say you were, again?"

I had not in fact said how old I was previously, but I told him 13. He pointed to himself. "Ten."

He walked to the window. The moon produced some light, but the woods were dark. "It's curious what you do and don't recall from something that happened over half a century ago," he said. "All I remember from when my mother told me is I was wearing this sweater. This navy blue sweater she'd knitted for me. I had to wear it every day in winter for two years because of the wool rations. And it had this loose thread, and I kept pulling it and pulling it while she explained to me what sometimes happens to soldiers during wars, especially brave fighter pilots, and finally she screamed at me to stop it or my sweater would completely disappear."

"Sometimes people react in unpredictable ways when they hear about a death," I said.

"Did you?" Then he turned from the window. "You don't have to answer."

"No," I said. "I will."

I talked about how several of my relatives came to Doha from around Qatar for my 13th birthday. "But they were truly coming to visit my mother for one terminal time," I said, and I explained how she had breast cancer and the doctors had permitted us to move her to the apartment, which required transporting equipment and hiring a nurse. My father prepared much food the day before the party, including lamb, which was my mother's preferred meal. "It was hard for her to chew the lamb, so he made hareis, which is cooked slowly and therefore fragile," I said.

"I went to sleep stimulated about the party," I said. "My father came into my and my sister's bedroom that morning when it was still dark. Zahira was asleep. He said, 'Karim, come with me, please.' It was February and we did not have heating, so I was vibrating when I followed my father out of the bedroom and into the hallway. Then he told me, 'I am sorry, but we will not be having your birthday party tonight. We will be having a funeral.'"

Mr. Schrub was looking directly at me while I spoke, which typically would make me nervous, but now I was concentrating on the story and I forgot about his presence.

"I was quiet for a long time," I said. "And then I do not know why I did it, but I smiled. That is what I mean by unpredictable behavior, because of course I was not happy. My father asked, 'Why are you smiling?' and I did not know and did not answer, but he kept asking me and it kept making me smile more, and finally he slapped me on the left side of my face. Then I think I said, 'I do not want a birthday party anyway,' and ran away from him. I exited our apartment, even though I was in my nightwear and it was still dark, and ran through our courtyard to a big date tree behind the apartment complex that was there when we moved in. I sat underneath the date tree for a few minutes, but its skin hurt my back, and I turned around and punched it. It pained me, and because the tree did not move I punched it again and continued punching it for several minutes."

I paused. It was strange how I was remembering all these details I thought I had forgotten by talking about them for the first time.

"I was upset about many things," I said. "I think what upset me the most was that I never said good-bye to my mother, even though that might have been more painful to do. I do not even

remember what our last conversation was. It was probably something insignificant." I tried to remember it at that moment, but
as I always did, I failed.

"In a few minutes my father found me," I said. "He pulled
me away and I tried punching him instead but he restricted my
arms and I finally gave up. It was foolish to do, and sometimes
my right hand still pains me, e.g., when I play racquetball for too
long. But I came back inside with my father because I considered that someone had to tell my sister what happened in a way
that would protect at least some of her feelings."

I stopped. It was the most I had said nonstop to anyone since
I arrived in the U.S. I felt slightly humiliated for revealing so
much, but I also felt partially enhanced.

Mr. Schrub didn't say anything. He only nodded. I valued
that.

He picked up a glass of golden alcohol that looked even
more golden from his desk lamp and drank from it, then held his
hand under the lamp. "He had these hands, these huge hands.
Johnny Bench hands. Skin like a deer hide, calluses everywhere.
I always wondered when my hands would get to be that size,
feel that rough. And they never did. Dainty little things." He
inspected his hand more closely and laughed quietly. "I get a
manicure every two weeks."

I understood, because I remembered looking at my father's
hands the same way when I was young, but now my hands are of
equal size, although his skin is rougher.

"It's funny," he said. "You act a certain way, and you think
you're an absolutist, but every day there are these little shifts.
They're so small you don't even notice them. And one day you
look at yourself and aren't sure how you got there."

I said, "That is usually how change occurs. It is like physical growth. You cannot detect it on a daily basis."

"Like a physical growth," he said, although I had merely said "physical growth" and did not include the indefinite article. "Exactly. Like a tumor."

I didn't want to correct him, so I said nothing, and he looked at me and said, "I know listening to a drunken old man ramble on isn't your idea of a wild Saturday night. I'll let you hit the hay."

As I exited the office, he said, "Thanks for the talk."

I said, "You are welcome, Mr. Schrub," and then I felt even worse about spying.

I went to my room. Now I would have to return in the middle of the night for the voice recorder. I considered his statement about the little shifts and what Mrs. Schrub said about being different now from what she was at age 16. My mother always told me the best jobs helped others, but my skill set does not make me a good teacher, and although I am strong at memorizing, I had difficulty with biology and therefore would not be an efficient doctor, and I am not very interested in the legal system because it is man-made and elastic to different countries and not universal the way math or programming is. Of course I am creating and distributing wealth through Kapitoil, but I am only indirectly helping others. To reroute my brain I read *The Grapes of Wrath*, and I stayed awake until I completed it.

I initially became angry at Steinbeck when the character Rose of Sharon gives birth to a baby that is dead. It was as if he didn't want to write a happy ending, so he selected the unhappiest ending. But then she fed the dying man she didn't know at the true ending with the milk that she initially reserved for her baby, and I appreciated the previous negative charge. It was possibly the first time a book made me think differently about a subject not because of a logical argument. I felt like calling Zahira to tell her about it, but I didn't want to contact my father.

In addition, it was 2:30 a.m. and an optimal time to retrieve the voice recorder. If someone detected me, I would say I was making myself at home in the fridge.

I descended the stairs slowly. The house was muted, and the light under Mr. Schrub's office door was out. As I walked down the hallway, I heard voices outside the front door. If I stayed near his office I would be caught, and if I ran back upstairs it would look suspicious, so I quickly entered the kitchen.

The sounds were (1) the front door opening with difficulty; (2) Jeromy and Wilson whispering loudly; and (3) a female voice laughing with them.

Mr. Schrub's sons entered the kitchen with a female approximately their age. She was very tall and thin with blonde hair and a face that was slightly like a horse's and a white scarf tied around her neck. I wished I wasn't in my nightwear.

"Hey, what's going on, Karim?" Wilson said. He sniffed and rubbed his nose several times and said, "Karim works for my dad. This is George." I was surprised a female had the name George, but I didn't say anything. "What are you doing up, man? A little midnight snackage?"

"I already ate some baklava," I said.

"He already ate some baklava," Wilson said, and he laughed and again sniffed his nose, and George laughed also, even though there was nothing humorous or original in his statement. Then he said, "What, you don't like our country's cuisine?"

"I very much like American food," I said.

He asked, "And how do you like our house here?"

"I like it very much as well."

"So if I go to—where the fuck are you from, again?" he asked. I told him. "Qatar," he said. "Qatar. Qatar."

He got up and ran to a drawer and pulled out a knife and put it behind his back. Then he said, "Cut her, cut her," and returned to the table and grabbed George's arms behind her back and commanded me, "Cut her, Karim, cut her," and deposited the knife in my hand as he held her.

It was a knife for butter, so I knew he wasn't serious, and she pushed him off and said, "You are *such* a cock, Wilson," but she was laughing and then said, "And don't be mean to him," which was generous but made me feel like a child even though I was the oldest.

Wilson said, "But seriously, if I go to Qatar, you'll put me up? We'll hang?"

"Yes. Although we do not have as luxurious accommodations, I will try to show you the hospitality your family has shown me," I said.

He nodded and smiled. "I'm just fucking with you. The only thing that's going to cut her is a surgeon's knife." He compressed his hands over her breasts. "Give her a nice pair of D-cups."

George pushed him off again, but Wilson asked, "What do you think, Karim? Does she need an upgrade?"

Although her chest was in fact very minimal, and the rest of her body was so thin that I could see light blue veins every-where, I said, "I do not know."

"Why not?" he asked. "You don't swing that way?"

Jeromy said, "Come on, Wilson," but he ignored him.

"I have not been observing your girlfriend in that mode," I said.

"My *girlfriend*?" he said. "She's not my girlfriend. She's my *sister*." He kissed George with his tongue for several seconds until she again pushed him away. "This is what we do with our sisters in America. We keep it in the family. Family's important, don't you agree?"

The room and the house were quiet. "Family is very important," I said.

He put his hand on George's behind. "And you do this with your sisters in Qatar?"

"No," I said. "We treat our sisters with respect. If you truly had a sister, maybe you would understand."

Then we heard rapid footsteps like a clock ticking quickly and Jeromy said "Shit" and in a few seconds Mr. Schrub opened the kitchen door with force. He was wearing the same clothing as before and looked as if he had fallen asleep in his office.

"How did you get home?" he asked Wilson.

"Drove," Wilson said.

His face was as red as the hawk's shoulders. "You've been drinking?"

"No," Wilson said. "I had one drink. Maybe two."

Mr. Schrub breathed in deeply through his nostrils. "Would you mind taking a taxi home?" he asked George. She looked very afraid and said she didn't mind, and he gave her a $50 bill from his wallet and asked her to call for it and wait outside.

I didn't know if I should leave as well, but I was afraid to ask. I moved to the kitchen door but Mr. Schrub said, "You can stay, Karim."

Then he turned to his sons and commanded them to sit down. They both looked at the table as he spoke. I don't remember all his words, but at a high volume he told them that they should call a taxi if they had even one drink and he wasn't bailing them out for any more DUIs and they were irresponsible and he was fed up with them. In the middle of yelling at them he picked up the knife, which I had placed on the table, and he didn't pay attention to it in his hands, but when Wilson interrupted him once to say he was 21 years old and legally allowed to drink, Mr. Schrub yelled even louder and bent the knife approximately 30 degrees with his hands and Wilson didn't say anything else.

Mr. Schrub said one more thing that surprised me: "I'm furious with you two. You've really let me down." I wondered if this was something all fathers said to their children, or if it was just that my father and Mr. Schrub had similar philosophies, even though my father said he wasn't angry and Mr. Schrub said he was.

He walked to the door and stopped. "And if I ever, *ever* hear you talk to Karim, or anyone else, like that again, I'll be much more than furious."

Then he exited to the upstairs and I waited for 45 seconds while Wilson and Jeromy were mute before I returned to my bed.

I couldn't get the voice recorder now, and I couldn't fall asleep, so I looked out the window in my room at the light from the moon, which was half dark, and at the stars, which are invisible in New York and which I miss seeing when we visit our cousins in Al Khor. I'm not the class of person who believes that my mother is in the stars and observing me from there, but it's profitable to remember that sometimes your problems are minor and the universe is infinitely larger and ultimately careless of what happens on earth, especially to one person, which can simultaneously make you feel alone.

I still didn't fall asleep for several hours, and I woke up when Irma knocked on my door and told me it was time for brunch.

Everyone was waiting for me at the dining room table, and I apologized. Wilson and Jeromy both looked more fatigued than I was, so I didn't feel as guilty.

"How late did you stay up?" Mrs. Schrub asked.

Mr. Schrub quickly looked at me, then looked down, and Wilson also did. It was as if I knew all their secrets but couldn't say anything, even though I was the one with the real secret. "I stayed up late to read *The Grapes of Wrath* in my room," I said.

Mr. Schrub and Mrs. Schrub had drinks of tomato juice with vodka. Mr. Schrub was in a positive mood and made many jokes which even I understood.

Wilson and Jeromy said good-bye after brunch. I shook their hands and they avoided my eyes. Mrs. Schrub told me the car to return to New York could leave as soon as I was ready. My opportunity to get the voice recorder was the opposite of golden. I packed my luggage slowly, because I was hoping Mr. Schrub might leave the house before I did. But I went downstairs and his office was still closed. When I was a few feet past the office, the door opened and Mr. Schrub asked to borrow me for a minute.

I again became panicked that he had discovered me. But he said, "I apologize for the scene last night, and for my sons' behavior." I said he didn't need to apologize, and it was almost as if I could hear the voice recorder a few feet behind me.

Then he said, "Well, in better news, I have a proposal for you. My business people emailed it over this morning." He showed me two stacks of several papers. "I don't fully understand it, but apparently they want you to de-encrypt Kapitoil and allow our programmers access to the code, so they can make modifications to the algorithms, too. You'll still be the point man on all this, and you'll get a corresponding bump in salary." He pointed to the number. It was double my current salary. "As far as I can tell, it's a win-win for everyone."

He gave me one of the stacks, as they were duplicates. It looked normal to me, and the money would be hard to reject. But more than that, this was my chance to compensate for what I had done last night. "I will sign it," I said.

Mr. Schrub smiled and said he had a special pen for contracts, and he retrieved a Mont-Blanc pen from a holder on his desk. "Careful, it leaks easily," he said.

As I was about to write my name, I noticed in the right corner of the front page the date and time it had originally been printed: November 12 at 9:16 a.m., which was Friday morning. Mr. Schrub said they had emailed it to him this morning. Sometimes computers have incorrect dates, but it made me pause.

Then I had an idea. In fact it was a double idea, but I didn't have time to visualize the stars at night.

I started to sign my name, and I pressed very hard with the pen when writing the *K*. A large quantity of ink spilled and made the area for my signature a black puddle.

"I am sorry," I said.

"No harm, no foul," said Mr. Schrub. "I'll print you up a fresh back page."

Mr. Schrub worked on his computer. I walked back to the bookshelves to give him privacy. But I moved to *Democracy Through Prosperity* on the bookshelf.

Mr. Schrub was still clicking on the computer and the contract wasn't on the monitor yet. I reached behind the book for the voice recorder. But I didn't feel it.

The computer monitor now displayed the document.

I moved my fingers behind the books. Maybe he had already discovered it.

The printer began making feeding sounds like a car engine powering on. Then I felt something hard. I tried to pick up the voice recorder, but it was difficult because I had to reach over the line of books. It was similar to those machine games in which the user controls a device that retrieves stuffed animals with its metal talons. Zahira always wanted to play those when we were younger, and I had to tell her that they were designed to make the customer almost always lose money.

"Looking for something?" Mr. Schrub asked. His face was turned over his shoulder at me.

I moved my hand to the top of the book. "This book sounds interesting," I said.

"It's a free country, take a look," Mr. Schrub said. He observed me for several seconds, as if he were deciphering a complex problem. I couldn't remove it or he might see the voice recorder.

Then the printer beeped, and Mr. Schrub said, "Lousy printer," and it was a paper jam and he had to remove the malfunctioning sheet and restart the job.

I took down *Democracy Through Prosperity* with my left hand and with my right hand I reached for the voice recorder and pocketed it and my heart accelerated as much as if I were playing racquetball. The printer respooled. I returned to his desk and he handed me the complete contract again.

The new page had the current date and time.

I looked at it for several seconds. Mr. Schrub asked, "Something wrong?"

"Possibly I should review this further on my own," I said.

"Take your time," he said. "Just get back to George whenever you're ready."

Mr. Schrub said he had enjoyed my company, and I thanked him and his family for hosting me. He removed a business card from his wallet and said, "In case you ever need to contact me," although I knew I would be too afraid to contact him directly and would reach him only through his secretary.

During the car ride back to New York I couldn't listen to the voice recorder of course, because Mr. Schrub's driver, Patrick, was there. When we were static in traffic, Patrick called Mr. Schrub and told him he would be late returning to the house. After he disconnected, I asked how many days a week he had to work for Mr. Schrub.

"Just a few," he said. "Mr. Schrub's very generous with time off."

I considered deleting everything on the voice recorder at that moment. It wasn't my business and it was illegal. But sometimes even when you know the correct action, you can't force yourself to do it.

In addition I felt bad about distrusting Mr. Schrub. It was an obsolete printer, and possibly it or the computer merely malfunctioned and displayed the incorrect date, and Mr. Schrub was telling the truth that he had received it that morning.

Still, I tried to read the contract more thoroughly in the car. It is long and the language is difficult for me to interpret, however, so it will take some time.

When I got into my apartment I immediately listened to the voice recorder, as if it were a present I couldn't wait to open. I had to rewind through some sounds in the night the voice recorder had powered on for, and then I heard our conversation from last night.

The remainder of the recording was just our conversation in the morning. I don't know what I was expecting to discover, but I was relieved it was nothing. I still saved our two conversations on the voice recorder. It was rare to have both a personal dialogue and a business conversation with Mr. Schrub within a few hours, and I always want to remember them.

acclimate = adjust to

at your earliest convenience = polite way of requesting a response ASAP

birding = observing birds

borrow a person = have that person's attention briefly

bowl a person over = significantly impress that person

call dibs = claim ownership

DUI = charge for Driving Under the Influence (of alcohol)

full clearance = 100% permission

heliport = airport for helicopters

Johnny Bench = baseball player known for having large hands

made my bitch = defeated = conquered = subjugated = dominated = enslaved

no harm, no foul = no serious damage has been inflicted

notes = variations of flavor in wine

POV = point of view

retire = hit the hay = go to sleep

talons = a bird's feet that are used for containing a smaller animal

we're not in Kansas anymore = revised line from *The Wizard of Oz* that indicates being in a new environment that is different and frightening

I bought a quality card with plant and bird designs and thanked Mr. and Mrs. Schrub for their hospitality, and mailed it to their home address in New York. I didn't receive a response, so on Thursday I emailed his secretary to thank him again, and added:

> Please also pass on my wishes for a happy Thanksgiving next week for the Schrubs. It is a holiday I do not know well, but I know that Americans use it to give thanks for what they have, and I am thankful for the opportunity Mr. Schrub has provided me.

The office would be closed next Thursday, and although the stock market was open on Friday, Schrub was giving the day off to most employees, including me. Everyone else was stimulated about having four days off from work, but I was anxious. I didn't have anything to do or anywhere to go. I hadn't needed to do much work on Kapitoil lately, because it was mostly self-running, and for the first time my work was slightly boring to me. Even the Y2K project required more problem-solving skills. Mr. Ray had told me I could use the time to work on new programs, but ever since I started finessing Kapitoil I wasn't having any original ideas that stimulated me. So I hoped Mr. Schrub would possibly invite me back to Connecticut for Thanksgiving.

I saw Rebecca in the coffee room and asked about her Thanksgiving plans.

"I'm not really doing Thanksgiving this year," she said. "It's hard to justify flying to my mother's just for a few days."

I asked, "Where does your father live?" and then I remembered I shouldn't ask about him because she didn't mention him previously.

"New Jersey." She poured herself more coffee even though her cup was almost full, and we discussed the Y2K project briefly before we divided.

On Friday Mr. Ray visited me in my office. "Just wanted to let you know we're still thrilled with Kapitoil's results," he said. "Are you working on anything new?"

"I am continuously updating the algorithms," I said.

"I meant any new programs."

I said, "No, I have not innovated anything." I should have said, e.g., "I am batting around some ideas," as I heard Jefferson say to a supervisor one time, which is strategic because it is undefined and the listener will probably not ask for more details. But I am unskilled at that class of speaking.

Mr. Ray said, "Ah. Well, let me know if you're struck by lightning with anything." At the door he added, "And Mr. Schrub mentioned something about a contract?"

I had been attempting to read it over the week, but I couldn't decipher most of its contents, and I couldn't ask Jefferson or Dan or even Rebecca for help. So I said, "I am still reviewing it." He said that was fine and he would recheck with me later.

I went to a bookstore on Saturday and bought another novel by John Steinbeck, *Of Mice and Men*. I read it all in one day, and I liked it even more than *The Grapes of Wrath*, because it made a similar economic argument and had equal emotional power in a more efficient length. I emailed Zahira and recommended that she read it after her winter exams were over.

That night there was news of a small bombing in Pakistan

on an oil refinery. Five people died as well. It would make the markets volatile and Kapitoil would profit on the vacillations. It was the class of event that happened infrequently, but when it did I tried to reroute my brain.

So I thought about Zahira some more, and wondered if she would pursue biology and possibly become a doctor, and if so if she would be a doctor who did clinical research to boot and attempted to cure diseases or simply a doctor who treated diseases. If I were a doctor I would prefer to do clinical work, as it's more beneficial to prevent diseases before they develop than merely treat them after they have made an impact, and I would also be less valuable as a regular doctor because my interpersonal skills are weak.

Then I was struck by lightning.

What if I could apply the idea of using news reports, and an updated version of Kapitoil's algorithm, to predict the spread of disease? The stock market functions like other systems of controlled chaos, such as viruses and epidemiology. Some diseases, e.g., cancer, are not possible to predict, because they occur independently of world events, but possibly I could anticipate how the flu virus or malaria spreads, or other diseases that relate to variables like poverty and sanitation and also political unrest that are discussed in the news.

But I will test out my hypothesis and create a prototype program to certify it has merit before I propose it to Mr. Ray or Mr. Schrub.

do a holiday = observe a holiday 100% by spending it with family

struck by lightning = innovate a major idea

On Monday I received an email reply from Mr. Schrub's secretary:

> Mr. Schrub was pleased to have you as his guest, and he wishes you a happy Thanksgiving as well.

That was all. I was foolish to think he would invite me to Connecticut. He had his own family and other friends and business acquaintances. I was not an integral part of his life. "Pleased" was a word with such minimal weight. And possibly Mr. Ray told him I didn't have any new ideas and therefore didn't merit an invitation. I almost wrote to the secretary that I had a new idea about Kapitoil, but of course Kapitoil was still highly privileged information, and I had not even started testing out my new idea yet.

On Wednesday I went into my former pod and said good-bye to Rebecca. She was still working, and it was rare for me to exit work before she did. She had dark shadows under her eyes. I said, "Possibly you should not work so hard."

Her mouth turned up slightly and she told me to have a good Thanksgiving. I asked if she was celebrating it with her roommate, but she said Jessica had gone home to California the previous day.

That night I watched television without truly selecting a program, which I don't like doing. I considered finally calling one of the people in New York our family friends knew, the Bashar family. I opened my cellular and scrolled through the few numbers I had inputted so far, but stopped before I reached them.

"Hello?" Barron said.

"Hello, Mr. Wright. This is Karim Issar. I am the Schrub Equities employee you have previously driven from JFK Airport to my apartment, from the Schrub office to game four of the World Series between the Yankees and the Atlanta Braves, and from—"

"Yeah, yeah, I know," he said. "What time and where?"

"I do not require transportation," I said. "I would merely like to give thanks to you for the previous rides."

He paused for a few seconds, then laughed. "You're welcome. It's my job."

"Also, I would like to wish you and your family a happy Thanksgiving." He reciprocated, and I asked, "Are you having a large Thanksgiving dinner?"

"Just having a few friends and relatives over, nothing too fancy," he said.

"That sounds enjoyable."

There was another pause, and he said, "You?"

"I do not have any current plans," I said.

I could hear Barron intake his breath, and then he said, "Well, shit, like I said, it's nothing fancy, but you're welcome to come over here."

"I could not infringe on your hospitality."

"I wouldn't have invited you if it was an infringement," he said.

"Then I accept your offer, and I will bring some food with me as well." He gave me his contact information. "Mr. Wright, may I infringe on your hospitality and invite someone else?"

He laughed again. Barron created high pressure when he didn't speak, but when he laughed he depressurized the environment. He said why the hell not as long as I called him Barron and not Mr. Wright.

I called Rebecca, who picked up on the second ring. When I invited her to Barron's, she said, "You don't have to do that just because you feel sorry for me."

"It is all right," I said. "I was invited just because he felt sorry for me."

She laughed and accepted, and I hypothesized that she and Barron would partner well because they were the only two people in the U.S. who thought I had a sense of humor.

On Thanksgiving I cooked hareis. It is my preferred meal to cook because it is like writing a complex program: It takes a long time to produce such fragile meat, you can innovate with trial-and-error experiments with different spices (e.g., I use more cinnamon than most cooks do), and removing the bones at the end is even parallel to debugging. Then you have a full meal made from several ingredients that would not be independently edible, minus the lamb and rice, just as a program combines several functions that have less value when solitary.

I also blended a complex juice of bananas, strawberries, peaches, and kiwis, which *are* independently edible but preferable in collaboration.

Rebecca and I planned to meet at Barron's home in Jackson Heights, which I read was the most diverse area in the world. The subway was above the ground in Queens, and I tried counting the number of Spanish and Indian restaurants, but even I couldn't do it. I also saw very few stores with names I recognized. Before I came to New York I expected to see this class of neighborhood more, but I haven't found it in Manhattan.

Although I found this neighborhood intriguing, all the garbage on the streets suddenly made me wish I was in Connecticut with Mr. Schrub and his family and around trees and lawns and spacious houses.

I found a small brick house in a row of similar houses and rang the front door. A female with short black hair answered. She was Japanese.

I reviewed the number above the door. "I apologize," I said. "I think I have the incorrect home."

"For whom are you looking?" she asked.

"Is this the house of Barron Wright?"

"The house of Barron Wright and Cynthia Oharu, yes. Barron's my husband." She smiled, and I felt foolish for my original statement. "Karim, right? Please come in. And would you mind taking off your shoes?"

I said that was often the custom where I was from as well. She asked for the location, and I told her, and she made me guarantee to tell her more about Qatar later. Then she said my friend was waiting for me.

The living room had pictures on the walls of Barron and Cynthia and their daughter. Over a dozen adults and several children stood or sat on the two couches and multiple chairs. Everyone was black or Latin American, minus Cynthia, Rebecca, two white couples, and me.

Rebecca was eating and talking on one of the couches with another female. She told me to sit with them and introduced me. She introduced me to the people near us. She wasn't a networker in the office, but she was more skilled here, similar to how she was at her own party, although that was understandable because the guests there were her friends.

There was a table near the kitchen with food on top of it, like at the Yankees game, including the hareis, but all the guests served themselves, so I did the same. The food was not the Thanksgiving food I previously read about, which slightly disappointed me, but there were fish and vegetable pies and dishes I believe were Latin American.

Cynthia made everyone laugh and transferred between guests frequently. She reminded me slightly of my mother, who was also a robust host. I briefly considered asking Jefferson later if he wanted to meet her, but his interest in Japan was not 100% positive, and for him to meet Cynthia merely because she was Japanese was parallel to when I thought it wasn't Barron's house also because she was Japanese.

Barron was more like my father. He talked to a few of the guests at the party but remained in his seat, except at one point when he tickled his daughter, Michelle, which amused me, although of course I was not the target of the tickling. When I said hello to him, he shook my hand and thanked me for coming. This was more like my father when I was much younger. I don't remember the last time we had a party in our apartment.

I said, "I would like to thanks-give to you and your family for inviting me."

Barron's brother was next to him. "Thanks-give?" he asked as he laughed at me.

Barron turned to him with a look I had never seen on his face. "Shut the hell up," he said quietly. Then he said to me, "That suit still looks sharp on you," and I thanked him, but he was incorrect, as it was in fact a different suit from the one I wore in the car, although he was correct in that it did look sexy on me. I felt enhanced until I saw his gray sweater had a small hole under the shoulder.

Several people enjoyed the hareis, and although the other children drank soda instead, Michelle repeatedly requested more of my juice.

I didn't talk with Rebecca because Cynthia asked me much about Qatar and I also talked to a female social worker named Ana, who was originally from the Dominican Republic and who sometimes partnered with Cynthia's law firm. She asked me, "Have you had any trouble assimil—have you had any trouble adjusting to life here?"

I said, "I have had some difficulties assimilating and acclimating, but I am not having a very hard time dealing."

"I'm sorry. I didn't mean to imply you didn't know that word," she said.

"No harm, no foul," I said. "I did know it, but I enjoy learning new words."

Right after I said that, Cynthia said we should all play a game called Taboo. She explained the rules, which require a person to provide clues for his teammates to guess a specific word or phrase, but the person cannot state five other words, e.g., if the word is "baseball," you cannot say: "sport," "game," "pastime," "hitter," or "pitcher."

I would be very poor at this game, because I didn't even know the word "pastime," and if I didn't know the censored words then I wouldn't know the non-censored words either, and I would humiliate myself in front of everyone and Rebecca. So when Cynthia said we had an odd number of adults, I said I would not play. Rebecca tried to make me partner on her team, but I said I preferred to play with the children.

As the adults set up the game, I asked the children, "Who wants to play a game?"

All seven children approached me, and I said I had a fun game called Sleep Handshake. I explained the rules: "All the players walk around and shake hands, and one person also scratches one other person's hand with his finger," I said. "After several seconds, that other person 'falls asleep.' The other players must observe and guess who is the 'sleeper.'" I used to play this game with Zahira and her friends to teach them analytical skills of observation.

"I know that game," one of the older children said. "It's not called Sleep Handshake. It's called Murderer. And you don't fall asleep. You die."

"No," I said. "That is a different game. In this game you merely fall asleep. Now I will choose a sleeper." I shook everyone's hand and scratched Michelle's hand.

While we played, I listened to the adults play Taboo. They were all laughing and shouting with friendly competition. Because I am an adept multitasker with low-level problems, I studied the various strategies they used. The weaker players tried to describe the clues in elongated ways, but the stronger players, like Rebecca and Cynthia, used outside-the-box thinking to innovate clues and were more efficient.

The children enjoyed themselves as well, and at one point I saw Rebecca looking at us. Soon one of the adults said he had to leave.

"Karim, we need a sub," Rebecca said.

Michelle put another child to sleep. "The children require supervision."

"They'll be fine," Cynthia said. "Barron, move your fat ass."

I was on the same team as Rebecca, which relieved me, as I didn't want my teammates to become upset if I failed, and Rebecca was not the class of person to do that.

I studied more intensely as the other players provided clues, and because of that I didn't try to answer any clues. I was very nervous just before my turn, but then I became calm when I remembered I must think outside the box, which is easy for me.

My first phrase was "Holiday Inn." I could not say "hotel," "motel," "vacation," "room," "lodge." I said: "A place you reside in overnight; non-work schedule plus non-out."

Immediately Rebecca said "Holiday Inn!"

I used a similar strategy for the next phrase, "World Series" (I said "global iterations," although I almost said "I attended this athletic event with Mr. Schrub"), and again Rebecca guessed it. When she correctly answered my third clue, Barron said, "You two married or something?" and I was slightly humiliated but remained focused.

My team guessed eight of my clues, which was the most of anyone, and Rebecca claimed responsibility for five of them. She was across from me, but she made her mouth move mutely so I could understand the words: "Nice job, Karim."

It was strange to hear this compliment outside of the office, but it felt as good as when a higher-up praised me at work.

And I didn't wish I was at Mr. Schrub's house anymore.

The one time that was false was a few minutes after the game, when my stomach became turbulent. Probably it was from the large quantities of different foods I had consumed. I perspired, and Rebecca even asked if I was all right, and I said I was and that I had to make a telephone call, but instead I went to the restroom and turned on the water loudly so no one would hear me. I finished the toilet paper before I was completed, which panicked me, but then I located more under the sink.

We stayed until the other guests started leaving, and then Rebecca again moved her mouth to ask "Should we go?" I moved my mouth to say, "This is a strategic juncture to depart," but she didn't understand, so I nodded.

Because it was a holiday there were almost zero commuters. Rebecca talked nonstop about how much she had enjoyed it and continued thanking me for inviting her.

We reached Rebecca's platform for the G train, which was empty. She again thanked me, and I said, "That is the sixth time you have thanked me."

"I guess I'm a little thrown off by a Thanksgiving that doesn't end in mutual recriminations fueled by gallons of cheap red wine," she said.

We stood there for a few seconds without saying anything, and I heard her train approaching, and I said, "It is unsafe for you to travel home tonight because there are very few passengers. I will accompany you to your subway stop."

"I'm a big girl," she said. "Besides, it's out of your way."

I thought she was referring to her size, which was not thin but not big either, and then I understood, so I said, "That is true, but I would enjoy the company anyway." She again said it was out of my way, but I maintained my position, and we boarded the train.

It was empty, minus a man and female at the other end. Their appearances and clothing were almost equal. The female rested her head on the man's shoulder and he had his arm around her, and their eyes were closed. Rebecca and I sat next to each other, and on the trip we discussed nonwork subjects, e.g., Barron and Cynthia and Thanksgiving, but the entire time I was thinking how I wanted us to be in the same position as the couple.

Although no one was looking, I was too afraid to do anything. As we approached Rebecca's stop, I said, "Rebecca," and she asked, "What?" but I responded, "I should consult the map," and I went to the middle of the train to investigate how to get back, even though I knew from the party at Rebecca's apartment how to return to Manhattan and also I had memorized most of the subway system before I left Doha.

Rebecca's stop at Fulton St. was next, and I had to stay on one more stop to transfer, and we didn't talk as we decelerated into the station. I walked with Rebecca to the doors and she again thanked me and said, "Sorry, number seven." This was the optimal time. Her fingers touched her hair and she looked through the windows of the doors at the station's columns that passed by us like pictures in a slide projector.

I continued thinking I should kiss her, and commanded myself to do it, but the doors dinged and opened and she said good night and stepped out and the doors closed.

I watched her on the other side of the doors with her back to me, and I also saw myself in the window. I looked foolish standing there. And then the doors dinged again and reopened, as they sometimes do, and I thought this was a golden opportunity and not a random accident, and without thinking I said "Rebecca" as I did before, and she rotated and I leaned across the vertical plane of the train doors and kissed her, and she reciprocated, and I touched her hand, and we remained there for several seconds.

I could still taste the sugary milk from the Tres Leches cake she had eaten multiple pieces of, and the inside of her mouth was warm and the outside skin was cold, and my eyes remained open but hers were closed, and I wanted to remain in that position for much longer, but the doors dinged again and began closing and I pulled back so we would not get compressed.

Then the train moved and I watched her through the window as she looked down at her shoes, and I could not see if she was smiling or worried, and soon I was in the tunnel again. The entire trip back to my apartment I wondered if I should call her or not, and if I should, when I should do it and what to say. It wasn't like a mathematics problem with a definite solution, and I had difficulty deciphering an answer. I couldn't consult with my father and especially not Zahira. Possibly my mother would have been helpful for this situation, but I wasn't old enough when she died to know.

a big girl (boy) = an independent female (man)
look sharp = clothing appears sexy
mutual recriminations = reciprocal insults
pastime = a leisure activity

Because I didn't know what to do in this situation, and because possibly Rebecca did, I waited for her to initiate a dialogue with me that weekend. But she didn't call.

I tried to reroute my brain by spending more time on my idea about Kapitoil and epidemiology. Typically I can force myself to concentrate, but whenever I looked at the text on the monitor, I thought of looking at Rebecca's closed eyes when we kissed, and whenever I moved my mouse I thought instead of touching her hand, and in my brain I smelled her watermelon shampoo and remembered the feel of her lips like two small pillows.

Then on Sunday I did something I have never previously done. I was using my computer's painting program to diagram an object-oriented classes of viruses, but instead I tried to draw Rebecca's face. However, I'm not a skilled artist on paper, and I'm even inferior on the computer, so it didn't look like her. And then I was struck by lightning, although it was different from my typical class of lightning.

I employed one of the algorithms in Kapitoil and programmed a macro for it to utilize the painting program. Of course it didn't draw a face, but a random piece of art like abstract expressionism that derived from a picture of a watermelon on the Internet. Except I knew it wasn't random, because it was based on an algorithm, and when I analyzed it closely I could see the causes behind its decisions. I thought Jackson Pollock would green-light my design, and I titled it *R #1*.

And then the design *did* seem Rebecca-esque, as sometimes one object can mirror another one not because they look precisely equal, but because something more tangential feels similar, e.g., much of the painting utilized the visible spectrum near indigo, and if I think of a color to represent Rebecca, it would be indigo, because (1) of her personality; (2) most people cannot identify indigo between blue and violet, parallel to how some people might not notice Rebecca; and (3) I once saw a CD of hers by a female band with the word "Indigo" in its name.

On Monday morning I still had not heard from Rebecca, and I was afraid we were both acting like negotiating holdouts and not making an offer to increase our value. Although I knew I should wait longer, later that morning I emailed her:

Rebecca,
May I request a meeting at your earliest convenience in the coffee room to discuss certain subjects?
Sincerely,
Karim

She replied:

Mr. Issar:
Yes, but only if we can talk like that the whole time. See you in five minutes.
Formally yours,
Ms. Goldman

I didn't know if she was teasing me or not, but when I reached the coffee room she was already sitting at the small table and tapping her right foot on the ground repeatedly as if she were timing a song.

"Would you like to begin?" I asked.

"I'm not dying to," she said.

This was problematic, because I had hoped she would start and I could respond. I began talking without a clear plan, which is a tactic I would never use in business.

"I enjoyed spending Thanksgiving with you," I said. "And the subway ride."

"But?" she interrupted.

"What do you mean?" I said.

"You enjoyed it, but . . ." she said again.

I didn't know if she meant she had an objection to my enjoyment, or if she was predicting I had an objection planned. So I said, "This is not a 'but' statement. I merely enjoyed it."

She looked like she didn't know what else to say. The periodicity of her foot's taps was decreasing.

Another employee who always looks like he is asleep even when he is walking entered for coffee. Rebecca and I didn't say anything the entire time he was there. When he spent approximately 30 seconds deciding between real sugar and false sugar, I had to restrict myself from commanding him to take both packets and decide at his desk.

He finally left. "In my experience, it is beneficial to repeat events that are enjoyable. Do you agree?" I asked.

She said, "In my experience, that's also true."

"I am available to repeat events on Saturday."

"So am I," she said. "Wait, am I supposed to say I'm not, to play hard to get?"

"I do not understand." At times like this I wish I had more mastery of English, but possibly these kinds of exchanges are challenging even for fluent speakers. "Are you available or unavailable?"

She said she was available. I said, "I will shoot you an email with further details," and she consented, and when she left I couldn't stop myself from smiling, and in my office I even slightly punched the air with stimulation, although I contacted my fist on my desk and it hurt because I'm not used to punching, but the pain didn't bother me, and in fact it felt good to be feeling sensations, even unpleasant sensations.

I spent Monday brainstorming for our date. Now that I had more money I could afford to take Rebecca someplace classy. Jefferson probably knew of good places, but I couldn't ask him. So I researched places on the Internet that might impress Rebecca and made a list with pros and cons about different restaurants, e.g.:

Bavarian Haus

PRO	CON
Received 3 stars	Most non-Germans evaluate German food as low quality

It was more difficult than programming in many ways, because in programming if you can't predict results, you can still test out new variables and use trial and error to arrive at a solution, but with people you typically have one opportunity and their motivations and reactions are more difficult to understand, especially with females.

By Tuesday afternoon I still didn't know what to do. So I forced myself to work on my new Kapitoil-esque project instead. I made some progress, and soon I forgot about my nervousness with Rebecca and reentered the world of programming where I have ultimate control, and I worked through the night in my office, and I remembered how enjoyable it is to concentrate on a project that stimulates me, and by the end of the night I had hurdled some obstacles and received encouraging results, and once I finalize my program and presentation I will propose the concept to Mr. Schrub. If he was impressed with me initially, then this will bowl him over.

not dying to = not stimulated to proceed with an action
play hard to get = create the impression of limited supply to raise external demand

DECEMBER

I worked on the epidemiology project, but by Friday I still had no ideas for what to do with Rebecca. And then I decided to yield to my difficulties: I would simply not plan anything. It had the potential to be a growth experience. So I emailed Rebecca and told her to meet me in Central Park on Saturday at noon.

We met in Sheep Meadow. Rebecca blocked her eyes from the sun with her hand and asked, "What's the plan, Stan?"

"I do not have a plan, Dan," I said, because I thought she was doing a play on words with me and the only other American name I could think of that rhymed with "plan" was Dan. To boot, I now had a response for Dan when he called me "Karim the Dream." "I thought we could walk around Central Park." I had walked through parts of it before, but not much of it, and always by myself.

At first I wondered if we would discuss the events of Thanksgiving with each other, and because I was distracted our conversation was rigid, and I asked her several questions such as, "What did you do to entertain yourself last night?"

Rebecca said, "I know I always say this, but, really, you can let yourself go some. We're not in the office. You can curse or whatever."

I considered this, then said, "Fuck. Shit. Asshole."

Rebecca laughed, and that softened the rigidity of our dialogue, and then we talked about a play she had seen the previous night that her roommate acted in, and about her brother and how he had joined his university's newspaper, and then about how that might interest Zahira as well, as she was an excellent writer.

We entered an area called the Ramble which is known for birding. We spent several minutes watching different species, many of which we didn't know the names of, but Rebecca made interesting analytical observations, e.g., how multiple birds frequently partner on a tree after a few birds first land there, as if the first birds are scouting to certify the tree's safety. Although I didn't learn as much as when I was with Mr. Schrub, it was more stimulating because I prefer problem solving to receiving data passively.

When we reached the end of the Ramble, we decided to progress to the reservoir at 96th St. By then I forgot about what happened on Thanksgiving and it was like we were still coworkers at adjacent desks, although we weren't talking about work anymore.

At the Reservoir, Rebecca asked if I had anything else I wanted to do. "I am enjoying this," I said. "Would you like to continue walking around?"

She said she would, and we shifted over to Riverside Park on the West Side and walked along the blue and green and gray water of the Hudson River, and through the Upper West Side aggregated with Jewish families and Asian restaurants, and finally all the way down to Chelsea and the variably angled streets and cafes of Greenwich Village and the classy and minimal clothing stores in SoHo and the less clean streets and caged athletics areas of the Lower East Side and the East Village. And although we ended up spending almost no money, minus water and some snacks (e.g., in Chinatown, where we ate dumplings and something called red-bean-paste bun), that's not why I wanted to do it, but I'm glad we did that instead of paying for external entertainment. Sometimes merely partnering on a walk is sufficient.

When we were on Sullivan St., she was discussing her brother and the art classes he was taking at university, and I was asking her questions about art. "You know, there may be a bit of a language barrier, but you're pretty easy to talk to," she said. "Most people here, their conversations are intellectualized middle-school sarcasm. They're just trying to prove how intelligent or cool they are. You're not like that." At first I thought she meant I wasn't intelligent or cool, but then I understood she meant that I didn't try to prove I had those qualities, and although I believe I am intelligent in certain modes, I'm of course not cool in any modes, so that part remains true.

We were both exhausted at 6:30 p.m. Rebecca asked if I was hungry, and I was, but so far restaurants in New York had caused problems for me with questions about halal food, and also I didn't enjoy waiters serving me. So I proposed cooking dinner, and Rebecca suggested we do it in Brooklyn because groceries were cheaper there.

We discussed what to cook on the way there. Rebecca said she was trying to become a vegetarian, so we shouldn't buy meat. She added, "And I'm not just saying that because it'll be harder to find halal meat." I told her I was glad she'd said that, and how I disliked it when Americans corrected their behavior around me. She didn't say anything else about it.

We selected pasta with peppers and cauliflowers and a salad and divided the cost equally and took the food back to her apartment. Her roommate was out at her play. Rebecca asked if I wanted to hear music while we cooked.

"I liked the musician you played for me before," I said. "The one who sings the line 'Your hair upon the pillow like a sleepy golden storm.'"

"I remember," she said.

This time she played a song called "Suzanne," and it was equal in quality to the song she had played in her room. The line that intrigued me most was "And she shows you where to look among the garbage and the flowers," because sometimes there is no difference between garbage and flowers, and things that people discard or ignore or forget or lose often contain the most valuable material or data, as Rebecca once said.

"Are you a good singer?" I asked.

"Yes," she said. "If you consider the anguished cries of a fatally wounded dolphin 'good.'"

She opened a bottle of white wine and poured herself a glass but she didn't make any comments about how I could have some if I wanted. So I finished my glass of water and poured myself some as well.

We ate dinner in her living room, and when we finished we drank more wine, although I was careful to drink just a small amount. I discovered if I drank at the rate of 0.75 glasses/hour it slightly relaxed me but didn't negate my control, which was optimal, especially in a situation like this.

In fact, I was still very nervous. When I kissed her previously, it happened because I temporarily didn't strategize. Now I was strategizing too much, with ideas such as (1) the lighting was too bright; (2) we were both holding glasses of wine and a sudden movement could spill them (even though it was white wine and therefore less permanent); and (3) we were one foot apart from each other on the couch and moving closer to her would take too long.

I understood why movies about romance, such as the one I partially watched on television on Monday night, are so popular in the U.S., because they present high quantities of conflict, although I typically dislike the way those movies depict romantic conflicts, as they result either from simple misunderstandings or because the two main characters initially hate each other before falling in love, and although I am a novice at these situations, even I know that that conversion is illogical. In fact, frequently it is the opposite: People fall in love soon after they meet, and over time they lose it.

I said, "This wine has some pear notes."

She smiled slightly and didn't respond, and I had no other evaluations of the wine. Then I remembered my gift. "I have something for you," I told her, and I retrieved my coat and de-pocketed *R #1*.

"It is an algorithmic drawing," I said. "I created it using the discrete Fourier transform, by mapping each spatial frequency band of a picture of a watermelon to its own color—"

She linked her arms around my neck and said, "Thank you."

I was still nervous about what to do, but then I thought: You have to accept responsibility for your own decisions. She may reject you, but you will not know until you try, and if you do not even try, then it is as if you are rejecting yourself.

And then I shifted my head and kissed her, and she kissed me, and we stayed like that for a long time on the soft couch, and I thought how strange it was that two people could enjoy contacting their lips and tongues and hands for so long when most of the time we avoid contact.

She brought me to her bedroom, and our actions didn't equal what I did on Halloween, but it was still stimulating. We enjoyed each other's bodies but we didn't say anything about it, as I did with Melissa. Rebecca wasn't as thin as Melissa, but I preferred that. In addition, when I had difficulty releasing her bra, she whispered "It's okay," and did it herself. I also accidentally crashed my hand against her glasses at one point and they became asymmetrical on her nose. I apologized and was slightly humiliated by my poor dexterity, but she said "Look," and intentionally made the glasses even more asymmetrical, then put her hands out in the air and rotated her head and eyes rapidly as if she could not see anything and was panicked. It was humorous, so I laughed, and she said, "Thank God glasses are sort of in now and being a nerd is almost cool. It was a rough stretch there in high school for people like us, right?" Initially I disliked how she accurately classified me as a nerd, but then I valued how she did not mind calling herself one and therefore I was careless that I was a nerd as well.

When we were finished we didn't say anything for a few minutes, until I asked, "Goldman is a Jewish surname, correct?"

"Yeah," she said. "My family isn't really religious, though. Is yours?"

"We are. My father is the most," I said. "Both your parents are Jewish?"

"Just my father," she said. "But he's not really anything."

"What is his job?"

She yawned and turned her body away from me. "He's a surgeon."

I was asking about a subject that wasn't my business, but I didn't stop. "Why do you not see him anymore?"

"Are you trying to find out if I have daddy issues?" she said.

I said I didn't know what daddy issues were, and that I merely wanted to know why she didn't see him, but if she didn't want to discuss it, then I understood.

She turned to face me again. "He wasn't abusive, he wasn't an alcoholic, he wasn't a philanderer," she said. "Hope I'm not disappointing you with a mundane tale of middle-class neglect. He was a workaholic and never really paid attention to my mother, or my brother, or me. Sorry—he paid attention when he thought I would become a doctor, and when I accidentally-on-purpose failed bio, he gave up. They finally divorced when I was seventeen, which made for a fun senior year, we moved in with my grandmother in Wisconsin, he remarried, and I stopped talking to him four years ago because he never really seemed to care about talking to me. Satisfied?"

I didn't say anything for a while. Then I said, "I have some daddy issues as well, although they are different." I didn't say anything about my mother, though, because it would seem like we were exchanging personal data for the sake of exchanging it. I would also ask her another time about why she took Zoloft, which I had researched and learned was for depression and/or anxiety, because it was not necessarily caused by her relationship with her father, e.g., that is why I don't tell people about my mother, because they might think everything I do is caused by that, when human actions are the result of infinite factors and are complex and sometimes impossible to decipher.

connoisseur = expert in a field

daddy issues = conflict with one's father

philanderer = a husband who is disloyal to his wife

workaholic = someone who works constantly to avoid the remainder of his life

Rebecca and I didn't see each other at all the next few days, as I was busy with Kapitoil and the Y2K project was ramping up. My test results were enhanced, and I believed that with some additional work and more specific knowledge of epidemiology, which I lack, it might truly have value.

However, to apply it to other fields would require opening up the code and the idea to others who have more specialized knowledge, e.g., via an academic paper. And this would mean the termination of Kapitoil, because Schrub would no longer have a monopoly on it, and if everyone had access to the same predictive patterns, then they would cancel out on the market.

I considered that (1) I was performing very well with Schrub now and was getting to know Mr. Schrub more; (2) possibly it would be foolish to interrupt my progress with an idea that might hurt the company's prospects; and (3) Kapitoil, for oil futures, was the best program I had ever created, and even if it worked well in another area, I would destroy its perfect value for oil futures, and it is rare for something so ideal to exist in the world.

So I decided to be quiet about my program for now, and if I was 100% certain it functioned and I felt I was close enough to Mr. Schrub later, then I would bring it up.

Shortly after 5:00 p.m. on December 7 there was a small bombing in Jordan at a U.S.-owned hotel. Ramadan had just started there. Kapitoil would benefit again from the volatility in the market.

The next night I went to the mosque after work to pray. December 8 was also the day John Lennon was killed. At home I played some of his Beatles and non-Beatles songs, including

"Imagine," which my mother adored. I enjoyed it, as I always did, but when I heard the line "Nothing to kill or die for, and no religion too," I replayed it several times. Lennon was correct in that religion has caused some wars, but it has also created alliances where there might have been *other* wars, in the same way that countries fight with each other, but they also restrict potential fighting within their borders.

Zahira called at 4:00 a.m. in Doha. "Why are you calling so early?" I asked.

"Because he is still asleep," she whispered.

"Oh," I said.

"We had an argument last night," she said. "About my studies."

He and I had agreed always to conference about her academics before talking to her about them. I tried to lower my volume. "What about them?"

"He thinks I should not consider a career as a scientist."

"What does he want you to do? Work in the store with him?"

"No. He wants me to change my classes next semester and apply to the Nursing Technical Secondary School for next year."

"That is foolish. Nursing is valuable work, but your skill set should be applied to science."

"That's what I said, but he won't listen to me!" Her voice divided and she started crying.

"Stop crying," I said. "You are stronger than that."

It took her almost a minute to stabilize. It was difficult for me to listen to over the telephone.

Finally she stopped and inhaled and asked, "Will you talk to him for me?"

She didn't know he and I had had a fight. But I said, "Of course I will," and told her I would call him tomorrow while he was at work, and that she should call me again tomorrow night at the same time to discuss it.

I tried to relax, but I couldn't. Zahira and I had both worked too hard for her not to become something like a scientist. He may have contributed equally to her tuition, but it was not his decision to make.

The next morning I called my father after I arrived at the office. "What is it?" he asked after I greeted him.

"It's pleasant to hear from you as well," I said. "Zahira says you want her to think about a different profession."

"I told her there was a nursing shortage in Qatar," he said.

"She said you asked her to change her classes and apply to the nursing school."

"If she is going to pursue it, she needs to begin now," he said. "Nursing is a growth profession, the Women's Hospital is an excellent facility, it does not require additional schooling, and she can stay in Doha very easily to find work."

"Stay in Doha?" I asked. "Why is that important?"

"It's not safe for a young female to work in a foreign country the way you are doing. You underestimate how many problems she could encounter."

"I thought we agreed to discuss her academics together before making any major decisions," I said.

He said, "Well, you're not here now."

"That is unrelated. You can easily call me or email me."

"I don't have email," he said. "You're the one who loves computers so much."

I forced my voice to remain calm. "We're both contributing

to her tuition. If you prefer, you can pay all of it and then you will not have to consult with me at all. Or I can pay all of it, and then you will not have to be involved."

He laughed. "You think money is the solution to everything? I can pay for her tuition next semester. I'm her father. She grew up in my home. You are her brother. Just because you earn more money now doesn't mean you are in charge of her."

"I know I'm not in charge of her," I said. "I am letting *her* be in charge. I am only trying to keep her options open for her future."

"She has no significant options that I am closing off," he said. My upper and lower teeth compressed.

"She possibly has more options than I do, and she certainly has more options than you," I said. "You have no right to restrict her. And I hope you do not let your own backward position destroy her life." I disconnected. My hand holding the telephone was vibrating.

I did very little work the rest of the day. Zahira called me at night, and I asked if she had talked to our father.

"I studied in the library all night to avoid him," she said. "What happened?"

"He said . . ."

"Tell me," she said.

I was about to tell her that our father was illogical and had obsolete values, but increasing her anger with him wouldn't result in any net gain. It's an issue I often have to resolve, because although she did grow up in his home, I truly partnered with him in raising her, and I sometimes oppose his ideas, but I have always tried not to reveal our conflicts to Zahira and to make it as peaceful an environment as possible.

"Some of what he says is logical," I said. "Being a scientist is a difficult profession and requires graduate school and does not pay well. There is always a need for nurses, especially in Doha now."

"Are you serious?" she said.

"It is necessary to have a backup plan. You should take preparatory classes next semester, and maybe you will discover you prefer nursing. It is an integral job." My voice sounded deeper and quieter and slower than normal. I had to say something else, so I added, "If you disagree with him, you must talk to him. I cannot do it for you. You are an adult now."

"He doesn't treat me as an adult!" she said. "That is exactly the problem!"

"I am sorry, Zahira," I said.

She made an angry sound by exhaling loudly through her teeth and said, "I thought I had a good brother," which was the worst thing she could have said to me, because while I am not boastful about much, I am proud of my skills as a brother. Then she did to me what I did to my father: She disconnected.

She didn't call back. I felt doubly bad, for (1) not defending her against our father and (2) lying to her. When I returned home, I could talk to him again and try to convince him. I could resolve to pay for her entire tuition, but she would remain in his home, and he might still reject the idea, and in fact it would probably make him even more certain. It's even more difficult to change someone's mind on a subject they have strong beliefs about than it is to make someone interested in a subject they are careless of.

I was about to call her to tell her this, but I hypothesized that she was still upset and my predicted outcomes weren't very optimistic, so I decided to wait for her to stabilize and let her initiate contact with me when she was ready.

In bed that night I kept replaying what my father said about me not being in charge. I always thought earning a high salary would delete the lion's share of problems for our family. But some problems are problematic independent of finances, and he was in fact correct: Money was not the solution to everything.

I didn't see Rebecca again until late on Friday night. We had dinner to break my fast, and I was even more inferior at conversation than normal because I was focused on Zahira and also on Kapitoil and whether it meant Schrub leveraged other people's problems even if we weren't the source of the problems.

In her room she asked if I knew the musician Bob Dylan.

"I do not know most musicians, except for the Beatles," I said.

"Why's that?" She started playing a CD. "Are they big in Qatar?"

"No," I said. "I merely know them well."

It was enjoyable even though his voice was not as luxurious as John Lennon's, and we kissed while we listened. He played a song called "Sad-Eyed Lady of the Lowlands." The melody was beautiful, but some of the words didn't make sense, especially the line in the chorus "My warehouse eyes, my Arabian drums."

I paid attention the first time I heard it because of the word "Arabian," but "warehouse eyes" frustrated me for two reasons: (1) A noun ("warehouse") modifies another noun ("eyes"), which is grammatically poor, and (2) what does "warehouse eyes" mean? It does not present a logical visual analog for the listener.

So I asked Rebecca what "warehouse eyes" meant, and she said, "It's a metaphor. But sometimes it's just about the sound."

I listened to the rest of the song, although it frustrated me that a musician could write something that he wants to be indecipherable, but then I remembered that Pollock's paintings frustrated me initially before I adopted new strategies for viewing them. So I listened without analyzing the meaning in my conventional mode. And the fifth time he sang it, I suddenly had a mental tableau of a warehouse with two lighted windows, and even if my analysis was not parallel to Dylan's original plan, his method now seemed like a slightly more valid way to write a song.

By the time the song was over, all our clothing was on the floor. I told myself it was incorrect behavior for Ramadan, but my body defeated my brain.

The CD changer switched and soon the song "With God on Our Side" played, and I continued listening. Like Lennon, Dylan was arguing that religion had caused many wars and made people act foolishly, e.g., "And you never ask questions, when God's on your side." Lennon and Dylan assumed that all religious people don't evaluate what their religion tells them to do, when in fact some of the most thoughtful people I know are the most religious, because religion focuses not exclusively on spirituality but also on morality, which many people forget to consider.

And then I considered where I was: in bed with an American female, with both of us naked. I didn't feel the way I did with Melissa, when it was as if I had committed a major crime, but possibly that was not a positive development. I remembered what Mr. Schrub said about how every day there are shifts that are so small you do not identify them, and finally you become a different person without even recognizing it.

I was truly not doing Ramadan this year.

"I should go home," I said. She didn't respond, so I exited the bed and replaced the white sheets partially over her body. "I am planning to be at the mosque all day tomorrow and will need to retire for a full night of sleep."

She was quiet for a minute. Then she said, "Usually guys want to leave *after*."

I didn't want to explain why I wanted to leave, but I also didn't want to make her feel bad, and I heard her incorrectly and thought she said "*Usual* guys," so I said, "Well, I am an unusual guy." It didn't make her laugh, although I was uncertain if it was because (1) the logic of the joke was flawed from the launch; (2) she was not in the proper mood to laugh; or (3) it was merely humorless.

I told her I would call her soon, and left before I further damaged our relationship. It was a long subway ride home, and whenever the doors opened, the cold air entered the train like a strong punch to my body. The whole time I was thinking how I could instead be warm in bed with her, but I couldn't go back. It was like wanting to return the suits after I purchased them. Once you make a significant decision, it is difficult or sometimes impossible to reverse it.

I was afraid that if I called her she'd still be upset with me and I would say other foolish things, and she would wonder why she had consented to be with me originally, and then reject me. I also wondered why she was with me. I didn't possess the very handsome face of someone like Jefferson (although I knew Rebecca wouldn't want to be with someone like Jefferson), or the knowledge base of music and movies and original clothing like her male friends, and I made many foolish errors in conversation, and now I was causing problems in other ways.

But some of it was possibly her fault, e.g., she didn't truly consider how I might feel about seeing her during Ramadan. And in fact most Americans I had met only thought about my religion in relation to food or alcohol, not about the spiritual areas. I walked around my living room in a rectangular pattern, and the more I thought about this, the more upset I grew, and I decided to write an email. It wasn't to Rebecca, however:

> Mr. Ray, I am responding to Mr. Schrub's request about a contract he has for me to sign. Can you please tell him I am available to meet him at his earliest convenience?

big in = popular in

warehouse eyes = an example of a metaphor that may not have a directly logical meaning

Rebecca didn't contact me the remainder of the weekend, and on Monday I avoided her in the office. In the morning I received a response from Mr. Ray that Mr. Schrub could meet me that afternoon for lunch. I was nervous of course, but I also felt confident that my epidemiology proposal would intrigue him.

The restaurant had an Italian name and was in the Financial District, so I walked there. Every table was full of businesspeople, but it was also very quiet and partially dark even though it was lunchtime.

I waited for Mr. Schrub at the bar and ordered a Coke, and in ten minutes he arrived and the main guard led us to a long table in a private section behind a door. Most of the eaters watched him as we walked past but pretended not to, and I felt their eyes observing me as well, and although attention usually makes me feel uncomfortable, now I felt stronger and sexier.

"I already arranged to do the chef's menu," Mr. Schrub told me. "And I made sure your food is vegetarian and otherwise appropriate."

I reminded myself how much he had given me and that he was considering my needs and how luxurious the room we were in was, with paintings of apples and pears on the wall and a very white tablecloth that was simultaneously rigid and soft, and I told him I appreciated it.

Our waiter was probably the same age as Mr. Schrub, although he looked older. After he gave Mr. Schrub the wine menu, I said, "I have a new idea relating to Kapitoil."

He put down the menu. "George said you hadn't come up with anything."

I felt foolish that Mr. Ray had said that, and it validated my fear that they were less impressed with me now, so I quickly explained how the epidemiology program would work and how my test results were robust so far.

Then, to conclude on another positive, I said, "I believe its applications are something your wife would find especially intriguing, as it can significantly enhance quality of life in the Third World."

"How would you develop the program if, as you say, you don't know much about epidemiology?" he asked.

"I would write the concept and reveal the algorithms for Kapitoil in an academic paper and release it to the public." I turned my eyes to the wallpaper's complex repeating pattern design of flower petals. "This means we would lose our monopoly on the program and it would no longer be valuable on the oil futures market."

The waiter returned. "I don't like to talk business over good food," Mr. Schrub said quietly to me. "We'll discuss it after the meal."

He continued looking at the menu, and after 20 seconds the waiter said, "We have an '88 Chianti that perfectly complements chef's menu."

Mr. Schrub didn't look up from the menu, but his facial muscles compressed and he said, "If I wanted a recommendation I would have asked for one."

The waiter's face was already pale, but it seemed to turn paler. "I apologize, sir," he said.

Mr. Schrub ordered a different wine I had never heard of, and the waiter said "Excellent choice," and exited quickly.

Mr. Schrub didn't discuss the contract at all while we ate,

and he didn't even talk about finance. Instead, he told me about the food we were eating. He and Mrs. Schrub owned a house in Tuscany and they went there every summer for at least a week and bought food at local markets and cooked together. "I recently cooked my first Italian meal," I said. Then I added, "I taught myself."

When I ate several gnocchi and grilled zucchini ASAP, he said, "Don't just gulp it down like a philistine. You have to rotate between the flavors, savor them." I decelerated my pace and was afraid he would find other flaws in my method of consuming and that it would somehow hurt my chances of convincing him to pursue the epidemiology project. "Break the taste apart into discrete essences—the fresh sweetness of the basil against the earthiness of the gnocchi." This is why I could never be a restaurant critic, because my only descriptions for food I liked were "delicious" or "flavorful" or simple adjectives in that class, and if you lack specific vocabulary to describe something, it is almost as if you are also restricted from specific thoughts, parallel to how if you do not know a coding command, not only are you prevented from implementing the idea, but you may not even innovate the idea initially.

After we received coffee I thought we were finally going to discuss my idea, but the owner of the restaurant entered and greeted Mr. Schrub.

"You must be a very important young man if you're lunching with Mr. Schrub," the owner said after Mr. Schrub introduced me, and I did feel like a VIYM again.

"He's only as important as I let him be," Mr. Schrub said. They both laughed, and the owner asked about our meal. Mr. Schrub said the food was excellent. "The waiter was perhaps a little big for his britches. You may want to have a word."

The owner apologized and said he would speak with him, then left us to drink our coffee. Mr. Schrub didn't say anything for almost a minute as he breathed on his coffee, and I was afraid of deleting the silence. He was like Barron in that way, because when they were mute I knew they were having thoughts they were withholding but I didn't know what the thoughts were, except Barron usually made me feel relieved after.

I finally said, "Have you thought about—"

He put up a finger as he poured milk into his cup. After he tasted it and licked his lips and dried them with his napkin and replaced his napkin on his lap, he said, "The epidemiology proposal sounds like a brilliant idea. But before we do something that rash, I think we should investigate further. Why don't you give my programmers access to the code, they can bring it up with some confidential partners who know more about this subject, and we can figure out if this thing really does have a fighting chance." He retrieved the contracts from his briefcase. "We've also gotten you some more money."

There was something about his "Why don't you" sentence that bothered me besides the fact that it was less a question and more a statement. I looked at the contracts that I still didn't 100% understand on the rigid white tablecloth. The solitary thing I did understand was the amount of money, which was boldfaced and double the initial amount.

"If it is all right with you, I prefer to update my prototype further before I release it to your programmers," I said.

He replaced the contracts in his briefcase as efficiently as if he was a printer feeding paper. "I understand," he said. "You're a perfectionist. So am I." He discussed the snowstorm expected next weekend, and we finished our coffee and he refused to permit me to pay for my share and told me to recontact him when I was ready.

I walked slowly back to the office. I replayed his sentence that bothered me, and I deciphered what caused turmoil for me: He used the phrase "my programmers," but *I* was also technically one of his programmers. Later in the sentence he said "we can figure out," so he should have also said "our programmers." It was a minor word choice, but it indicated something negative to me.

I had to consult with someone. There was only one person I could think of who was not upset with me now and who I thought could help me.

"No, you're not bothering me," Barron said on the telephone after I told him I didn't require a ride. "How's your lady friend?"

I said Rebecca was fine. But I truly wanted to speak about Mr. Schrub, although of course I couldn't reveal the full details of the situation to Barron. So I said, "Barron, what do you advise in a situation like this: Another party has given one great trust, and one would like to trust the other party, but one slightly believes one possibly should not trust everything about the other party."

Barron said, "Slow the hell down. If you say the words 'trust' and 'one' and 'the other party' one more time, I'm going to hang up. This is about Rebecca, right?"

This would be a convenient way to discuss Mr. Schrub, but I didn't want to lie to Barron. So I said, "I would not like to identify the party or parties involved."

"You don't make this easy," he said. "Let me ask you: Are you the kind of guy who doesn't usually trust people?"

I stood in the middle of a cluster of businesspeople waiting to cross Pine St. "No, I believe most people have positive values and goals and merit faith."

"That's a nice attitude, but it's dangerous. Especially in this city—it's full of phonies." I asked what phonies were. "Fakes, frauds, exploiters, if that's a word. You've got to watch your back. And if you think someone's trying to stab it, you have to turn around and confront them."

I was afraid Barron would say this. Typically people know what the correct answer is when they search for advice, but they need someone else to state it first. It is similar to flipping a coin to make a decision but knowing what decision you want to make independent of the outcome. Or possibly of praying for an outcome that ultimately you have the power to influence.

"On the other hand, Rebecca is no phony," he said.

"Rebecca is not the other party. Please do not hang up." It was time to ask him for a major-league favor. "I have a contract someone wants me to sign, and I am uncertain about its contents. Are you skilled at deciphering legal language?"

"What, because I'm a cabbie I can't read?" he asked.

"No, I only meant that the language is—"

"I'm messing around with you. You don't always have to fear the wrath of the black man," he said. "I'm okay with that stuff. But my wife deals with it all the time. You could fax it to her."

"I would prefer not to transmit it via fax." I thought for a few seconds. "Would you and your family like to come to my apartment for dinner?"

"Your place?" he asked.

"Well, shit, like I said, it's nothing fancy, but you're welcome to come over here." He was surprised and confused by my words.

"That is the same sentence you used when you permitted me to do Thanksgiving at your place. I was messing around with you as well."

He whistled and said, "You've got a steel-trap mind there." He told me he would have to check with his wife but he was fairly certain they could come. I gave him my address, because he drives so many people around and therefore does not have a steel-trap mind for that.

I prepared the same pasta meal I had cooked with Rebecca but utilized gnocchi this time and also blended the multi-fruit juice Michelle enjoyed at Thanksgiving. Barron and Cynthia brought nondairy cupcakes for dessert. It pleased me to be utilizing all four chairs for the first time. We had a pleasant conversation until they discussed what instrument Michelle should learn next year in school.

"Barron wants her to take saxophone," Cynthia said. "He used to play it. Horribly."

"And you'd rather have her learn the flute?" Barron said.

"I didn't say it had to be the flute," she said. "I said a *woodwind*."

"The saxophone *is* a woodwind!" Barron said. Michelle was creating scalene triangles by lining up pieces of gnocchi on her plate. "I don't want my daughter playing the flute. The flute is . . ." He shook his head and cleaned his mouth with his napkin.

"What?" she said. "Say it."

He removed the napkin. "It's bougie," he said. "It's a bougie instrument for bougie music that bougie people listen to."

"*I* listen to classical music," Cynthia said.

"I'm not attacking you. But we do enough bougie shit already. And I never complain. You want to spend a grand on a couch,

I don't complain. You want to fly to Paris for Christmas, I don't complain. This is the one thing I'm asking for."

"Daddy's *asking* for," Michelle said, which was illogical, but children often repeat statements they hear without consideration, even if they are illogical and lacking context. Frequently I had to correct Zahira.

Cynthia was quiet. Then she said, "Let's talk about this later."

"No, let's talk about this now," Barron said. "Let's ask Karim what he thinks."

"Don't bring him into this," Cynthia said, and I mutely agreed with her, but Barron was looking at me and I felt I had to provide some input because I was asking them for help as well.

Michelle was resuming her triangles. "Possibly it is best to present her both options, and see which she is interested in and excels at," I said.

"And she'll be interested in the sax, like any intelligent person," Barron said. "Good advice, Karim." Cynthia looked upset. "Fine, we'll discuss it later," he added. "Okay?" Cynthia quietly said okay. It wasn't the ideal parenting technique, but in some ways it is preferable for both parties to state their opinions, even if it produces arguments.

I said loudly, "I hope the gnocchi has enough earthiness." No one responded for a few seconds until Cynthia said it was very tasty.

After the cupcakes, I made tea and Cynthia read my contract and I discussed politics with Barron, who knew much about American history and taught me about the 1960s political movements, which was another area I wanted to broaden my knowledge of.

Finally Cynthia said, "The language is complicated, but it looks to me like if you sign this, you're transferring ownership of the intellectual property to the company."

She explained the details, but I didn't 100% listen to them. I was mute for several seconds before I remembered to thank her. I didn't want them to ask more questions about what the intellectual property was, and fortunately Michelle yawned and Barron said they should get going. I walked them to the door and closed it behind them and sat down on my floor for several minutes.

Mr. Schrub had lied to me, or he had not told me the complete truth. And possibly he had only invited me to spend time with him not because he liked me, but because he wanted me to trust him enough to sign the contract.

I thought of what Barron said about confrontation. I emailed Mr. Ray again:

Please tell Mr. Schrub I would like to proceed with my own proposal and meet with him again to discuss it.

Then I understood that although Barron's advice wasn't about Rebecca, and although she wasn't a phony like Mr. Schrub was, it was applicable to her to boot. It was cowardly of me to not contact her. You have to confront obstacles and not hope they will be resolved without hard work.

I was going to shoot her an email, but even that was cowardly, so I called her. She answered in a flat voice.

"Rebecca, this is Karim," I said. I hadn't strategized, which was possibly foolish, but sometimes it results in saying truer things. "It is my bad for the other night. I have some issues that are independent of you."

She said, "Uh-huh."

"Let us see if we can't resolve this problem," I said.

"What exactly *is* your problem?" Rebecca asked.

I hoped she would already understand, but I said, "It is difficult to explain."

"I can handle it," she said. "You don't want to see me anymore."

"No," I said. "I mean, 'No, that is false,' not 'No, I don't want to see you.'" I find the usage of "no" as a prefix confusing because it's not always clear what the negative applies to. Then I told her my recent thoughts about Ramadan.

"Uh-huh," she said again, and I could tell she was uncomfortable, but she asked me more about Ramadan and how I felt about it, and how I felt about being with her during it and in general.

I said I didn't feel good about it but I enjoyed being with her. It was difficult both to decipher my feelings and to state them initially, but the more I did it, the easier it was. "Possibly I should learn not to view my values as a series of binaries and instead find a compromise," I said.

"That's what relationships are about, right?" she said. "According to my last issue of *Cosmo*."

"Do you classify this as a relationship?" I asked.

"I don't really know," she said. "It's just been a couple of weeks."

"We are not in Kansas anymore," I said.

"What?"

"I have not been in a relationship previously," I said, "so I do not know the appropriate amount of time before it is technically considered one." When I said it, I realized it was the class of statement that someone like Angela from Cathedral would reject me for, but I hoped Rebecca would be careless.

"I'm no expert, either. But this is pretty quick," she said, and my heart slightly plummeted, but then she added, "Though we could keep seeing how it works. And I'm joking. I don't read *Cosmo*."

"I do not even know what *Cosmo* is," I said.

We made plans to see each other after work on Wednesday night, and for a little while I forgot about Mr. Schrub and Kapitoil, but only a little while.

big for one's britches = lacking humility with a higher-up

bougie = bourgeois; middle-class or materialistic

chef = used without an article, the term for a chef at a classy restaurant

Cosmo = *Cosmopolitan*, a magazine for females that frequently analyzes romantic relationships

exploiter = someone who leverages; this is a word

lady friend = either female friend or romantic partner

philistine = someone ignorant of quality culture

phonies = false people

stab someone's back = practice deception

steel-trap mind = a brain that does not forget many things

Mr. Ray replied and told me that Mr. Schrub would be very busy over the next week but he would contact me when he was free.

I should have said I was ready to sign the contract but that I wanted to meet with Mr. Schrub directly first. Now they knew I had reservations about the contract, and they were forcing me to wait so that I might reconsider. My father frequently negotiated with suppliers who used similar tactics, and I have read several business manuals on negotiating, although this was the first time I had ever had a real-world negotiating opportunity, which was why I made an error.

Of course I could simply write my proposal and try to publish it in an academic paper without telling Mr. Schrub, but he would fire me instantly for being too big for my britches and I would never have a chance to work for him again. Possibly if I waited and got him to see the idea from my POV, we could compromise.

I was relieved that Rebecca planned our date for Wednesday, which was to see her friend's rock-and-roll band's concert on the Lower East Side. The friend was the man from her party with long hair named James. He sang and played guitar, and although the crowd was not very bottlenecked in the dark room, several females stood in the front and watched him nonstop. People danced merely by rotating back and forth on an axis over their feet and not truly moving, so I didn't have to worry about dancing poorly and looking foolish. I asked if Rebecca wanted a beer. She said, "Sure, but you don't need to buy it for me," and I said I would purchase this first set and she could purchase the second set. "It's called 'buying a round,'" she said.

By the time we were on Rebecca's round, James's band was done. After they put away their equipment, he located us at the bar and hugged Rebecca. "Thanks for coming, Becks," he said. "Looks like you're the only one who made it."

She nodded at the females. "You've got plenty of groupies."

"They're a pale mimesis of you," he said as he compressed her around the shoulders with his arm.

Rebecca retracted very slightly, just a few inches. "You remember Karim from my party, right?"

"No, nice to meet you," James said, and shook my hand with great force. It was very loud in the bar, and I heard him say, "You a fan of Indian rock?"

"I am not Indian," I said. "I am from Qatar."

James's upper lip rotated to the left when he laughed via his nose, but Rebecca didn't and she said, "No, 'indie rock'—it's short for independent. Music not released on big record labels."

"In that case, yours is the first band I have heard that is in that class, and I did enjoy your music," I said, even though I didn't truly enjoy his music and thought his voice was impure, unlike that of Leonard Cohen or John Lennon or even Bob Dylan, whose voice is impure but intriguing.

James said he could obtain free alcohol for us, and soon he had three small glasses of whiskey and three cans of a beer that tasted mostly like water, and we drank the whiskey and then the beer to reduce the burning, and after we finished the beers he produced a second round and we repeated our actions.

I was slightly dizzy, but Rebecca was very unstable, and when she almost became imbalanced James held her and her body became fragile in his arms, and he said, "Your hair always smells so fucking good, like strawberries," which doubly angered me because it smells in fact like watermelons, and then he slowly danced with her even though the band was playing a fast song.

I wanted to leave so I wouldn't have to see what was happening, but I was afraid that if I left James would attempt even more. So I stood by the bar and watched them dance in the middle of the room and felt my body heat up like a microwave at James every time he whispered something in her ear and also at Rebecca for frequently laughing at what he said and for acting like this directly in front of me while we were on a romantic date.

When James lighted a cigarette for himself and let Rebecca inhale from it as well, I decided that if this was what she wanted to do, then it was her choice, and I left.

Outside the wind burned my ears as I determined the location of the subway. Before I walked away, Rebecca exited the bar and almost fell. "Wait," she said.

I rotated but didn't speak. "Why are you leaving?" she asked. Some of her words blended together.

"You do not seem to require my presence," I said.

She leaned against the wall of the bar. "I don't normally act this way," she said.

"Then why are you doing it now?" I asked.

"I don't know. For attention," she said. "Sometimes. When I drink. Even from sleazeballs like James."

"But why do you want attention from James when I am already paying it to you?" I asked.

"Because," she said, and she decelerated her words. "I really like you."

I leaned against the wall next to her. "Then those are not logical actions," I said.

She collapsed but I hugged her before she fell. She pocketed her hands inside my coat to keep them warm and got close to me and our breath was the only non-cold thing near our faces, and she kissed me and it made my entire body feel hotter, but not like the temperature spike of a digital microwave as before, as it was more like an analog toaster with gradual heat. "You want to come home with me?" she asked.

"Of course I want to," I said. First we went into a store and I bought her a large bottle of water. She nearly crashed into a stand that stored snacks. When I helped her outside she almost fell again, and I said, "Maybe we should go home independently tonight." She nodded. I retrieved a taxi and gave the driver $30 and wrote down his car's ID number and said if he made her pay I would contact his employer.

After I linked Rebecca's seat belt, I told her I would call later to certify her safety. She pulled my tie and body close to her and said, "You can hate me if you want."

"I do not hate you," I said. "Obviously, I also really like you." She asked, "Yeah?" and I said yes again, and then kissed her on her hand. She smiled when I did that and touched the spot with her other hand, and I closed the door and watched her drive away.

When I returned home I had an email waiting for me from Mr. Schrub's secretary. My heart became stimulated because I thought it would be about a meeting with Mr. Schrub, but she was forwarding me a message from Mrs. Schrub that read:

Dear Karim,

Would you care to attend a holiday fund-raising event next Wednesday the 22nd that I'm organizing?

The event was to raise money for refugees from Kosovo. I knew she hadn't told Mr. Schrub she was inviting me, because if he was there he would not have wanted me to also be there after my last email to Mr. Ray. And this would be my best opportunity to confront him again about my proposal.

buying a round = purchasing alcoholic drinks in bulk for several people
groupies = females who desire musicians
indie = independent
mimesis = imitation
sleazeball = James

On Friday afternoon a few small white objects fell from the sky, and for a moment I thought someone was ejecting shredded paper from a window above me. I opened a window and put my hand out to touch the snowflakes, but they deleted almost instantly on my hands. I wanted Zahira to be able to see them.

I called home. My father picked up. I disconnected.

Rebecca had invited me to go out to a bar with some of her friends and Jessica that night in Brooklyn, because she was leaving for Wisconsin on Tuesday for almost a week to work remotely on the Y2K preparations. We had to go to her apartment first to drop off some of her possessions, and we decided to eat something there first. When she looked out the window after we finished, she said, "You mind if we ditch the bar and stay in with this weather?"

"I am not dying to go to the bar," I said. I didn't feel like talking to new people, even though I liked Rebecca's friends, minus James, and I also understood why Rebecca once said she liked Jessica but didn't 100% connect with her.

She had a selection of board games, and I chose one that I thought would enhance my English: Scrabble. I would lose but I didn't mind playing poorly in front of Rebecca.

She explained the rules to me and we started as we sat on the carpet next to her coffee table. "We can listen to some indie rock that's better than James's band," she said, which made me smile to myself, "or this CD of '50s songs." I said I was unfamiliar with music from the 1950s so I would prefer that, and she said, "Me, too. There's only so many scratchy-voiced tales of postgraduate alienation a girl can take." I didn't always understand Rebecca's ideas, but I valued the way she stated them.

I was robust at understanding the structure of the game, although my limited English restricted me, and Rebecca won the first game easily.

We replayed, and when Rebecca created the word "C-A-N-C-E-R-S" she clapped her hands and said, "Bingo plus triple-word score!" She laughed as she counted her points. I didn't say anything, and she looked up and said, "What's wrong? Afraid of getting blown out a second time?" It reminded me of what Mr. Schrub said after he won a point in racquetball. Americans enjoy boasting when they are winning competitions.

"I do not mind losing the game," I said. "Your word made me think of my mother."

She stopped scoring her move. "What about her?"

Before she could say something such as how she was sorry, I explained the basic facts of my mother's death. I didn't discuss the night of my birthday.

She didn't say anything the entire time, just as Mr. Schrub didn't. When it was over, she said, "I think you're the first decent guy I've actually liked."

"Decent means 'average,' correct?" I asked, because it did not seem like a compliment.

"No, not average," she said. "Unusual."

Suddenly I wanted to feel close to her in a way I hadn't yet. I took her hand and we walked to her bedroom. It felt simultaneously familiar and new, which was an intriguing combination, and I thought that is how all experiences should feel, or how you should make them feel to you, but often they feel too familiar or we desire something exclusively because it is new. After a few minutes she said, "Do you want me to get a condom?" and I said yes, and she retrieved one from the bottom shelf of her clothing drawer.

My performance was slightly better than the time with Melissa. I paid attention to which actions produced no effect and which yielded a net gain, as in a boosting algorithm, and I utilized the strong ones in variable patterns so they wouldn't become predictable, but after a period of time I merely let myself enjoy our actions, even if I wasn't the cream of the cream partner. At one point we stopped moving and looked at each other at highly magnified range and she removed the perspiration from my forehead with her hand and I did the same for her and we both smiled, and I knew what it was like to know that your happiness was making someone else happy and have reciprocity for it, which was a true example of something that wasn't a zero-sum game.

When I terminated, I lay down and was ready to fall asleep, but Rebecca took my hand and guided it on her body and instructed me on what to do until she also terminated. After that, she turned her back to me but placed my left arm around her body and my hand over her right breast, but soon she reversed and made a motion for me to reverse as well, with her arm around my body, and we fell asleep and remained that way, as if we were two open parentheses.

When I woke up in the morning, she was gone. The snow was several inches high on her windowsill and growing. She and Jessica were in the kitchen making pancakes.

"It's pretty miserable out, and the trains are running a Saturday schedule," Rebecca said as I served myself coffee. "So if you wanted to spend the night again."

"You do not need to make external excuses for why I should stay," I said. "I would like to even if it were pleasant out and the trains ran a non-Saturday schedule."

Jessica laughed as she deposited chocolate chips in some of the pancakes. "Does he always talk like that?" she asked. But it didn't make me feel bad. In fact, it made me feel unique, as when Barron said I had a sense of humor.

We stayed inside all day while it snowed and watched movies they owned and listened to music and read. I told Rebecca I had enjoyed the two Steinbeck books and she scanned her bookshelf and selected *The Great Gatsby*. F. Scott Fitzgerald's sentences were more complex than Steinbeck's and my progress was slow, but she told me to keep it until I finished. We played more board games and cooked a large lunch and dinner. It was one of the most enjoyable days I had spent in New York so far, even though nothing we did was exclusive to New York, but Rebecca and Jessica weren't the class of people I would meet in Doha.

Jessica left at night, but Rebecca and I watched the movie *Platoon* on television. When it was over, I said it was interesting to observe the deviations from *Three Kings* in that they were about the U.S.'s two most recent wars, and of course the Gulf War movie was more optimistic, but they shared some parallels, especially in the way the male characters related to each other.

"Yeah," she said. "Though they threw in a female in *Three Kings* and the Other is depicted in a much more generous light—concessions to PC tastes and Hollywood sensibility. Yet they both affirm the dominance of patriarchy and masculine excess transferred from father to son in warfare."

After I asked her to define several of the words she used and to clarify her idea, I said it was very intelligent, and she said, "Good film critics borrow; great film critics steal." I asked her to reclarify, and she said, "I lifted it from an essay I read in college. I'll show you."

She took me into her room and retrieved a book of essays on movies from a large bookshelf that incorporated, in decreasing quantity, books on history and culture, novels, computer science, finance, and poetry.

I tried reading the beginning of the essay, but it contained many larger words I didn't know. Then Rebecca said, "It's been a while since I've looked at it myself. Want to read it together?"

We sat on her bed and Rebecca read the first paragraph. Then she defined each larger word and explained the argument, and asked what I thought about it. We did this for each paragraph. The essay was 20 pages long, and it took us almost two hours. However, by the end I understood the idea very well and had gained some new vocabulary from it and the dictionary in the rear, e.g., "mise-en-scène" and "phallologocentric," although I'm uncertain how valuable some of the words will be to know.

When we finished I said, "Rebecca, you will be a good teacher someday."

She was quiet for a few seconds, then said "Thanks." Similar to me, Rebecca doesn't like to look boastful when she has performed well at something she truly is invested in, but I believe she was proud.

I also think she enjoyed that night's activities more, because my skills were enhancing and I wasn't as nervous about making an error.

The next morning it stopped snowing, but there were over eight inches on the ground. We read the Sunday *New York Times*, which was the solitary time the whole weekend I thought of Kapitoil, until Jessica suggested we go to Prospect Park.

The park was like a lake with thick white waves that were static. Many children rode sleds down a hill and built statues with the snow and some threw snow at each other, which caused at least two children to cry. Jessica worked as a waitress and had taken an orange tray from her restaurant, and we used it on the hill. It was one of the more stimulating exercises of my life, much more than racquetball, and Rebecca also said she missed doing winter activities in Wisconsin.

Jessica had to leave early to meet someone, but Rebecca and I stayed longer. We sat under a tree on a rock and cleared the snow off it and watched the sun set until just a few children remained. I wasn't wearing my watch, and the only way to estimate the time was from the sun, and I wished we could spend several more days like this. It was as if time didn't truly exist outside of us, which reversed how I always felt at work, when the world moves forward with or without you and you have to maintain progress with it.

The sun made the field of white look pink like the clouds at sunset, and the sylvan trees without branches were like the hands of elderly people. I told Rebecca it would be nice to take a picture.

"I don't own a camera," she said. "I don't really think visually."

So I looked around at everything and at Rebecca and removed my left glove and put my hand inside her glove next to hers and inhaled the air and listened to the sounds of the children, and closed my eyes and saved all the different sensations to my nonvisual memory.

But then I wanted to save the emotions I was feeling, and it was more difficult to classify and categorize them, so I concentrated exclusively on the feeling I received from the cold air that removed all odor except for a minimal amount of Rebecca's watermelon shampoo, and it was still complex to classify it, but I tried anyway.

When I opened my eyes, the sun was almost 100% down and it was time for the Salatu-l-Maghrib prayer. Rebecca asked if she could watch. I consented, and afterward I taught her about the different prayer positions and the translations of what I was saying. Then, because she seemed interested, I discussed a few other subjects, e.g., the Five Pillars. "I'm pretty ignorant about this stuff," she said.

"As a parallel, I now see I did not truly know much about the U.S. before I came here," I said. "And I am ignorant about movies and music and books."

We were quiet for a few minutes until she received a telephone call from her brother. She gave him advice on where to search for an airplane ticket and how much to spend. When she disconnected, I asked if he was visiting her.

She shook her head and picked up some snow and compressed it with both hands. "He always flies the day after Christmas to see our father."

"I did not realize he still spoke with him," I said.

"They have a little more in common than I do. Though not much. But David tries, and when my father isn't caught up with his family, he deigns to let him visit a couple times a year," she said. "He's got a lot of lingering anger at our father. I mean, I do, too, but I'm aware of it, thanks to several hundred hours of therapy. I'm not sure he's really conscious of how upset he is."

She continued compressing the snow into a sphere. "I think I understand what you mean," I said.

Her body vibrated from the wind, and she said it was getting late and that we should return. She was about to throw the sphere, but contained it in her glove, and it remained there as we walked home in silence until she dropped it outside her apartment where it blended with all the other snow.

decent = possessing positive values

deign = lower yourself to do something

ditch an event = do not attend an event

mise-en-scène = visual arrangement within a movie

Other = term for people who are not the majority

patriarchy = a society controlled by men, or a family controlled by the father

PC = Politically Correct; fearful of offending the Other

phallologocentric = I still do not understand what this means

After burning the midnight oil for several days, I completed a draft of the epidemiology paper at the office on Wednesday. The writing was Karim-esque, but it stated the central ideas clearly and the math and programming examples were elegant. It could be a strong launch pad from which connoisseurs in the field might refine Kapitoil.

That night, as I put on the rented tuxedo Mrs. Schrub had delivered to me at my apartment, I debated ditching the party. I was not 100% certain that Mr. Schrub was being dishonest with me, and I was also not 100% certain my epidemiology idea would function. At significant crisis moments some people feel confident about themselves and some people lack confidence, and although I ultimately trust my skills, I do not think I will ever be the class of person who is infinitely certain of himself.

The fund-raising event was at a hotel near the Schrubs' apartment. It was in the ballroom, and when the young female guard asked for my name, I identified myself, and she said, "Issar . . . I don't see you here." I became nervous and I spelled my name in case she didn't see it. Then she said, "My mistake—you're on the special guest list of Helena Schrub. Go on in, sir." The people behind me on line paid more attention to me as she allowed me to enter.

The ballroom was littered with men in tuxedos and females in black dresses but no fur coats like there were at Mr. Schrub's luxury box in Yankee Stadium. There were also many waiters carrying food, and since I didn't see Mr. or Mrs. Schrub, I ate some stuffed vegetarian grape leaves.

Then I saw Mrs. Schrub in the middle of a cluster. She waved for me to come over. "Karim, I'm so glad you could make it," she said. She introduced me to the five people with her, who were all her age or older. "Karim is from Qatar, and he's worked his way up to a top position at Schrub Equities in just a few months. Derek says he's one of his most gifted employees."

Even though Mr. Schrub made a similar statement at the Yankees game, I didn't know he had said this, which sounded much more impressive because he said it to his wife and not to his associate. The only thing that bothered me is that she pronounced it "Ka-tar" instead of "cutter," which most Americans do, so I am typically careless, but I had used the correct pronunciation with her several times in Greenwich.

Two of the men in the circle also worked in finance at other firms, and soon we launched our own conversation. I was surprised that they wanted my opinion, especially on the 1,000-mile view of e-commerce.

"There are golden opportunities now," I said, "but I believe investors are overestimating the value of the Internet. At the end of the day, consumers still sometimes prefer the human interaction that machines cannot deliver."

Two other men joined us, and they continued asking for my theories, and soon I forgot why I was at the fund-raiser. When a waiter brought us a tray of small pastries containing cream, I took one without thinking, and it was so delicious that I remembered it was haraam but I couldn't restrict myself and I consumed two more.

I was talking so much about my ideas that I was unprepared when one of the men, who was the senior member of our cluster and ran a rival hedge fund which was less powerful than Schrub, said, "Your boy Karim is giving away all your secrets," and Mr.

Schrub placed his hand on the back of my neck and said, "Not all, I hope," and winked at me and compressed his hand slightly harder than necessary.

I didn't know how to approach asking to speak to him privately, so I didn't say anything as he greeted the other men. They all moved back a few inches to let him center himself.

"I take it Karim's been tutoring all you dinosaurs on millennial advancements?" he asked. "This kid is the future. He's got brains and vision." I had to bite the inside of my lip so that I wouldn't smile.

Then he said, "Just goes to show, being smart and hardworking still counts for something in America. You don't need to come from a wealthy family or go to an Ivy, or even have a business degree." Even though he was overall complimenting me, I quickly felt less like a VIP again, and I wondered if all the men now thought my previous ideas lacked value because of my poor qualifications.

Soon a female started speaking on a microphone. She thanked everyone for coming and spoke about her organization's goals. One of Mr. Schrub's friends, who was the youngest and whose name was Mr. Slagle, motioned for a waiter. The waiter was a Mexican man who waited as Mr. Slagle selected three dates contained inside bacon. After he consumed them he had a remainder of three toothpicks, and since we weren't near a trash bin or a table and the waiter had left, he dropped them on the floor.

Mr. Schrub whispered to his friends, "Remind me who we're giving our money away to for this one?"

Mr. Slagle said, "Kosovo."

"Kosovo," Mr. Schrub said. "It's beautiful there. They don't need any money."

Mr. Slagle laughed. Mr. Schrub looked at him. "You find that humorous, Dick?" His tone of voice was as serious as when he yelled at his sons.

Mr. Slagle's eyes rotated to the others. "Sure," he said.

"Well, it's not," Mr. Schrub said. "My great-grandfather was from there."

His friends looked uncomfortable. "Hey, I'm sorry, Derek," Mr. Slagle said.

"You're sorry?" Mr. Schrub asked.

Mr. Slagle looked at the others as if he required help. "Honestly, I don't know what to say," he said. "I thought you were making a joke."

The female finished her speech and the crowd applauded, but Mr. Schrub remained silent. I wanted to say something to help Mr. Slagle, but I didn't know what I could say and of course I was afraid.

Then Mr. Schrub said, "I'm just joking, Dick," and he contacted him on his shoulder and smiled. "What do you take me for, some kind of monster?"

Mr. Schrub laughed and then Mr. Slagle did and the other men followed, and the tension around them deleted. However, my muscles still felt restricted, as if I were exercising with weights. It reminded me of when Dan pretended he had cancer.

The others began talking again, and Mr. Schrub seemed to be in a positive mood, so I said to him quietly, "I am ready to discuss the contract."

He looked at me and said, "Let's go to my car." He told his friends he would see them later, and he called Patrick to bring the car around. We exited the ballroom together. Walking with him was again parallel to walking through the restaurant: People pretended not to observe him, but they were all doing it.

We had to wait a minute on the street for the car, and I didn't know what to say, and Mr. Schrub said nothing either, and I again felt a lack of confidence and wished I hadn't told him I was ready to discuss the contract, but now I was there and I had to continue my plan.

The limo arrived and we got inside and Mr. Schrub told Patrick to drive us around the area for a few minutes. Mr. Schrub raised the internal divider between us and Patrick, and the world outside muted. The windows were also cloudy from the combination of interior heat and exterior cold, so it was as if we were contained inside a small egg with no sounds and few lights as we drove down 5th Ave.

"So?" he asked. It is difficult to proceed when someone launches a conversation with that.

I commanded myself to be strong and said, "I have finished the epidemiology paper. But I am not signing the contract, because I believe it transfers ownership to you."

The lights of the luxury stores and their neon Christmas decorations passed by our dark windows in undefined shapes. "It transfers ownership so we can improve it," he said. "You still get a healthy raise and plenty of stock. You're not getting a raw deal here in any way."

"It is not about the money," I said. "Kapitoil has already independently outpaced quants revenues from all of last year by 3%. Possibly this can help people."

"You already are helping people," he said. "This is not a zero-sum game, Karim. Do you know how many people in our office would be looking for jobs now if not for Kapitoil? Or how many other people it's created opportunities for?" I didn't say anything. "Look, I want to help people, too. But I'm a realist. The program might work for predicting the spread of diseases. But it definitely works for predicting oil futures. You don't cut open the goose that lays golden eggs."

"I understand I am helping some people," I said. "But Kapitoil is a zero-sum game. It leverages problems elsewhere and transforms a loss into financial gain."

He shook his head. "If we don't do it, someone else will. Maybe you wish otherwise, but those are the rules of the game. If you can't play by them—well, then, you're not man enough to be in this business. And I had you pegged wrong."

The car stopped quickly, and to stabilize myself I placed my hand on the window and deleted a section of the moisture. It was interesting how by making something clear I simultaneously left a mark. Through the small hole was St. Patrick's Cathedral and its two tall towers in the front that looked like antennae.

"I've discussed with George promoting you and giving you a raise," he continued. Then he stated a figure I never expected to earn in my life.

"Don't answer now," he said. "I'll be away for Christmas, but my secretary will set up a meeting on the 30th with a new contract and all the terms spelled out clearly."

He asked if I wanted to return to the fund-raiser, but I said I could walk home. Before I exited, he said, "Remember what I said about the goose, Karim."

But as I walked home, instead of considering the goose or the rules of the game or if I was cut out to be in business, I thought about the toothpicks Mr. Slagle had deposited on the ground, and I wondered how long it would take until someone located them and picked them up, and how they would probably remain hidden for weeks or months with small pieces of dates and bacon on them and turn rotten. It was not the correct subject to be thinking about, but sometimes it's difficult to control where your brain routes itself.

in the ballpark = an estimated value
man enough = possessing the strength and power to succeed
raw deal = a deal that is unfavorable for one party

The next day I still didn't know what to do. I could consult with Barron, but (1) I still didn't want to reveal what Kapitoil was, and (2) I was afraid he would think I was greedy for considering taking the money. And I had already not told the 100% truth to Rebecca and couldn't disclose to her all the details.

My mother would have also been a valuable advisor in this situation. She would not have judged me like my father would. And she would not have been as inexperienced as Zahira is in subjects like this. She also would be able to see multiple POVs, e.g., maybe the epidemiology proposal wouldn't function and I might lose this program that would certify Zahira and I had sufficient funds for the future, or maybe it would function and some ventures like this merited the risk.

On the day of Christmas Eve I watched television for several hours. Most channels displayed shows or movies with Christmas as the subject. In one, a family invited a homeless man to their Christmas dinner, even though they were poor themselves. In the end he revealed that he was in fact a millionaire, and for their generosity he rewarded them. It was unrealistic and false although it still made me feel slightly enhanced at the end, but the more I thought about it after, the less I liked it.

By nighttime I felt quarantined in my apartment. I had seen advertisements on the news the entire day about Midnight Mass at St. Patrick's Cathedral, and driving past it with Mr. Schrub had already made me think about attending it, and I had nothing else to do.

I walked along 50th St. to the cathedral. The black sky was littered with snowflakes like rays of sun underwater. I thought of how they would melt and sink into the ground for trees, and then the trees would eject water vapor, which produces more rain in return. The world can be so elegant when it is left alone to itself.

I wished I could share that moment and that thought with Rebecca, or with Zahira.

On a large monitor a few blocks from the cathedral, an anchorman was discussing a story about a famous female singer who sang for soldiers at an American base on Christmas Eve. Below it the scrolling font displayed: INSIDERS PREDICT "ANY GIVEN SUNDAY" WILL WIN HOLIDAY WEEKEND BOX OFFICE . . .

I followed the crowd entering the cathedral and powered off my cellular. The interior had long white pillars that curved at the top to form a ceiling that reminded me of the New York mosque's dome. White lights looked like the snowflakes from the nighttime sky, and the blue glass windows were like the daytime sky. Although it wasn't midnight yet, members of the church wearing white robes that looked like the class men wear in Qatar were singing in the front in Latin. There were no open seats, so I stood in the rear and closed my eyes and listened to the singing for several minutes. Of course it was a foreign language, but it was simultaneously not foreign at all.

The rest of the service was a combination of music, reading from the Bible, and rituals with candles. I imitated the people around me, and different religious ceremonies usually follow similar classes of algorithms and procedures, and although I looked different, I believe I merged well with the Christians, except when they launched the ritual of communion and I remained in the rear.

When I left, it was snowing more heavily and the frozen ground looked like a clean tablecloth. I didn't want to ruin it, so I walked only in the paths other people had produced.

I woke up on the morning of Christmas and remembered I had powered off my cellular. I had two messages.

I was surprised to hear my father's voice on the first one. He sounded volatile and all he said was to call him back ASAP. The next message was also from him and provided a different number.

I called, and a female voice answered "Hamad General Hospital," and my lungs inhaled air too rapidly.

It took me several seconds to ask for my father. In a minute he was on the telephone.

"There has been an accident with Zahira," he said.

I could not speak. My brain produced a series of images similar to the ones from the bad dreams I sometimes have about her.

A small bomb had exploded in a trash bin in the Mall early in the morning, he said, and Zahira was there. The bomb did not hurt her, but the explosion knocked her against a wall and she hit her head. She had a concussion and was taken to the emergency room.

"Is there any serious damage?" I finally asked.

"Not from the concussion," he said. "But the doctors say they found something abnormal with her blood and are running additional tests."

"What is it?" I asked.

"I do not know," he said. "The way they speak, it is impossible to understand. We are allowed to talk to her in a few hours."

I didn't know what else to say. So I asked, "What was the reason for the bomb?"

He spoke slowly. "They say it was a group here that is protesting the development of new malls in Qatar."

"Did anyone—" I paused. "Did anyone else get hurt?"

"A few other people had minor injuries," he said. "But there was a boy standing between Zahira and the trash bin."

"What happened to him?" I asked, and immediately I wished I hadn't.

His voice became very quiet. "I think he was taken to the burn unit."

We were mute for a while. I asked him to have Zahira call me at her earliest convenience.

I disconnected, then sat up in bed and looked out my window. The Schrub monitor displayed: MERRY XMAS . . . BRONCOS VS. LIONS 4:15 P.M. KICKOFF . . . MIX OF FREEZING DRIZZLE AND LIGHT SLEET THROUGH DAY . . . I watched for several minutes, but there was nothing about the bombing.

My eyes moved up to the neon-green Schrub hawk against the gray sky. It was strange. I always thought of it as setting down the S and E, but now it looked as if it were picking them up in its talons.

The solitary positive was that Zahira was too young to remember which hospital it was.

I didn't leave the apartment because I wanted to certify Zahira could reach me. I prayed, but not for Zahira's health, because I know that only frustrates you when it fails. Finally my cellular rang in the afternoon.

"It is me," Zahira said when I answered it. She sounded exhausted.

"Are you okay?" I asked.

"I've felt healthier," she said, "but I'm okay."

"Father said they were running tests," I said.

"That is why I am calling," she said, and again my stomach rotated. "They think I have something called ulcerative colitis. It's a disease in the colon. I have been losing weight for several months, and this is why."

I closed my eyes with force. "How serious is it?"

"Because they found it early, they're going to put me on medication, and they believe it will help," she said. "If they had discovered it later, it could have required removal of the colon."

I opened my eyes again. Three of the chairs at the table were in order, but the fourth one was out of line, and the asymmetry bothered me. "What causes it?"

"No one knows," she said. "It's just poor luck."

"Maybe you have been losing weight because you have been studying so much. When I work hard I sometimes forget to eat well."

"No. I have been eating less because everything I eat makes me feel ill," she said. "I did not tell anyone what was happening to me because I was humiliated."

"You should get a second opinion," I said.

"Three different doctors here all agree."

"Still, doctors are sometimes wrong."

"I have it!" she said. "All right? I have it."

I aligned the fourth chair with the other three and sat in it. "This is not right. It is not fair for you to get this."

"Stop it, Karim. Don't make me sad about this."

"I'm not trying to make you sad. I am upset for you."

"Well, don't be!" she said. "I'm trying to see the better side. It could have been worse. They could have discovered this in six months and I could be preparing to lose my colon. Or the accident could have been worse. I could have been that boy." She stopped.

"I am going to fly home tomorrow," I said.

"No," she said. "I can handle this. They say I am anemic and require a blood transfusion and they want to observe me here for a few more days. The visiting hours are short and there is no need for you to miss your last week of work if you are already coming home on the 31st."

I hadn't told her that if I signed a new contract, Schrub would therefore probably extend my stay beyond my initial departure date. We argued more about it, but finally I said I would call her each day. Then I asked, "How is father?"

"Haami and Maysaa are with him now," she said. "It is hard to tell with him. He has been very quiet."

Before the nurse made us disconnect, I asked, "Zahira, why were you in the Mall?"

"I was buying a gift," she said.

"Who was it for?"

She paused. "It was for myself."

It was difficult to continue talking, but I said, "I have missed our conversations."

She said, "So have I."

At night I called Rebecca. "We have family friends over, so I can't talk long," she said.

"Okay," I said.

She talked about the activities like cross-country skiing she had done with her family and the many milkshakes she had consumed and a class of cheese she enjoys that she consumes there. "I may even need to set foot in a gym to shed these 30 new pounds," she said. I didn't respond, and she laughed and said, "That's an exaggeration. I'll never go to a gym."

I said, "My sister has had some health issues."

She immediately said she was very sorry and asked how she was. I told her, but I didn't include the bombing. "What about you?" she asked. "You all right?"

"It does not matter how I am," I said.

"Okay," she said. "Is it a good hospital?"

I felt pressure behind my eyes as I did in Rebecca's bedroom at her party, and my throat began restricting itself. My voice was unstable as I said, "I am receiving another call. It may be my family."

"Take it."

"Good-bye," I said, and now my voice was very volatile.

"Bye," she said. "I guess I'll touch base with you when I'm back."

I disconnected and stood there for several minutes with my eyes closed until my body stabilized. When I opened them, my black table and its four ordered chairs looked very spacious and voided.

touch base = reestablish contact

I talked to Zahira each day. She was still fatigued, but her mood was enhanced, and she told me everything about her disease that she had learned from the doctors and her own research. She used many jargon terms I had never heard before, and I had difficulty following her, although I didn't want to tell her that while she was stimulated, but when she started discussing a chromosome named "1p36" in English, I finally had to confess that I didn't understand.

"I think that is the first time you have admitted you don't know something," she said.

Normally I would be slightly angry, but I could tell she was smiling, so I merely said, "You are skilled at biology, and I am skilled at computers. If you studied computers you would excel in them, and if I studied biology I would excel at that," although that is false, as I was never strong at biology.

Talking to her distracted me, but I was still uncertain about what to do at my meeting with Mr. Schrub on Thursday afternoon.

Rebecca was working overtime in preparation for Y2K and was too exhausted to see me, but I went to her apartment on Wednesday night. Jessica was there with a man she had recently launched a relationship with named Colin who had almost parallel facial features to her, and the four of us cooked a dinner of couscous and vegetables and a stew together. When Jessica couldn't find their blender (which was inferior to my Juicinator) and I found it in a cabinet, she said, "Time for you to move in with us," which simultaneously humiliated and delighted me.

Colin and I partnered to purchase olive oil at the market. He asked how long I had been dating Rebecca. "Since Thanksgiving, so five weeks minus one day, although I have known her for almost three months," I said.

"You seem to really like each other," he said.

"We are very different in some ways, but similar in others, and I have not met anyone like her before," I said. Although I always attempt not to be boastful, I added, "And I believe she has not met anyone like me."

After dinner we played poker and bet quarters. I played well, as did Rebecca, although I was cautious and only bet when I knew I had a high percentage of winning. At the end Rebecca and I continually raised each other, and Jessica and Colin exited the game. I had two pairs, but Rebecca raised so rapidly that I began to question the relative value of my cards, and finally, even though the money was insignificant to me, I exited as well, because it's still always preferable to minimize losses. Jessica asked what we both had. Rebecca showed her cards, which were valueless. "Just my ability to bullshit," she said as she aggregated the quarters. "You've got to learn how to bluff if you're going to be a card shark, Karim."

We divided into the two bedrooms. I selected a CD by Bob Dylan without asking her permission and reclined on the bed with my head on her stomach and listened to it while she petted my hair. My preferred song was called "Don't Think Twice, It's All Right," which was a strong example of the art I had been enjoying the last few months in that it blended positive emotions with negative ones. I still of course appreciate art that boosts positive emotions, because that is rare and necessary, and although the Beatles will always be special to me because of my memories and because their instrumental and vocal skills are the highest quality, musicians like Bob Dylan and Leonard

Cohen are also appealing because they sing about subjects that reject binaries and are mysterious in the way math can be mysterious, e.g., sometimes you locate an answer and the universe becomes almost magical because in the middle of chaos there is still order, and sometimes there is no answer, and because of that the universe is even more magical since it has secrets that humans can never understand.

I told Rebecca this, and she said, "You're turning into a real postmodernist," which I understood from the movie essay even if I still didn't 100% understand the concept of postmodernism.

"You haven't mentioned Zahira," she also said.

I told her what I had learned about her disease from her, and that the doctors believed she could control it with medication.

"If you have your health and family, nothing else really matters," she said. "My apologies for turning into a human Hallmark card."

Without evaluating it, I asked her, "What would you think if I created a computer program that might have a significant impact on health in developing countries?"

"Is that what you've been working on?" she asked.

"Yes, but if I pursue it, I may need to leave the country for several months," I said. I was regretting telling her this much already. Even explaining further a partial detail such as how I would need to leave the country temporarily, because Schrub would fire me and I would have to find a new employer in the U.S. to sponsor my visa, would require full disclosure about Kapitoil.

"So it's like a fellowship?"

I looked at one of her brother's paintings and its strange colors. "It is similar to that," I said.

The music compensated for our muteness. Then she said, "If it's something you want to do, don't let me hold you back."

I was hoping she wouldn't want me to go, to facilitate my decision, but I said, "I will know what I am doing in a few days."

She received a call, and I asked if she wanted me to exit to give her privacy, but she said it was her mother and she would require just a few minutes. She talked in a different voice to her on the telephone from with me. I heard her mother ask a question, and Rebecca slightly rotated her head away from me and she said a little more quietly, "I can't really say right now." Now I felt I was being invasive, but if I left the room it would appear that I was aware of my infringement, so I moved to the bookshelf and examined her books but couldn't restrict myself from listening.

The volume of her voice lowered even more. "It's far from that stage yet, so you don't have to worry about it. In fact, it's not even your place to worry about at all." She listened more. "Fine. *Yes*, fine."

She said good-bye and disconnected and made an angry animal sound with her throat. I went to the restroom to give her some time to stabilize. When I returned, she was drawing lines with her finger against the cold glass of her window. "Are you all right?" I asked.

"Hmm?" she said. "Yeah, she's just . . . I don't know."

We listened to the remainder of the CD without talking. Our bodies were in contact on the bed, but it felt again like we were magnets with similar poles.

She fell asleep before I did, and when I petted her arm I felt a square object under her sleeve. I lifted it and recognized from advertisements a nicotine patch. I hadn't seen her smoke or smelled it on her clothing recently. I was happy to see the patch, but I had two other thoughts: (1) It is hard for me to understand why someone needs to rely on any drug to resolve a problem (which is the same reason I find it hard to understand why Rebecca requires Zoloft), although I know that not everyone is like I am and wants to problem-solve independently, and (2) it is intriguing that to overcome an addiction to a substance, the addict frequently requires a certain amount of the substance before she can 100% remove it. It supports my theory that extreme reactions aren't necessary and are often less efficient than moderate approaches.

I removed my arm from under her head without waking her, which was difficult because her head seemed so soft to me, even the small bump centered on the back under her hair, and I exited to the living room window and looked at the yellow streetlights on the snow and dialed my cellular.

My father answered at his store. I asked how Zahira looked.

"Not good," he said. "Although that is temporary. But this disease will still make it difficult."

"It will make what difficult?"

"Finding her a husband," he said.

It was a mistake to call him. "I cannot believe that is what concerns you," I said.

"Her health concerns me as well. But this presents an additional problem."

"If a man is foolish enough not to be interested in her because of this, then he does not merit her anyway."

"Is that all you called to say?" he asked. "That I'm an old man who doesn't understand how the modern world works? I'm merely looking out for her."

"That isn't looking out for her." The few lights of the buildings in the neighborhood produced yellow constellations against the black sky. "And she doesn't need you to do so."

"Then I should let her go where she pleases, and maybe next time she will end up in the burn unit as well?"

"Unless you quarantine her in a room, there are too many dangers in the world to defend her against," I said. "And even if you quarantine her, there are still some dangers you cannot prevent."

He didn't say anything. "Is the hospital room comfortable for her?" I asked.

"It has been updated since I was last here, but it still has a certain smell I dislike," he said. "And the doctors speak to me as if I am a child."

"That must be very frustrating for you," I said.

"Yes," he said.

"She tells me the doctors are informing her well, and that she is doing her own research."

"Yes," he said again.

"Is she explaining the concepts to you?"

"And to Haami," he said. "Which is even more difficult."

I almost laughed, but I interrupted myself. "It is unfortunate the doctors there do not possess the communication skills she has," I said.

"Yes," he said for a third time.

The door to Rebecca's room was still closed.

I said, "I am in a relationship here with a Jewish female."

He was mute for such a long time that I thought we might be disconnected. Finally he said, "It is not my preference. But I cannot quarantine you in a room."

Then he added one word: "Either."

That word was an important one. And when I heard it, I knew what I had to do the next day.

There was some noise, and he said he had a customer. I said, "I have one question." It was difficult for me to ask, but I forced myself to state it as if it were a strategy question in a business conference: "Do you remember the Beatles song mother often used to sing to me when I went to sleep?"

I heard him ask the customer to wait. My eyes became fatigued, and the lights of the buildings across the street spread out like gold dust.

Then he said, "I do not remember it, but I know the title was a female's name." The customer yelled at him, and we disconnected.

I put down my cellular. I still couldn't remember the song.

My eyes refocused and the yellow lights outside sharpened into small squares and one room powered off its lights while another one near it simultaneously powered on.

This line entered my brain:

Her hair of floating sky is shimmering, glimmering, in the sun.

And the metaphor of floating sky suddenly made me access a brief memory of my mother singing that part of the song "Julia" to me while sitting on the side of my bed. That was all I could recall. Then I lost the memory of the sound and image. But at least I had it for a few moments, and I remembered that the Beatles also sang about blended emotions, and the pressure bottlenecked behind my eyes again, and I told myself to be strong and to repress it, but then I considered that maybe it was in fact stronger to allow it to happen, so I let myself release, and for several minutes I could not control it, which typically panics me but now it didn't because it wasn't exclusively sad, it was also blended, and Rebecca entered the living room and petted my back in a circular pattern with her hand and we stood there mutely for several minutes until I stabilized, and she kept her hand on my back and we returned to her bed and remained mute, which I valued.

bluff = display confidence when your holdings are valueless to leverage the ignorance of the other party

card shark = a card player who bluffs and succeeds

The day of my meeting with Mr. Schrub I let Kapitoil run on autopilot. The scrolling white numbers on the black monitor blurred like a snowstorm the entire morning.

In the afternoon I walked all the way uptown through the snow to Mr. Schrub's apartment. My external concentration was so low that a garbage truck almost crashed into me on Broadway. It was almost amusing to me how you can be so focused on macro concerns, but it requires only a micro event like that to impact everything.

When I arrived at Mr. Schrub's apartment, I had to check in as before. The receptionist called upstairs and then told me that Mr. Schrub was coming downstairs. I waited 20 minutes, however, and each minute I grew more panicked. But I reminded myself that this was possibly part of his negotiation strategy.

Finally Mr. Schrub arrived with his briefcase. "Let's take a walk," he said. "I've been cooped up all day."

We crossed the street to Central Park without talking. As we passed a white horse with black markings attached to a carriage, Mr. Schrub asked, "Feel like a carriage ride? I'm always up for one, but Helena says it's cruel to the animals."

I consented, and he arranged a ride with the driver, an Indian man with glasses that were highly concave.

We covered ourselves with blankets and the horse pulled us into the park, away from all the dirty snow where people had walked and onto a clean interior path. Our breath made small clouds in front of our faces like exhaust from a car.

Mr. Schrub put his briefcase on his lap over the blanket and opened it. "I've got the contract ready. You can sign now, but we'll wait until you have a lawyer cosign it so you can be sure

you understand all its terms. I think you'll find it very generous."

He handed me the stack of papers. In bolded font was the
price for the program. It was even higher than what he said at
the fund-raiser. Something happens when you see a number
attached to a currency symbol, instead of just thinking about
it. It becomes more real. Sometimes I enjoy examining my
bank account for that reason: Unless I observe evidence, I still
don't believe someone is paying me for what I would also do
for free.

There was a division in the path, and Mr. Schrub asked the
driver to turn left, but because it was windy and we were behind
him and the horse made so much noise, Mr. Schrub had to yell
at him three times before he finally heard, and the horse angled
northwest. Its body was perspiring even though the temperature
was below freezing.

Mr. Schrub added, "And we'll give you a team of programmers to direct. Any resource you want, you'll get. We're going to
groom you for a leadership position."

I considered my options:

1. This was of course what I wanted most of all when I arrived
   here in October;
      A. and in some ways it was what I still wanted;
      B. and as a leader at Schrub I could make some en-
         hancements in business practices;
2. but Kapitoil would still operate and exploit problems elsewhere;
      A. and as Mr. Schrub said about himself, I would
         change slightly daily in ways I wouldn't notice;

    B. and one day I would be a different person and no
        longer Karim-esque;
        i. and possibly being Karim-esque, although
            it is not confident or experienced or a strong
            negotiator or many other factors that make a
            skilled businessman, is still a positive class of
            being;
        ii. and is in fact superior to being Schrub-esque;
            1. and I knew that if I signed the contract
               and told my father what I had done, he
               would be disappointed.

I folded the contract in half.

"I cannot sign this," I said.

"Is it a money issue?" he asked. "We can get more."

I shook my head. "I will be publishing my paper."

"What if we confidentially provided the code to a few select partners in the sectors you're interested in, and continued running Kapitoil?"

I had already evaluated this idea. "The code must be on the open market for the best people to utilize it. And there may be applications we have not thought of. The only way to know is if it is available to everyone," I said. "I have made my decision."

He exhaled with force through his nostrils. His muteness made me nervous, as it always did.

Then he said, "Kapitoil was fully funded by the company and written on company time. We could take you to court and easily block you from disclosing it to others, and my programmers could get access to the code or write a version of it on their own.

You wouldn't come away with a cent. We're offering you a lot of money to avoid that."

Although the horse accelerated on an empty path and the wind sliced my cheeks, my body heated up under the blanket. I couldn't believe I was so foolish that I hadn't asked Cynthia about this. I hadn't 100% created the program on company time as he stated, but they had funded me. He had the best lawyers in the country, and the solitary one I knew was Cynthia.

Mr. Schrub was correct: Possibly I wasn't man enough to be in business.

And I could make my family secure for years, not months, if I merely signed the contract.

He was the more skilled player. He knew how to leverage the rules of the game.

The horse slowed down and stopped as a large cluster of Asian tourists crossed the path in front of us. I looked down the side of the carriage as we waited. A small piece of bread sat on top of the snow like a topping on a cake with icing, and dozens of ants were aggregating around it. It again wasn't the correct subject to be thinking about at the time, but it made me happy that such a small piece of food was sufficient for so many ants.

The other incorrect subject to be thinking about was Mr. Schrub's comment that his programmers could innovate their own version of Kapitoil. It was a complex and beautiful program, and although Schrub has the cream of the cream programmers, I don't believe anyone else could write a parallel program, even launching from the proposal I presented to Mr. Ray, and it angered me that he thought other people could.

But maybe he didn't truly think his employees could rewrite Kapitoil. Schrub had continued to offer me more and more money to have access to the code. They had probably attempted to create their own version and failed, and they knew that their only opportunity was to buy the program from me.

Then I thought of Rebecca's advice from our poker game and had an idea. And it was as if I were observing the entire galaxy of stars while I was simultaneously struck by lightning.

I retrieved my voice recorder and accessed the saved recordings folder and selected a short file and pressed play.

Mr. Schrub's voice came on: "Well, in better news, I have a proposal for you. My business people emailed it over this morning . . . I don't fully understand it, but apparently they want you to de-encrypt Kapitoil and allow our programmers access to the code, so they can make modifications to the algorithms, too. You'll still be the point man on all this, and you'll get a corresponding bump in salary . . . As far as I can tell, it's a win-win for everyone."

I pressed the stop button. The skin around Mr. Schrub's eyes trisected.

I said, "That is proof you tried to mislead me about the original contract." Then I bluffed. "I can sue you for that. My lawyer has a copy of this recording, and because I did not in fact create Kapitoil on company time but on my own time, and it is copyrighted in my name, she says that the rights are mine. You will have a few more months to use the program until the paper is published and before the algorithmic signal loses its power." I added something that I didn't believe, but maybe Mr. Schrub would: "And if you take us to court, the concept of the program will be revealed to the public immediately and someone else will gain enough information to create a similar program and Kapitoil will be valueless for the futures market, and *you* will not come away with a cent."

Then I was mute, and for once I could tell he was the nervous negotiator. He rotated his head and observed the snowy trees that looked like cauliflowers. "I'd like you to turn off the recorder for a moment," he said.

I powered it off and showed him.

He watched the Asian tourists, who were stopping to take photographs and still blocking our progress. He quietly said, "Do you know what a cipher is?"

I said, "It is a jargon term for an algorithm that encrypts or decrypts."

"No," he said, even though my statement was true. "A cipher is a zero. A nothing. It doesn't exist." Finally he turned his head to me, and his face was slightly red from the wind, although his voice still remained quiet. "You, Karim—you are a cipher. You are a nothing. A nobody. You don't exist. You don't make a difference."

And for a few seconds, his words truly made me feel like I didn't exist, which is possibly the worst feeling to have about yourself.

"People from your area of the world can encounter visa problems very easily," he said. "Sometimes they can't reenter the U.S. after they leave. Forever."

His face returned to normal color and he looked relaxed again, as if he had hit a strong racquetball shot and knew I had little chance of returning it. My legs lost strength, and it felt like knives were stabbing my back. I also knew he had the power to do this to me. But Mr. Schrub's warning didn't target precisely what he thought he was targeting: that I could never work at a company in the U.S. again. That wasn't what I was most invested in anymore.

He was forcing me to make a zero-sum decision, as the lion's share of business transactions are.

A pigeon rapidly descended by my side to the ground. It stabbed the piece of bread with its beak and in a second it was deleted, and just as quickly the pigeon vibrated its wings and left behind the ants.

I rotated my eyes toward Mr. Schrub's hands on top of the blanket. Although he had no cuts or scars on them, his skin had spots and looked as fragile and wrinkled as a used banknote. It seemed like the only thing he could do with them was type on a computer or use a pen. Most of his nails were trimmed, but the one on the second finger of his right hand was slightly longer than the others and slightly yellow and acutely angled.

I wasn't afraid anymore. Instead, I was very sad, as if I were watching somebody, or something, die in front of me. And although he had insulted and threatened me, I felt almost sorry for him. He was more like his sons than he wanted to believe. They were driven only by having a good time. He was driven only by winning. And he could not see that one party's victory always causes another party's defeat.

"Good-bye, Mr. Schrub," I said.

I pushed the blanket off me and jumped out of the carriage and merged with the Asian tourists just before the carriage restarted.

I walked with them for several feet as the carriage resumed down the path and Mr. Schrub turned back to watch me, and then I ran ahead of the tourists and deeper into the park.

My body was strong. I continued running northwest, even though it was difficult on the snow in my shoes, but I could not stop. I felt as if I could run infinitely. When I reached the Ramble after several minutes, I was the solitary person around, and I finally decelerated, and it was peaceful hearing exclusively the sounds of ice and snow crunching under my feet like almonds in teeth and of squirrels running and a few birds chirping.

I found a stone bridge with a small arch entryway just a few feet wide at its base. Inside the arch, I stood and put my hands on the walls and closed my eyes for a long time. I listened to the wind and inhaled the air and finally deleted my mind of thoughts in a way I had not been able to achieve in all my time in New York.

When I reopened my eyes, I didn't know how much time had passed, but the sun was setting. I used the snow to wash myself as efficiently as I could, and the coldness of the snow somehow warmed me, and I performed the Maghrib prayer under the arch. The air smelled clean, as if the world had refreshed itself.

I finished and called Rebecca at the office. "I have to leave on my flight tomorrow morning," I said.

I could hear Dan talking to Jefferson in the background. "You took the fellowship?" she asked.

"I will give you details later," I said, and I asked her to meet me at my apartment after work. Then I called Barron and arranged for him to drive me to the airport the next morning.

Packing was simple, as my additional possessions were exclusively my new shirts and suits and my juicer. I had to retrieve a cardboard box from the doorman to store the extra suits and juicer.

Rebecca arrived and apologized for being late. I asked her to sit on the couch. It took me a long time to initiate my sentence, and she said, "The suspense is killing me."

Then I told her everything about Kapitoil and the epidemiology project I was still going to move forward with, and how I had rejected Mr. Schrub's offer, and that I was fired.

At the end she asked, "Well, can't you find another job here?"

I explained what Mr. Schrub was going to do.

"Oh," she said. "Oh."

Then she took off her glasses and rubbed her eyes and while they were closed said, "This is maybe a moronic idea, but what if—I can't believe I'm suggesting this, of all people—but what if we got a quickie marriage tomorrow to keep you in the country?"

My body's interior felt an electric charge. "You would marry me?" I asked.

She removed her hands from her eyes and looked down. "It's not necessarily how I always daydreamed about my wedding day, but I could do worse." She laughed slightly. "For the record, I've never had a daydream about my wedding." Then her eyes angled to me and were large and serious. "But, yeah," she said, and she smiled for an instant before returning to a non-smile.

I knew she was not proposing a fully authentic marriage, but she would not have done it if her feelings were not at least partially authentic. And my feelings for her were authentic. In fact, except for Zahira, I was most Karim-esque around Rebecca, and to boot, I was even learning to be Rebecca-esque, which was possibly what relationships were about more than they were merely about compromise.

I thought about how happy I would be if I went to sleep and woke up next to her daily, and how much I would learn from her, and possibly how much I could teach her, and what it would be like for her to meet Zahira and for me to meet her brother.

Then I wondered what it would be like for her to meet my father, or for me to meet her mother, or to walk around Doha with her. And we had other differences that might make us incompatible for a long-term partnership.

However, Rebecca and I were both intelligent problem solvers, and even though emotions and relationships were in many ways more complex than programs and mathematics equations, I had developed my skill set significantly in these areas in the last few months. Possibly it could work.

But I put my hand on her arm and said, "I value that idea very much. But Mr. Schrub probably has the power to prevent it from helping anyway, and I do not want this to cause problems for you as well." She replaced her glasses. "And although it is an idea I like, this is not the method to be together. It is like an arranged marriage." Then I added, "Love cannot be produced by force. It should come from itself," which is the idea I had when I smoked marijuana at her party, and it surprised me that I stated it now, because most ideas created with the help of drugs aren't sound, but I truly believed this one.

She nodded and looked at my hand on her arm. "I'm going to quit, too, by the way. Don't worry, it's not just about you. But you finally motivated me to get the hell out of Dodge," she said. "It's an idiom for leaving a place you don't want to be."

"What will you do?" I asked.

"There's still enough time to sign up for spring classes in a Master of Ed program somewhere," she said. "In a couple years

I can teach high school history in the city. Some idiot once told me I'd make a good teacher."

I said, "You should be careful about taking advice from an idiot, but I also support your decision."

I asked her to sleep over, and we talked for a little longer. When she was half sleeping, I touched her left ear on the soft part above her dolphin earring and said quietly, "I am afraid you will find someone else and forget about me."

Her eyes were closed and I believe she slightly heard me but she was almost unconscious so she only said something I couldn't understand and put her arm around me tighter, but I decided it didn't matter, because if what I said was true, that love comes from itself and is the ultimate self-starter, then if we were meant to be together we would be together, and if she was meant to be with someone else, then I had to be an adult and accept my loss and instead try to remember the additions she made to my life.

When my alarm powered on in the morning, Rebecca and I were still linked and it was dark outside. I told her she could sleep longer and even stay after I left, and prepared in the restroom.

She was standing by the bed when I returned. "I'll leave with you," she said.

We went downstairs with my luggage and waited outside as snow fell on us from the gray sky like a shower. We didn't say very much. It is always difficult when you know you are about to leave someone and you cannot prevent it.

Soon Barron parked his car in front, and he helped me store my luggage and the cardboard box in the trunk. He said hello to Rebecca, then sat in the car and waited.

"I almost forgot this," she said, and she retrieved from her bag a CD. "I made this over Christmas. It's a mix."

She had written "Songs for Karim" on it. I liked how she didn't have to write "From Rebecca" on it. I told her I would listen to it when I arrived home.

She bit her lip and the skin of her forehead compressed in the middle, and then she removed her own CD player from her bag and gave it to me. "Listen to it on the plane," she said. I remembered I still had her copy of *The Great Gatsby* and had not finished it yet, but she told me to keep it as well, and I said I felt foolish that I had no gifts for her, but she said she didn't enjoy receiving gifts anyway although she was framing the picture I made for her and was going to hang it in her room.

"I hate good-byes," said Rebecca.

"I do as well," I said.

"I just realized that, even more than I hate good-byes, I hate people who say 'I hate good-byes.'"

I said, "I do not, but I understand what you mean."

"You'll be checking email over there?" she asked.

"No," I said. "But I will send you a stone with symbols on it."

"Your sense of humor is getting better," she said. "I mean, 'enhancing.'"

I thanked her, but instead of saying "You're welcome" she said, "I don't want to watch you go." So I rotated her glasses on her face asymmetrically, and she put out her hands as if she couldn't see me for a few seconds, and I laughed, and then she took them off 100% and hugged me and opened the front door of the car and squeezed my hand one more time and kissed it, which no one else has ever done for me, and before she closed the door she said, "Take care of yourself, kiddo."

We drove away and she walked carefully on the icy sidewalk until she disappeared through the snow and into the subway. Although we said we'd remain in contact, I knew that our emails would decrease in frequency over the next few months, and I wasn't skilled on the telephone so we wouldn't converse much, and we would discuss her traveling to Qatar or meeting in another country, although that would probably not happen, and then maybe we would email exclusively on holidays or birthdays, and finally we would go so long without communication that it would be too difficult to relaunch it, and our relationship would terminate.

I didn't want my last memory of Rebecca to be of her entering the subway with that thought in my brain, so I recalled being with her in Prospect Park in the snow and the odor of her watermelon shampoo in the cold air. I hoped that would be how she would remember me as well. It wasn't a hard copy, but for this I trusted more the power of my memory.

And possibly my prediction about us was incorrect. Human emotions and behavior often deny conventional analysis. People cannot always be quantified.

Barron was mute until we reached the tunnel for Queens. Then he said, "She's good people," and even though he omitted the indefinite article and used the incorrect plural, I said, "That is true."

"I take it things worked out with that contract?" he asked.

I said, "I am satisfied with the results."

He exited the tunnel and we accelerated on the highway. In the mirror, Manhattan's tall buildings minimized until they looked like gray toothpicks. "So, you going back to your old job?"

I remembered what Jefferson had said about Dan: that he had a "narrow worldview." With experience and training, possibly I could broaden my worldview and utilize computers in a nonfinancial form, as I was trying to do with the epidemiology project. And if Zahira's skill set deepened with biology, we could even partner in the future.

But that would require me to master new subjects. Now I could afford to enroll in daytime university classes, although it was too late to register for classes in the spring and therefore I could not start until August. While I waited, I would need to find another job. I could do something with computers, but it would be difficult to find an employer who would hire me for just a few months. And my solitary professional experience was in finance.

"No," I said at a low volume.

We didn't talk the remainder of the ride as I considered what else I had the qualifications for. The roads weren't bottlenecked because it was so early, and we arrived at the airport in a few minutes and I took out a $50 bill. Just before he took it, he pushed my hand away and said, "It's on the house."

He defined the expression, and I thanked him and said I could retrieve my luggage myself. We shook hands inside the car and said good-bye and I gave him my English business card. "Wait," I said, and I crossed out my Schrub contact data and wrote my home telephone and personal email address.

I removed my luggage from the rear. As I took out the box with my extra suits and juicer, I had a quick mental tableau of Barron in one of my suits making juice for his daughter, and although I was stimulated to show the juicer to Zahira, the image made me so happy that I took out a pen and wrote, "(4) suits and (1) juicer for Barron and Michelle," and replaced it. I closed the trunk and stayed where I was and waved at Barron while he drove away so he couldn't see that I didn't possess the box anymore.

Inside the airport, the airline employee behind the counter checked me in for my flight. "And would you like to purchase an upgrade to first class, Mr. Issar?" she asked.

"No, thank you," I said.

She pressed some keys on her computer and observed my suit. "Will you be traveling to Qatar for work?"

All around me, businesspeople in clothing like mine handed over passports and swiped credit cards and deposited pieces of luggage that moved along the rubber tracks before they disappeared into the void.

"No," I said again.

I know what I will be doing. I will float through the sky one quarter of the earth's circumference to the east. I will land and retrieve my possessions. I will visit my sister in the hospital that once held my mother. I will sleep at night in the home where she died.

And then, in the morning, I will wake up, eat breakfast, walk to the place where I have spent more hours than at any other job, and go to work for my father.

ACKNOWLEDGMENTS

I would like to thank my deeply loyal and supportive agent, Rosalie Siegel; my astute, gracious editor, Jeanette Perez; Amy Baker, Erica Barmash, Jane Beirn, Milan Bozic, Tom Cherwin, Mary Beth Constant, Carrie Kania, Greg Kubie, Cal Morgan, and everyone else at Harper Perennial; Professors Kathryn Davis, Kathleen Finneran, Marshall Klimasewiski, and Kellie Wells and the Writing Program at Washington University in St. Louis; my readers Vaqar Ahsan, Angela Hur, Eric Lundgren, Nathaniel Popper, Brad Stoler, Greg Wayne, and especially Sarah Buishas; various editors who have given me opportunities over the years, in particular George Kalogerakis, Christopher Monks, Mike Sacks, and John Warner; Clara Boyd, Julia Boyd, Ryan Chapman, Andrew Epstein, Daniel Feiner, Maja Groff, Eileen G'Sell, Olivia Harman, Mayme Hostetter, Melissa Johnson, Jesse Lerner-Kinglake, Felix Brandon Lloyd, Catherine Meeks, Christi Mladic, Lev Moscow, Jessica Pantzer, Alex Quinlan, Lauren Schnipper, Jesse Ann Lorraine Gunderson and the rest of the Gunderson/Brady clan; and my family.

About the author

About the book

Read on

Insights,
Interviews
& More...

A Conversation with Teddy Wayne

Rory Gunderson

Let's start simple—where are you from?

I grew up first in Yonkers, New York, then in Riverdale, a suburb in the Bronx. I went to a nearby high school attended predominantly by Manhattanites, and spent a good deal of time in the city, so I had somewhat of a hybrid suburban-urban upbringing.

When did you start writing?

I decided I wanted to be a writer sometime in elementary school, but until college I was much more of a reader than a writer (which I think is better training for writing, anyway). I wrote a handful of (angst-ridden) stories in high school, and in my senior year I wrote an (unproduced) television script for *Seinfeld*, which I suppose was the start of my interest in humor writing. In college, I dabbled first in plays, then fruitlessly in screenplays for a while, while very intermittently writing (embarrassingly bad) poems and stories. At 24, it was finally time to write a (mediocre)

> ❝ I decided I wanted to be a writer sometime in elementary school, but until college I was much more of a reader than a writer (which I think is better training for writing, anyway). ❞

novel. It didn't get published, thankfully, but it got me into graduate school.

Do you remember the first book you fell in love with and why it affected you so strongly?

As a child, I was very attracted to stories with talking animals in them, but the first book that had a profound impact on me was one with non-talking animals: Wilson Rawls's *Where the Red Fern Grows*. Stories about humble protagonists singularly dedicated to achieving a goal important to them (but not necessarily to others) have always appealed to me—*Kapitoil* can be read as a variant on this narrative—and the young boy's dedication to and love for his hunting dogs tore me up; I'm not ashamed to admit that the ending made me cry more than once. I reread it as an adult. I might have had something in my eye by the final pages.

Who are some of your writing influences?

They'd all be insulted to be named as influences, but some writers whose work I've loved over the years include, in childhood, Roald Dahl; in adolescence, Salinger, Nabokov, Hemingway; in college, Joyce, DeLillo, David Foster Wallace, Bob Dylan; since then, too many to name, and I still feel highly malleable.

What's the best writing advice you've ever received?

Hemingway advised stopping writing for the day midsentence so that you have something to return to the next session. Midsentence seems a little abrupt, but I usually stop when I haven't completely emptied my tank. He dispensed that nugget to me personally in Paris in 1926. ▶

> 66 Stories about humble protagonists singularly dedicated to achieving a goal important to them (but not necessarily to others) have always appealed to me. 99

A Conversation with Teddy Wayne *(continued)*

On a craft level, seek out the unfamiliar, surprising, yet still relevant detail; self-consciously contrarian flourishes are themselves a form of cliché.

When you're writing, do you have an audience in mind? Are you writing for someone in particular?

For fiction, you should always write something that you yourself would want to read, and hope that others out there share your tastes—it's too intimate, difficult, and low-paying a profession to do anything else. That said, self-indulgent writing is the worst kind; there has to be some acknowledgment that another person is taking the time to read your work and choosing it over more digestible forms of media, and if you don't meet the reader halfway, he may not want to investigate whatever you have to offer.

When writing for different publications, I absolutely tailor my writing to their audiences—everyone else in the world has to do some work they don't always want to, and I don't think I'm exempt. I have to adjust my voice least when writing for *McSweeney's*; its audience is most similar to me in cultural interests and sensibility.

In many of your articles and essays, and certainly in Kapitoil, you take on a persona that is extremely different from your own. How much does your background, whether it be the city you grew up in, your family, or your experiences, make its way into your writing? Or do you find that your writing and subjects are completely outside of your personal experiences?

Many writers have something tangibly prominent in their histories or identities that serves as a touchstone for all their work, whether it be their race, gender, religion, sexuality, region, family dynamic, a tragedy. To reduce it to these basic statistics, I'm a white male secular heterosexual New Yorker with a mildly interesting family and a life that's been visited by some pain, but which is nothing compared to what some people go through—and, thus, I don't mine my own background for much material. In terms of a concrete subject for fiction, however, what probably interests me most is class. I grew up and live in New York, a city deeply stratified by wealth but geographically crammed together, where millionaires have to step around homeless men to hail cabs and prep school students get mugged on the subway because their monogrammed L.L.Bean backpacks make them easy marks.

What informs my writing more personally is my position as an interloper who never feels comfortable within any subculture or with any specific designations and who, because of that, has to forge connections without the benefit of prefabricated bonds. From those labels above, I'm aware that I've been dealt a very good hand by fate, so I don't expect anyone to feel sorry for me and, likewise, I don't think semiautobiographical depictions of my so-called plight would tempt many readers. For *Kapitoil*, then, I turned simultaneously outward and inward, writing about a character who seems to share little with me on the surface but who is also (more conspicuously) an alienated outsider, both in the local environment of New York City finance and on a more global level. Underneath the veils of my far more ironic social persona and through the thornbushes of my cynicism, I'm not all that different from Karim. A few select details from the novel originate from my experiences, and some of the worlds and characters he traverses and encounters—nightclubbing bankers, liberal-arts Brooklynites, multicultural potlucks, masters of the universe—are ones I'm familiar with to greater or lesser extents.

New York plays a prominent role in Kapitoil *and almost acts like a* character in and of itself. Having grown up there, did you always know you wanted to set your first novel in New York? You spent your grad school years in St. Louis; how did your experience in the Midwest change the way you looked at New York?

My first failed novel was not set in New York, but that may be because when I wrote it I hadn't yet spent enough time there as an adult to know it well enough. By now, I think I have an anecdote for just about every street in downtown Manhattan.

I have fond memories of St. Louis, but living there was a culture shock akin in some ways to living in a foreign country. I made some close friends from the Midwest and the South, areas of the country I had spent little to no time in and from where I hardly knew anyone. And while some of the stereotypes about Midwestern life are true— a lot of people smoke incessantly in bars, eat fried food, and drive to the mall five blocks away—I found numerous exceptions, especially in a city like St. Louis, which is big enough to sustain a variety of thriving subcultures.

When I would return to New York, however, the outsider status I've always been keenly aware of was underscored. I'd grown accustomed to the slower pace of life in modest Missouri, and the frenetic ambitions ▶

of Manhattan were suddenly alien and terrifying. Everything I loved and hated about the city—and there's much in both columns—was amplified and, consequently, made it easier to write from the perspective of a foreigner.

Since moving back, I've somewhat adjusted, but although New York is what I know best, I'll never feel entirely at home here—which isn't necessarily a bad thing.

There are some great comedic elements to Kapitoil, *and much of your other writing consists of satire and humor pieces. How do you feel humor writing compares to traditional writing? Do you have any advice for humor writers?*

Humor writing, by which I don't mean comic fiction but, rather, work that aims primarily to provoke laughter, is probably as distinct from fiction writing as is nonfiction writing. Like any kind of prose, humor writing requires meticulous attention to craft, because when it fails, it fails very obviously—the reader simply doesn't find it funny. Aside from general writing rules, there are all sorts of tricks: use lists of threes with a dissonant final example; end sentences on the funniest word; examine the latency phase origins of your sexual fetishes. The main difference is that humor writing comes from a highly conceptual place that's later elaborated upon with detail (I first knew I wanted that third example to be absurd, and then rooted around for the detail), whereas fiction feels most authentic and visceral when the profusion of details accretes and transforms the concept itself.

Humor in fiction is challenging, which is the main reason I think a lot of writers rarely employ it, though most writers I know have excellent senses of humor. The average half-hour sitcom will make me laugh out loud more times than most 400-page comic novels. For *Kapitoil*, I was hoping to stir neither mild bemusement with overdetermined one-liners nor knowing chuckles due to exaggeratedly satirical send-ups (both of which I'm used to shooting for in my other humor writing), but to write a realist novel whose comedy derived from its humanity—and, yes, that would make me, at least, laugh more than that sitcom. I'm certain it doesn't work for everyone, but I tried; humor is a great consolation, and to neglect it in literature is to ignore one of our essential mechanisms for emotional survival.

My advice to humor writers is to absorb textual and visual comedic material with a critical eye, but not to limit themselves to what's solely funny—also read and watch serious literature and films. It'll make you a better writer overall, and that will trickle down to your humor writing.

Also, pun whenever possible. People love puns.

Kapitoil *is set in 1999 at the tail end of the dot-com boom, yet many of the issues of greed and corporate responsibility you present are relevant during our current financial crisis. Did you write with the current crisis in mind? Do you see Karim's decision as a lesson for bankers today?*

I didn't have the crisis in mind when I began the book in early 2006, when no one but the most clairvoyant of analysts was predicting the financial meltdown of 2008; I set the action in 1999 for other political reasons. But it's not shocking that an era of unchecked avarice and a lack of corporate ethics resulted in economic devastation a few years later. I don't know how many bankers will (a) read *Kapitoil* and (b) undergo any epiphanies from it, and I tried not to moralize too explicitly. Yet one of my ambitions was not to preach simply to the choir, but draw in and inspire some readers in financial fields who had practiced their professions without much reflection to meditate a little more on what their jobs mean, both for themselves and for the world.

I'll let you know if I get audited. ༶

A Pre-9/11 Novel
by Teddy Wayne

KAPITOIL BEGAN with the voice of Karim, and the voice of Karim began with a job.

For almost three rudderless years after college, my main source of income was editing graduate-school application essays through a website I won't name here. The majority of the applications were to American business schools, and most of these came from China, Japan, and South Korea. For several hours a day, I repaired the sometimes-mangled English in clients' responses to eternal questions such as "What are your short- and long-term business goals?" and "How have you grown from a workplace challenge?" It was, needless to say, a childhood dream job come true.

While many of the essays had grammatical problems, nearly all the English as a Second Language writers had remarkably extensive vocabularies for financial and technological jargon. Phrases such as "broaden my knowledge base" and "leverage toxic assets" peppered their prose like standard idiomatic expressions. This was how they had learned and understood English: filtered through the dissonant poetry of corporate-speak.

The dubious ethical implications of editing strangers' essays over the Internet aside (not to mention the possible legal implications of occasionally emailing friends snippets of the most amusing thesaurus-aided butchery—"He said that I should earnestly brush communication skills, including chaffering each other and patience to hear other party's yawping to their heart's content"), the job offered one potential reward: I had always been a fan of idiosyncratically narrated novels (more on this later), and I hoped that, for my own

> **“** While many of the essays had grammatical problems, nearly all the English as a Second Language writers had remarkably extensive vocabularies for financial and technological jargon. **”**

long-term literary goal, I might transform the hundreds of essays I hacked through into something truly worth reading.

Beyond providing me some verbal insights into finance-minded ESL speakers, I also developed a fuller appreciation for the character of businesspeople. It is simple for someone pursuing a less remunerative career path to judge those who elect moneymaking professions as materialistic, venal, and anti-intellectual, but many of the applicants sincerely seemed to care about improving quality of life for others through business and were stimulated by their work. Granted, they were showcasing their best sides, but most of them were doing far more good for the world than was I, putting my college degree to waste by mindlessly editing essays in my boxers. (Not to mention that an application essay by me in French would stir up even greater mirth in my Parisian editorial counterpart as he smoked Gauloises in his blue-and-white-striped underwear.)

I was eventually fired via email for lapsing into slipshod work, a dismissal that was probably best for all parties.

Fast-forward a few years to 2006 and the end of my first year of graduate school at Washington University in St. Louis, for an MFA, not an MBA. After several false starts, I began writing in a composite, more refined voice inspired by my clients. I compiled a running glossary for all the substituted technofinancial words. I decided that a character with such a mathematically precise mind would, in fact, use nearly impeccable grammar (besides which, mocking his grammar felt condescending and too familiar). The more I wrote, the less I needed to refer to my glossary, and the voice took on new registers, sounding less robotic, deploying words not necessarily connected to business, at times even approaching ▶

> 66 It is simple for someone pursuing a less remunerative career path to judge those who elect moneymaking professions as materialistic, venal, and anti-intellectual, but many of the applicants sincerely seemed to care about improving quality of life for others. 99

A Pre-9/11 Novel (*continued*)

lyricism. Eventually, I was inside the head of Karim Issar: a young man deeply engaged with and informed by finance and computers who also has—this was my aim—an equally sensitive soul.

I had a character; now I needed a story. Around the same time, my younger brother, Greg, a neuroscientist and programmer, developed with a friend a program they believed would predict the stock market's vicissitudes (which had nothing to do with news articles) and make them multimillionaires by 25. To make a long story short, my brother is still living off his grad student stipend, but the idea and ambition seemed apposite to Karim's makeup. (It helped, too, that I had temped in dozens of offices by this point, from sterile insurance agencies to glossy gossip magazines, and had something of a feel for the quiet desperation of the modern workplace, though this was a literary conceit I took pains not to overstate.)

Again, this was 2006—we were dwelling in the nadir of George W. Bush's presidency, and the American empire was on its way to collapse. Rather than apply a predictive program to the entire stock market, I narrowed it down to the commodity that had galvanized the biggest headlines—Iraq, Halliburton, global warming, gas prices—over the past few years: oil.

But I was wary of a new genre that had proliferated alongside the same doomsday headlines—the 9/11 novel. There are certainly a few exceptional novels that address post-9/11 America as their subject, but many, to me, exploit national tragedy as mere backdrop. Other than people directly affected by loss of life from September 11th (I am not one of them, and cannot imagine what it must be like), most Americans were seized with vulnerability, terrified to open envelopes and step onto airplanes, and jolted into geopolitical awareness—for a few months, until they moved on to watch reality shows and reelect the president whose negligence and arrogance had abetted and emboldened our sworn enemies.

To write about the anxieties of well-heeled Upper East Siders after the World Trade Center attacks, then, felt like a redoubling of the solipsism for which I was criticizing them. Similar strife occurs weekly around the globe; why were we so special? What mattered most about 9/11 to the world at large was the seismic shift in American foreign policy, the blank check it issued to the Bush administration to start two disastrous major wars, at least one of which was a highly carcinogenic smokescreen for economic interests. But chronicling these issues as they happen is often best left to nonfiction writers—you literally can't make this stuff up— and I feared that such an explicitly topical fiction would risk the polemical fervor and heavy-handedness of this essay. Moreover, writing about a young Muslim man in newly xenophobic America was a very different kind of novel, and as a young white man whom no one ever looked at askance boarding the subway or an airplane, I had even less authority to ventriloquize as such.

Hence, the temporal subterfuge of following Karim's adventures in New York before Osama bin Laden, Enron, the Patriot Act, Afghanistan, Iraq, Guantánamo, Katrina, and the economic crisis (it was a fun ride while it lasted, huh?), in an era when the trickiest political question was unpacking what the meaning of the word "is" is; and when, with hindsight, we might be able to glean how we landed in the historic mess we made a few years later.

Hence, too, *Kapitoil*: what I like to call a "pre-9/11 novel."

And that is how I grew from a workplace challenge. ❧

Author's Picks
Ten Idiosyncratically Narrated Books About Alienation

I THINK THAT ANY NOVEL narrated in the first person should bear, to some degree, the label "idiosyncratic." Its point of view need not be as overtly nonnormative as Karim's, but if we're entering the limited consciousness of the protagonist, as opposed to the more flexible perspective of a third-person narrator, it should be because something about that consciousness is uniquely slanted. And, quite often, that slant suggests some alienation on the part of the narrator. Here are ten books, in chronological order of publication, that in some form influenced *Kapitoil* and the voice of Karim:

Ulysses by James Joyce

The pioneering Modernist stream-of-consciousness used here has been widely imitated, though Joycean chaos is much more ordered than it seems—a coherent fragmentation.

The Sun Also Rises by Ernest Hemingway

Jake Barnes's spare, economical narration perfectly evokes Lost Generation disillusionment, and Hemingway's minimalism has become the lingua franca of all alienated narrators, from hard-boiled detectives to misunderstood youth.

The Catcher in the Rye by J. D. Salinger

Speaking of misunderstood youth, their urtext captures what's essential to the bildungsroman: Holden Caulfield's unconventional voice highlights his

> " I think that any novel narrated in the first person should bear, to some degree, the label 'idiosyncratic.' "

spiritual estrangement from bourgeois postwar society.

Lolita by Vladimir Nabokov

It's hard to classify as idiosyncratic what many consider to be the most beautifully written novel ever, but Humbert Humbert's erudite and fancy prose style marks him as a European outsider in tacky 1950s America.

A Clockwork Orange by Anthony Burgess

I first read this in high school with the aid of the glossary for Burgess's invented language, Nadsat, included in the back of the American edition (against the author's wishes). He was right to object; the reader doesn't require it after a few pages, and eventually becomes fluent in Nadsat and sees the dystopian future through the eyes of a young man with whom he would otherwise not identify—a reverse Holden Caulfield.

White Noise by Don DeLillo

I also hesitate to call this idiosyncratic, as DeLillo is a master stylist, but Jack Gladney's gemlike sentences are philosophical mini-treatises that counter the minimalism in vogue in American literature at the time.

Rule of the Bone by Russell Banks

Yet another novel tagged as a modern *Catcher in the Rye* and *Huck Finn*, this one deserves it, updating Holden's and Huck's slang for the late 20th century and making Bone's disaffected, run-on voice sound completely authentic.

A Supposedly Fun Thing I'll Never Do Again by David Foster Wallace

Infinite Jest is his legacy, but I first recommend this collection of essays to readers new to the late David Foster ▶

Author's Picks *(continued)*

Wallace; no one has ever written like him before, and even in his nonfiction, where he is only an observing presence, the singularity of his hyperkinetic, encyclopedic mind and prose is inimitable.

Pastoralia by George Saunders

Saunders is a master of deceptively simple prose that packs in both genuine humor and sadness; this collection of short stories is my favorite of his.

The Curious Incident of the Dog in the Night-time by Mark Haddon

This novel's hero, a British boy with Asperger's syndrome and savant-like math skills, shares much with Karim: a supreme understanding of the world of logic, but difficulty navigating the minefields of emotion and human relationships. It brilliantly inverts the conventional misunderstood youth into the misunderstanding youth. ∽

Kapitoil Troubleshooting Guide
by Teddy Wayne

I cannot open my book.

First, ensure you are opening the book from the right-hand side and not the left-hand, bound side. Next, make certain that the pages of the book are not stuck together with glue or another viscous agent, such as maple syrup. This may be the cause of the problem if you have been reading it frequently at IHOP, or are in the habit of leaving it lying around adult film sets.

Some resemblances in the book between persons living or dead do not seem entirely coincidental.

Are you suggesting that the characters contained herein are amalgams of imagination, personal history, and research? Or that, perhaps, the Shakespearean ideal of a fiction born completely of the mind, unfettered by the banalities of existence, may be an unattainable goal or, worse, one leached of authenticity and deeply felt experience? Or that you see yourself, generally speaking, in all of the characters, but, more specifically speaking, in exactly one of the characters, a particularly negatively drawn one, and that you are my ex-girlfriend from eighth grade currently filing a lawsuit against me for defamation? If so, I'm sorry, Janie, but you never should have dumped me for Chris in front of the whole school.

I am having problems organizing a folk music–filled hootenanny to commemorate the period marked by violent conflict between Northern Ireland and the IRA lasting from 1969 to 1998.

Please consult the "Troubles Hooting" Guide.

I am a screech owl with difficulties making sounds.

See above.

I find it hard to fire a gun at my tour leader.

Please consult the "Trouble Shooting Guide" Guide.

I need to write a five-paragraph essay on Kapitoil *for my English class. What are its major themes?* ▶

Kapitoil **Troubleshooting Guide** *(continued)*

The decline of the British aristocracy
following the Great War; the seduction
of Old Europe by Young America; the
self-destruction of monomaniacal whaling
quests. Be sure to cite evidence and
resummarize your thesis statement
in the conclusion.

*I was looking for a conventional reading
guide to direct my book club, but instead
I found this tired postmodern parody replete
with self-referential irony, misinformation,
and a series of increasingly bad puns.*

You may refer to the official reading guide
prepared for my forthcoming appearance
on Oprah's Book Club®, scheduled for
approximately never.

And in the meantime: Did you relate
to any of the characters, and why? If not,
why not?

*The ending failed to provide me with a sense
of closure.*